D1258478

Brown Harvest

Jay Russell

Four Walls Eight Windows
New York

Published in the United States by:
Four Walls Eight Windows
39 West 14th Street, room 503
New York, N.Y., 10011

Visit our website at http://www.4w8w.com

First printing October 2001.

Library of Congress Cataloging-in-Publication Data:
Russell, J., 1961–
Brown Harvest / by Jay Russell
p.   cm.
ISBN 1-56858-211-0
1. Characters and characteristics in literature—Fiction.
I. Title.
PS3568.U76667 B76 2001
813'.54—dc21   2001040344

 10 9 8 7 6 5 4 3 2 1

Printed in Canada
Typeset and designed by Dr. Prepress, Inc.

For
Gordon Van Gelder
&
for
all the smart kids who weren't quite smart enough

I. A Man in Brown and a Woman in White

It's my own stupid fault.

The needle was already kissing the red when I passed the last station six miles back, but I had it figured. Or so I thought. I know the precise capacity of the gas tank — I've measured it myself down to the milliliter — and I've charted fuel economy over a sufficiently long period of time, using a valid sample of branded and unbranded gasolines, to know the car's exact range under any variety of conditions. My calculations indicated that the last fill-up, back at the Interstate service stop with the filthy bathroom, would land me smack dab in the center of town, where I knew I'd find another station. It's a silly little game I play with myself; just something to occupy my mind and make the drive a little bit more interesting. Running on fumes. Life on the edge.

I was, of course, trusting to the accuracy of the gas pump; to the integrity of the manufacturer of the pump, and the station owner, and the inspector from the State Bureau of Weights and Measures — one Mr. E. Stratemeyer — whose oh-so-fancy John Hancock graced the official certificate plastered to the side of the pump.

But that gauge must have been off. Or Mr. Stratemeyer got it wrong. Or the station owner was a no good, cheating son-of-a-Bush.

1

In any case, whatever the explanation, I was out of gas.

Live and learn.

I know I sure have.

I managed to coast onto the soft shoulder as the engine kacked and died of thirst. I got out of the car and saw that I'd come to rest no more than ten yards away from the sign. I guess I was so flustered by my miscalculation that I hadn't even noticed the big sucker looming ahead of me. I walked up to it now, hardly believing what I saw.

WELCOME TO IDEAVILLE
Our past is your future
sponsored by Black X Software,
a Blackwell Unlimited Company

Ideaville.

They'd gone and changed the town's name to something out of some Stalinist wet dream.

It's not that I didn't know it had happened; I'd read about it and seen it on the maps, of course, but standing there by the side of the Old Post Road — a road I'd traveled so many times before on my bike or in my father's prowl car or just hiking with my friends — seeing it in stark black and white . . . well, it finally hit home.

Or what *used* to be home.

What's in a name? you might ask.

I know the answer, you see: everything. Every goddamn thing.

There's something startling, unsettling to the deepest part of your soul, to learn that the place where you grew up has changed its name. It sure as hell isn't something you expect to happen in America; even an America as changeable, as shockingly, commercially mutable as our own. After all, it's not like we're living in a post-colonial African nation or some southern hemisphere banana republic, subject to the whims and tides of foment and discontent and billionaire drug lords; changing its name with each incoming regime in order to make a statement against the prison and tragedy of its history. We're supposed to be proud of our past in America, emboldened and challenged by *our* history. We're taught that we have to live up to and exceed what our forefathers have achieved before us. A place, a name, is supposed to mean something, stand for something; speak to us about our past, in glory and ignominy, in our hearts and in our minds. A name — especially the name of the town where you were born — should be stamped on you, into your *essence*, like some indelible, spiritual tattoo. It should be as enduring as a sequoia, unyielding as a mountain, as important to the life of the soul as oxygen is to the life of the body.

Or so I'd always thought.

But then virtually no one, not even my best friends, ever called me by *my* true name. Few of them hardly even knew it.

So what the hell do I know?

Ideaville.

I shook my head at the sign. I felt mocked, laughed at, but what can you do? You get used to it. Believe me. No one had asked me to come back, and lord knows no one invited me. You pays your money and you takes your choice, as the man says.

And here I was.

I went back to the car and hauled my gear out of the back, then locked it up. In the town of my youth, you never had to think much about things like auto theft, but in a place called Ideaville, who knows? I wasn't about to see my radio ripped-off as some sentimental gesture to days gone by. I secured the steering wheel lock, too, 'cause you can't be too sure, and turned on the immobilizer. Something told me that crimes might not get solved as readily and inexorably as once they did.

Once upon a time, in the age of Boy Detectives.

I reckoned it was a good two miles to the main part of town. Not a bad walk, I suppose, but I felt tired from the long drive — two days to get here from the coast; amazing what you can do with a little determination, no one to distract you, and a case of caffeine-rich Mountain Dew by your side — and my bags were just heavy enough to make the prospect of the walk unappealing. There was a cruel snap of mid-western winter to come in the October afternoon, too, and though I zipped up my brown leather bomber jacket I felt a shiver run through me as I started down the Old Post Road.

Slinging the black case containing my notebook computer over my left shoulder, the half-empty garment bag over my right, I headed on past the big sign. I'd taken barely a dozen steps when I heard crunching gravel and turned to see a car pulling up on the shoulder behind me. A candy-apple red, vintage sixties Ford Mustang convertible screeched to a stop. The woman behind the wheel wore a tight nurse's uniform, white as bleached talc, with a shock of raven-black hair tucked beneath the cap. Her big eyes were as dark as her hair, but she had the reddest cheeks I've ever seen this side of an apple juice bottle. The Mustang's personalized license plate read: CHERRY.

Somehow I had my doubts.

"You okay there, hon?" she called out. She had a dazzler of a smile, equal parts girl-next-door and Playboy airbrush. The top two buttons of her blouse were undone and as she stood up, leaning over the windshield, I could see her lacy red bra underneath. I had to admit *I'd* never lived next door to anyone who looked quite like her.

"I'm fine, thanks. I could do with a ride into town, though," I said.

"That your car?"

"Afraid so."

"What's the matter with it?"

"Won't go," I said with a shrug.

"Too bad. I don't know a thing about 'em, except how to make 'em go fast."

"Me either," I lied and smiled. "And that they're big pains in the butt."

"Ain't that the hard living truth."

"Think I can cadge a ride with you?" I asked.

She flashed the smile at me again. "Indeed you *may*. Hop on in."

"Much obliged," I said. I tossed my bags on the back seat.

"You a consultant?" she asked.

"Pardon?"

"That black leather computer bag. You see 'em all over town. Usually it's the hired guns that carry 'em. Almost like doctors. Or hit men. Every fellah in every bar seems to have one tucked 'twixt his legs."

"Pretty sharp observation," I said.

"Bit of a hobby. So you a cyber jockey? Here to work for one of the big boys?"

"I suppose I am. Of sorts. But I don't work for anyone in particular. Purely independent."

"Must be nice. My momma always told me to find myself a fellow of independent means. I've found plenty of mean ones, but they're never all that independent. Well, buckle up and say your prayers," she warned. "Smoke 'em if you got 'em." She peeled out, sending gravel flying as she hopped the Mustang back onto the Old Post Road. She sure wasn't lying about driving fast.

"Not every woman would stop to help out a man on his own. It's very kind of you." I had to yell a bit to make myself heard over the fury of the wind.

"Life's an adventure, I always say. I figure you take a bite out of it, maybe it won't use its gnashers so bad on you." She took a long glance at me. "Besides, you look okay to me, and I am an angel of mercy. I mean, how dangerous can a fellow drives a Pacer be? American Motors, goddamn!"

I nodded. Her driving might be a little dodgy, but her powers of deduction were beyond reproach.

"You a nurse?" I asked.

She glanced at me, down at her uniform, then pityingly back at me. "Kind of a Sherlock Holmes yourself, ain't you? Sorry, honey, just jagging your wires. Yes sir, I work over at IG."

"IG?"

"Ideaville General? I'm assigned over the RSI unit. It's all the way the other side of town."

"Huh," was my response.

Town sprang up a lot sooner than I expected it to. Ideaville had grown a lot during my absence. I suppose that everything does, but it came as no less of a shock to see the first signs of what passes for that graceless thing we call *civilization* — fast-food temples, $39.95 do-your-secretary-at-lunch motels, giant warehouse discount stores selling cheaper by the gross — so far out of the heart of the quiet, little burg I had known. And the billboards! One after another, like ugly wallpaper down the length of the road. And every third one it seemed for some new computer game: SimHolocaust from Los Bros was getting the big push. I suppose Christmas wasn't all that far off.

Last time I'd been down the Old Post Road, on what I'd always thought was this life's final trip *out* of town, there'd been nothing but a few run-down farm stands, open according to season and the whims of the local farmers. And, of course, the burned-out ruins of Hellman Amusements. I can still remember the look of beaming pride on my father's face when I cracked the Hellman case and revealed the name of the fiend who'd

torched the place. I wonder if Old Lady Hellman's still alive or if she died in stir? The judge
who sentenced her swore that she would.

"So there's a hospital in town now, huh?"

"'Course. Two of 'em."

"Man alive," I said, shaking my head.

"What's that?"

"Nothing, nothing at all. It's just . . . it's so very
different. I can remember when there was only
Doc Clooney. And, of course, the free clinic run by
the county. But I never saw the inside of that."

"You from around here?" she asked.

"Yeah, once upon a time. A *long* time."

"I hardly been here a year myself. Got
recruited by the folks at Blackwell. Lived in Illi-
nois my whole life up to then. Hilton? It was all
right there, what with the family connections and
all, but they made this place sound like a slice of
heaven on earth."

"I can remember when I used to think that's
exactly what it was. But like I say that was a long
time ago in a galaxy far, far away. What's it like
now?" I asked.

"Oh, it's not so bad, I suppose. Little bit chi-
chi, maybe. Those software types make damn
good money — hell, what am I telling you, Mr.
Independent? — and it drives all the prices up.
Kind of a peculiar bunch, too, if you ask me. No
offense intended. That's why I live hell to gone
out of town. Rents are cheaper than here in Sili-
con Slit and the drive isn't too bad, though the
traffic can be a panic come Friday rush."

I laughed out loud.

"What's funny about that?"

"Sorry," I said, "but I can't imagine a rush hour in . . . Ideaville."

"Believe it, darling. Though where everybody's going, I don't know. Just another of the many mysteries of modern life. Like who put the ram in the ram-a-lam-a-ding-dong and why do birds suddenly appear. Yes sir, Ideaville is one happening place. Though it has its negatives."

"How so?"

"Teething pains, I suppose you'd call it. A place grows this fast, there's bound to be some frictions develop. The rise in Carpal Tunnel Syndrome alone'd make your hair stand on end. I double shift more than I care to say. Those bastards at Blackwell'd work me seven days a week if they could get away with it."

I was about to inquire further — and about life working for Blackwell Unlimited — but just then we passed a huge car dealership. I took a good look around and realized that it occupied the site of what had been the old town dump. A fleet of gleaming German luxury automobiles sat on an expanse of black tar macadam where I remembered a swampy waste. The dump had sat on the fringe of town, and the local bad boys would come out to shoot off their Wristrockets and air rifles. There had been an old graveyard nearby, too, where . . . now what had that case been about?

"So, what brings you back this way?"

"Huh?" I said. "What say?"

"I asked what brings you back to town? Business or pleasure?"

I considered that for a minute. "Neither, really. I'm here for . . . a funeral."

"Aw, hell, I'm sorry. Family?"

I had to think about that, too. "Friend," I finally muttered.

"That's rough. I'm a nurse, I know. Damned RSI. Somebody ought to do a telethon."

An old picture — the only kind I had — of Sandy coalesced in my mind. In the picture, I saw her racing ahead of me up Mile End Road on her big red bicycle, her muscular white legs and bony knees pumping like jackhammers beneath her flapping plaid school skirt, her dark hair trailing out behind her . . .

I blinked the image away.

"Into each life some shit must fall," I said.

The nurse cast me a frosty glance, but didn't say anything.

We came up to a set of lights at a vast traffic intersection. It took me a minute to realize that this was where the Old Post Road turned into Industry Street: the main drag through town in the good old days. There used to be nothing but a lonesome "Yield" sign to control the flow of cars; now there was a four-way traffic signal. Three of the corners were taken up by busy gas stations, the fourth featured a multi-plex cinema with eight screens. There'd only been the one movie theater in town in the old days, though it was big as a cathedral. I felt utterly at sea.

My vivacious chauffeuse made a right and pulled into the courtyard of one of the service stations: Swift Motors.

"Gonna let you off here, if that's all right. Too much traffic to drive through the center of town this time of day — I'll be late to work. These boys here service my 'Tang, and they're about as honest as grease monkeys get, which means they'll only charge you twice what they should for the work. Unlike those crooks opposite at Speedwell Auto. I'm sure they'll fetch your Pacer in for you and do the business on it. You still get parts for that thing?"

I nodded. "I like old stuff. There's a certain comfort to be taken in the past."

"Don't I know it, darling. Why else would I drive a gas-guzzling beast like this? You go on in and ask for Tom-Tom. Tell him that Cherry sent you, and he'll treat you right. But don't you believe what he says about me."

"Cherry's really your name?"

"It's what they've always called me. Named after my grandma, actually. Her name was Charity. Her sisters were Faith and Hope, believe it or not. But don't tell anyone," she said, and winked at me.

"Your secret's safe with me. And thanks again for the ride." I took my bags out of the rear.

"Not a thing to it. Sorry about your friend, sweetie. Hope you manage to have a nice homecoming anyway."

With another sexy wink and a peal of rubber she vanished in a red blur. I waited until the Mustang was out of sight, then walked out of the courtyard. I'd hardly need a mechanic to put gas in the tank. I'd take care of it myself later — I even keep an old gasoline can in the back of the car — but first I thought I'd take a walk around to try and regain my bearings and get a good whiff of the town where I'd grown up. Twenty years is a long time to be away, after all.

A nice homecoming.

Somehow, I don't think so.

The far end of Industry Street had been nothing but fields and forest when I knew it, and a narrow canal with the rusty wreck of an ancient Model-T at which the kids all hurled empty pop bottles. I recalled the time when some big city developer proposed building an "out of town" supermarket on the site, but the good citizens didn't like the idea, thought it would be bad for local businesses and the environment. The town council voted the plan down unanimously.

Dueling Wal-Mart and Barnes & Noble Superstores stood on opposite sides of the road now.

I walked on, past a panoply of near-identical mini-malls that would have done the San Fernando Valley proud. Clearly, the current population of Ideaville need never go in want of low-calorie frozen yogurt or blueberry bagels or one-hour photo processing (with double prints).

I never even ate a bagel when I was a kid, at least not until I ran away. (And bialies: forget about it!) There'd been two delis in town, sure, but you were about as likely to come across a bagel and lox as you were a Maori warrior. The Steins were the only Jewish family that we knew, and while Mr. Stein was a respected accountant, Mrs. Stein was famous in three counties for her Christmas ham and her ambrosia salad. Assimilation city!

Farther on, the new shopping nirvana mercifully gave way to a patch of green. I felt a rising
surge of hope that perhaps the main part of town
had been spared the ravages of concrete commercialism. Even the sidewalk petered out and I had
to walk along a neatly manicured grass verge. I
followed the narrowing stretch of green around a
bend, the cars whizzing past, the odd driver
scowling ferociously at the sight of an impudent
pedestrian. *Very* California. I suddenly realized
that I trod nothing less than Dead Man's Curve —
named after a carload of teens who crashed their
Corvair speeding around it about the time that I
was born, back when my father was still riding a
patrol car. Like all the kids, Sandy and I used to
race our bicycles out this way, daring each other
to see how fast we could take the curve and risk a
dead man's fate. My mom would have waxed
wroth if she'd known, and pathetically, it was
probably as rebellious an act as I ever engaged in.

On the other side of the bend, the anticipated
clover field where that legendary Corvair had
come to its fiery rest had been transformed into
an immense parking lot, and behind that stood a
hideous mirrored-glass office complex. It looked
like something built from a Girder & Panel set,
an architectural carbuncle on the green of the
land. The whole site was fenced off, though a
smattering of tiny white flowers, like Baby's
Breath, had been planted along the border in a
meager attempt at landscaping. There wasn't
even room to walk safely between the flower beds
and the road, so I dashed across the traffic to the
other side to continue my stroll. A steady stream

of cars came and went by way of the manned gate. The sign informed me that this was the head-quarters of Black X Software.

I felt my heart skip a beat.

On up Industry Street, I recognized nothing at all. The mom-and-pop storefronts of my youth had all given way to the familiar franchise names that litter main streets everywhere, offering the comfort of the dull, the easy, the familiar and monstrously corporate. A Vision Express had replaced Copper's E-Z Eyes Optometry. Old Mr. Copper had, himself, been cross-eyed, but that was half his charm. A Foot Locker, boasting three hundred different kinds of sneakers, stood on the site of Frankly Footwear, where my mom used to take me to buy PF Flyers at the start of every school year. (I counted no less than six "athletic shoe" shops on my wander through town.) The National Bank was now a Citibank. There used to only be four banks in town all told; I'd already passed more Citibank ATMs than that.

I remembered the one-armed security guard who used to work in the National, who likely couldn't have tied his own shoes (I suppose he must have worn loafers), much less stopped a rob-bery; for some reason the flap of the empty sleeve pinned to the shoulder of his neatly pressed uni-form used to terrify me when I was a little boy. At the peak of my investigative "career," and with Sandy's help, I helped to catch a no-good villain who had robbed the bank. The one-armed guard smiled and patted my head on the day of the award ceremony. (I got a certificate and a stack of

penny rolls — *empty* penny rolls — and was over-
joyed. What a bunch of cheapskates they were;
what an *asshole* I was.) I never admitted to anyone that the guard frightened me even then. Of
course, he was also the only black man I knew,
and I never did solve the mystery of where in
town he lived. Or what, exactly, had happened to
his arm.

The ubiquitous commercialism that had
changed the face of my old town shouldn't have
surprised me; there are probably few places left
in America that don't look largely the same these
days, that retain any sense of character or charm
not officially sanctioned by the multinational
behemoths who seem to rule the world under a
bewildering assortment of brand names and
trademarks. But beyond the boring storefronts
that now make up Anytown, USA, I saw, too, the
signs of the cyber-boom that had made Ideaville
"special," even in these post-bubble days: the software dealers and hardware merchants; the
glassy-eyed teens in YellowHat T-shirts stum-
bling out of gaudy VR arcades promising thrills
unseen in life as we know it; the faux art galleries
with their "limited edition" prints, the gadget
shops and Sharper Image stores hawking genuine retro lava lamps and twenty-first century X-
ray specs and all manner of gewgaw and doo-dad
that no one can figure exactly what the hell
they're supposed to gew or doo, but without which
we are supposedly unable to endure.

And patisserie after boulangerie after coffee
bar after fern-riddled café. Okay, I appreciate a

caffeine rush as much as the next Joe, but jumping Jesus on the java-jive, how much latte can
anyone drink?

As I approached Fleet Street, I could see the
clock tower of City Hall looming in front of me,
and I froze. I didn't think I was quite up to walking past there just yet. You never know exactly
who you might run into.

I walked up Pinkwater Avenue instead, tried
not get depressed by the enormous Blockbuster
Video that stood where a row of stores, including
the old taxidermy shop, used to be. Mr. Goldoni,
the Tony Perkins-dude who owned the place, once
gave me a stuffed vole for helping him nail a
shoplifter, but my mom made me throw it away
because she said it was infested. I offered to buy
a flea-collar for it, but she just wouldn't have it in
the house. My old pal Dink used to haunt the
alleyway in back of the store hoping to find discarded animal bits among the rubbish. Dink used
to collect "dead stuff." What a strange little fucker
Dink was; I wonder whatever became of him?

I walked around the corner to glance down
the alley — just for old times' sake — but as I
approached the entrance I jumped back when, as
if summoned by the memory of Dink's collection,
a little dog came running out carrying a human
hand in its mouth. As the mangy terrier emerged
unto the sunlight, I saw that it was only a plastic hand, off a mannequin perhaps. A short fat
man in the alley called out, "Jimbo. Yo, Jimbo!"
and the dog scurried back toward its master. It
left the hand at my feet, but I turned and walked
away.

Pinkwater Avenue terminated at the entrance to the park. The park had always been known as "the park;" it had no official name so far as I can remember. It was the only official park in town, and had a bandstand and a big statue of Abraham Lincoln in the center square to prove it. It was one of the two places kids went to play ball; the other was the field behind the school. You either went to "the park" or "the field," so your mom always knew where to find you.

A bronze plaque announced:

Benjamin Blackwell Sr. Memorial Park
(www.bbsmp.com)
Administered by
the Ideaville Parks Corporation
a Blackwell Unlimited Public Service Venture

I walked on up the path. A few young mothers smoked and gossiped while they watched their kids play on the swings and jungle gym, and the odd senior citizen sat reading the local paper, but it all felt very . . . sterile, somehow. The park seemed more paved over and fenced-off than I remembered. There were Keep Off The Grass signs posted all over, for Christ's sake — what the hell kind of park is it where you can't walk on the grass? I didn't even see any pigeons for the old folks to throw stale bread at.

I followed the path past the statue of our sixteenth president — at least that hadn't changed — but the bandstand had been torn down. The little duck pond was still there, too, so I went to take a closer look. I probably shouldn't have been surprised by the warnings not to feed the water fowl. Apparently, the ducks were on a strict, gluten-free diet.

The balloon-man used to stake out a prime spot by the pond on nice days. He sold his balloons for a dime each or three for a quarter, and if he liked you (and he liked *all* the kids with quarters in their pockets) he'd pull a couple of those special long balloons out of his pocket and twist them into the shape of a giraffe or dog for you. I wanted to believe that the balloon man might somehow have survived, even if the balloons weren't still three-for-a-quarter. I looked around for him in hope.

All I saw was a cappuccino and biscotti stand.

I made my way through the park and out again by way of the Rocky Beach Road exit. I don't know how many times I must have walked down Rocky Beach Road on my way home from playing ball. Given that the nearest real beach was a good six hundred miles away (and wasn't rocky at that), I always wondered how the street came by its name. In my younger, junior G-man days I even tried to find out: I checked all the town records, did library research, talked to anybody and everybody who might possibly know.

No one did.

I think the reason I was so curious about the name was that there was something hopeful in it. The fact that someone would call a nothing street in a landlocked little town Rocky Beach Road suggested a stubborn optimism to me, a refusal to be bound by nature or fate. Whoever named it must have *wanted* to live on a beach road real bad, and wasn't about to let the fact of the great American Midwest stand in the way of that dream. I can remember, as a child, thinking that if I followed Rocky Beach Road far enough, for long enough, it would take me to a real beach and the ocean itself. The sea is a powerful and dreamy lure when you grow up in the middle of a big country. Walking home from the park down Rocky Beach Road every day helped feed those dreams in its tiny way. And as I walked its length again, I was pleased to see that the street, at least, hadn't changed much in the years I'd been away.

Of course, I'd long since been to the sea, seen the ocean, walked the beach and smelled the salt air.

It was a huge disappointment.

I felt a tightness in my chest as I turned the corner onto Shortall Street and saw Sandy's house. Her old house. Sandy's family had moved out when we were fifteen, when her dad came into some serious money, to a bigger house on the other side of town. The *Blackwell* side of town. The old house had been repainted, god knows how many times, and a whole extension had been built over where the garage once stood. The lawn and shrubs in front were all different and the post with the mailbox at the foot of the path had been taken away.

But it was that house on Shortall Street that I'd always associate with her.

We were in fifth grade when Sandy's family moved to town, and life was never to be the same afterward. It was in the backyard of this old Cape Cod that she taught me — tried patiently,

futilely, to teach me — how to throw a curveball.
It was in the basement, playing Trouble ("Pop-a-
matic pops the dice, pop a six and you move
twice. . ."), that the solution to the Case of the
Cursed Wishbone came to me, inspired by something as seemingly inconsequential as Sandy's
broken watch stem. It was in her perfect pink
bedroom, third door on the left at the top of the
stairs, with the dolls staring down from the shelf
and the window you could reach from the
branches of the big Dutch elm, that together we
solved the Riddle of the Stinks.

I felt a shudder go through me. I walked
briskly down the street, staring only at the
stretch of sidewalk directly in front of my eyes.

And so I found myself on Primrose Avenue
before I even knew it.

That's a lie; I knew exactly where I was going,
precisely what I was doing.

I always do, you see. I always know.

A small boy played by himself on the front
lawn. He sat on the edge of a patch of overturned
soil that would no doubt be a vibrant patch of
flowers come spring. A traffic jam of toy cars and
trucks surrounded him. He had a watering can
with which he had created a little lake in the dirt.
In the middle of the lake, nose down, was a battered car, with a toy soldier precariously perched
on the bumper. The little boy held a helicopter in
his hand, a bit of string dangling off the end, and
he swooped it back and forth over the disaster
scene, trying to lasso the soldier in an emergency
rescue maneuver straight out of some David Has-
selhoff TV show. He made swooshing noises as he

circled the chopper and little screams of "help me, help me" in the voice of the soldier. He tried about a dozen times to catch the soldier's head in the loop of string, but couldn't quite snag it. Finally, he put the helicopter down, used both hands to tie the string around the plastic figure, then picked up the chopper again.

The soldier slid out of the loop and plopped head-first into the lake.

"Dickwad," the kid cursed. He screwed the soldier deeper into the muddy water, then stomped on it.

"That's not very nice," I said. He spun around and gawped up at me, open-mouthed. He was missing two teeth. I made him for about seven. "Besides, you cheated."

"Didn't," the kid muttered, but even he wasn't convinced.

"Shouldn't you be in school?"

"I'm sick," he said. And blew a big wad of snot out his nose to prove it.

I took a good look around. It was amazing, eerie even, how little the old place had changed. New windows and aluminum siding, sure, and some different plants set around the reland-scaped garden. The little apple tree, smaller than me, that I'd helped my mom plant was big enough now for this kid to climb. But the house, the street, didn't look any smaller to me. According to the clichés it's supposed to. In spite of all the hideous changes to Ideaville, it hardly looked different at all. The tightness in my chest wound-up another notch.

"Who are *you*?" the kid asked.

I ignored him and walked across the lawn. The kid followed me, helicopter still in hand. The garage at the side of the house — my old "office" — had been spruced up a bit, but even it looked the same. I wondered if the roof still leaked when it rained; if it smelled of turpentine inside.

"Do you know my pop?" the kid said.

I went around the side of the garage and scanned the rows of bricks. I couldn't be sure, but it didn't look as if it had been remortared anytime recently. I counted up from the bottom and across from the left, then got down on my haunches.

"Whatcha doing?"

The brick didn't budge. I counted a second time, saw I'd been one row off. I touched the brick and, sure enough, felt a hint of give.

"Do you like treasures?" I asked the kid.

His eyes went wide. He nodded his head ferociously. What kid doesn't?

"Can you keep a secret?"

Another nod.

"Cross your heart, hope to die, go and spit in your mother's eye?"

The kid put down the toy and crossed his heart.

I pulled at the brick. It stuck at first, but after a few good wiggles it slipped out. A dozen black beetles scurried out after it.

"Eeewwwwww," the kid said. "Cool."

I let the remaining bugs scuttle off, rolled up my sleeve and stuck my hand in the gap. It was kind of slimy in there — ancient insect burial grounds often are — but I could feel the tiny bit of cold metal. Gripping it between two fingertips,

I eased the old skate key out of its hidey-hole. It had once belonged to Sandy. She gave it to me long ago, before . . . it all went wrong. As a keepsake, I suppose. And in my own curious way, I *had* kept it. I almost wanted to cry.

The key was rusty and black now. I held it in my palm and showed it to my little buddy.

"Wo-o-o-ow. How'd you know that was there?"

I know lots of things, I wanted to say. Too many fucking things.

"I once saw it on a treasure map," I told him.

"What's it for?"

I held the key out to him. He reached for it, then hesitated, looking up at me. I could see the memory of his mom saying "Never take anything from strangers" flash across his features. I nodded at him, smiled, and he grabbed the key. Kids.

"It's for a treasure, of course." And that was the truth. "But you'll have to find *that* for yourself."

"What the hell are you doing?"

A burly, angry looking man in a stained jogging suit came up behind us. Pop, I presumed. He quickly stepped in front of the little boy, who was still admiring the key, in a manifestly protective manner. He saw the gap in the garage wall where I'd removed the brick.

"What the fuck you doing to my house?"

"Nothing," I said. "I was just . . ." How the hell could I explain? I should have, I know, but I found I suddenly didn't have the energy. The long drive, the walk around town — the sheer psychic strain of revisiting the past — had sucked most of the life out of me. "Nothing," I repeated.

"Get the hell off my property. What the fuck you doing with my kid?" He pulled his son out from behind him. A little harshly, I thought. "Did this man touch you? Did he do anything to you, go near your pee-pee? Tell me now."

The kid looked scared, but shook his head. The key was invisible in his closed fist. His father hadn't noticed it.

"Get inside," the father said. The kid obliged. But with his old man still watching me, he held up the key and nodded before disappearing around the side of the garage.

"Get the fuck out of here, you sonuvabitch."

I held my hands up, palms out. "No harm intended, pal. No harm at all."

"Walk. Now. Before I call the cops." The man took a step toward me, pointed toward the house and lowered his voice. "Or I'll get my goddamn shotgun and blow your baby-raping head off."

I could take a hint. I made for the sidewalk.

The happy owner of my childhood home watched me depart very carefully. When I stopped to take a final, wistful look at the place, he took another menacing step toward me. I started walking.

A nice homecoming? Somehow, I didn't think so.

How did I know?

II. The Little Sister

Hard to believe, but they'd opened a Sheraton in town. One of those big, ugly jobbers with the glass elevators that scamper up and down the outside like squirrels on a nut tree, and a conference center with three bars on different levels so they can let the hookers work one and still make out like the joint's got a touch of class. There was a Ramada and a Holiday Inn, two Best Westerns, a Comfort Inn, a Days Inn, a Quality Inn and out past Cherry's hospital, a Motel Six — damn, you know they really do leave the light on. And there must have been a good half-dozen Motel Six wannabes, too: cheap little prefab nightmares with stripped-down rooms and swimming pools no bigger than the bathtubs. Cable, too.

None of them felt quite right for me.

The Anchor Inn stood where I remembered it, just the other side of the railroad station, in what used to be as wrong a side of the tracks as existed in the town's and my younger days. I cracked a case there once. That is: *we* did. Me and Sandy. A case so simple a blind man could have seen the solution. Though, of course, my dad never did.

Or so I'd thought.

The hotel hadn't changed much over the years, though the neighborhood around it had perked up. Where there had been a messy salvage yard and an Earl Scheib $99.95, they'd built a Price

Club warehouse. The old bar next to the hotel that had no name, just a buzzing neon sign in the window that flashed BAR — like some generic can marked 'Beans' — had given way to a mock-Irish cyber-pub called Happy Hollister's, with unconvincing sawdust spilling out the front door, a dozen T1 Internet connections, and "real" Irish stout on tap. Uh-huh.

The pool hall across the street was, at least, still a pool hall. Way back when, it had been the hangout for a pack of local greasers who called themselves the Lions. They were a "gang" who were a few years older than me and were serious enough about juvenile delinquency (jeez, does anybody even use that phrase anymore? Other than me, I mean?) that even I knew better than to tangle with them. Of course, in the modern context of Crips and Bloods, with their Glocks and hookers and Colombian coke connections, the Lions' zip-guns seem as quaint as powder horns and muskets. I shook my head as I peered through the pool hall's smoky windows, marveling at all the fancy neon and chrome shining inside. Where once you wouldn't have dared walk into the place without a knuckle-duster or switchblade in your pocket, now they had valet parking and ladies' night every Thursday. It was all a bit hard to believe until I wandered over to a work site just past the hotel and saw the signs promoting *Old Ideaville*, courtesy of BU Construction (a Blackwell Unlimited company, natch). A community redevelopment project promising to bring me "the past through tomorrow."

I'd almost rather have the real thing.

The Anchor itself had been spruced up – some paint here, a new awning there — but remained shabby-looking enough to strike me as more old Ideaville than "Old Ideaville." It had been the closest thing the town had to a flophouse, and while it had definitely come up in the world, I don't reckon the manager at Motel Six, never mind the Sheraton, was sweating the competition. The hotel still had a revolving door in front, and same as it ever was, it still spun around the wrong way, as if the place sat in the southern hemisphere where toilets flush widdershins and winter is summer. The lobby looked like it might have been redecorated some time in recent memory, but the furniture was vintage Salvation Army. Though it wouldn't half surprise me if there were crazies out there who collect the stuff, like comic books or baseball cards or beanie babies. (Can *anyone* help me with that one?) There was a faint underscent of smoke — part tobacco, part failed arson — lingering about the lobby. No Smoking signs were plastered across the walls, though most of them had cigarette burns mock-punctuating the injunction. An old geezer sat in one of the big lobby armchairs, nose buried in a newspaper. I caught him peering around the edges of his *Daily Herald* at me, but didn't manage much of a look at him. Old people, babies and sitcom stars all look the same anyway.

I dropped my bags down in front of the reception desk. No one at home. A big old-fashioned mail rack took up most of the wall behind the desk and keys dangled from just about every slot. If Ideaville was booming, the Anchor didn't appear

to be sharing in the good times. I rang the bell for
service, like the little sign instructed, and waited,
but no one appeared. I rang it again, then a third
time until a muffled voice from somewhere
shouted something I couldn't make out, and I figured they'd be along soon enough.

I browsed through a stack of tourist
brochures sloppily stuffed into a wobbly metal
rack on the counter. They mostly promoted the
same pathetic "attractions" that can be found
just about anywhere: a local doll museum, a bird
park where you can get your picture taken with
a parrot shitting on your head, a would-be his-
toric manse that Abraham Lincoln once walked
past on his way to the hat store. And guided
tours of all three of the town's software giants:
Black X, YellowHat, and Los Bros. That must be
a thrill; what could there be to see? A bunch of
nerdy, twentysomething coders in dirty, Dilbert
T-shirts chug-a-lugging Jolt Cola and ragging on
Bill Gates? Thank you, no.

"Help you?"

A little guy with a bit of a limp walked around
behind the desk. He wore a pair of high-tide, JC
Penney polyester pants and a plain white shirt
with a clip-on bow tie. He looked a bit . . . creased,
like he'd been sitting in a drawer somewhere and
gone out of fashion in the interim. He had big,
square, welfare glasses which should have had
thicker lenses than they did, because he had an
ashen, Coke bottle-bottom complexion. Not to
mention a nasty facial tic. A tag on his pocket
identified him as D. Sturdy.

"Got a room?" I asked.

He actually seemed to think about it as he eyed me up. He frowned — and twitched — as he noted my computer case.

"We ain't hardwired. N-O."

"Beg pardon?"

"The hotel. She ain't hardwired. Gonna need a modem if you want to get on the Net. M-O-D-E-M."

"That's okay," I said. What the fuck was wrong with this guy?

"Most the other places in town are wired right on into BlackNet proper. Not us, though. Owner says N-O, he won't have it. Lots of people expect hardwired these days. They check in, find it ain't hardwired, check right back out. O-U-T exclamation point! Lots of paperwork for no damn good reason. Ink, too. Makes me mad. Just so's you know."

"I'm just looking for some clean sheets and a nice view."

That got him twitching.

"Can't speak for the view. Subjective, don't you see. Don't like to presume. P-R-E-S-U-M-E. Sheets are clean, though. I guarantee."

"C-L-E-A-N," I tried.

"That's the way we spell it," he said with a big smile. I think I made a friend. "Sign yourself in, why don't you."

I filled out the registration card. I never put my real name down, though I don't know why. Some kind of perverse anarchist streak, I suppose, left over from my hacker days. You can get away with it if you don't pay by credit card. Of course, in a place like the Anchor, they probably wouldn't even care about that.

"Mr. Peter Collinson," the clerk read.

"That's my name, don't wear it out."

D. Sturdy seemed to find that inordinately amusing. I sort of suspected he might. Probably thought squirting flowers and garlic gum were the height of wit.

"Well, let's see what we got for you."

He ran his finger back and forth across the mailboxes, but I interrupted him.

"How's about number 214?" I asked. The key was in the slot.

"Heh? Ain't much of a view. N-O, sir."

"That's all right. It's got . . . sentimental value to me."

"You stay here before?" he asked. With perfectly reasonable suspicion.

"Wouldn't consider anyplace else in Ideaville."

"Huh," he replied. But I paid him in cash so he handed me the key. He started to show me up to the room, but I told him I remembered the way.

"Some things you never forget," I said.

"Ain't that just the truth, Mr. Collinson. T-R-O-T-H."

He twitched at me again, so I gave him a reassuring smile. I picked up my gear and crossed the lobby toward the stairs.

"Pssst."

The old guy in the chair had lowered his paper and was gesturing at me. I walked over to where he was sitting.

"Hey there, sonny," he said. "The spelling bee still around, or is he gone?"

I glanced back toward the desk, but the clerk had disappeared back to whatever planet it was he had come from.

"No, all clear," I said.

"Phew," he sighed. "That boy makes me nervous sometimes. If you ask me he's F-U-C-Ked in the head. And I do mean *goofy*."

The old man watched me closely, but when I laughed he laughed along with me.

"Yeah," I said. "And he doesn't spell so good either."

"Awww, don't tell him. It'd break his heart."

"I think I can keep it to myself."

The old man was a queer looking duck. He had strong, angular features that had melted some with age, like a cubist portrait left out in the sun. The edges of his chin had gone to putty flab, but the nose could have cut plate glass. He had only thin wisps of hair on his square head, though the little that was left was so dark and deep a black that I could only think Grecian Formula. His eyes were almond slits with little pips of black that should have been cold as a raven's, but which registered a keen intellect within. His arthritic hands, I saw, shook with the effects of moderate Parkinson's. Or maybe it was from the weight of the enormous watch he wore on his left wrist: some godawful, red LED thing that should have stopped working in the seventies. Probably about the same time he had.

"Checking in?"

I nodded.

"Here on business?"

"Something like that," I said.

The old man's eyes went a little soft, like his chin. "None of my affair," he muttered, fluttering his paper. "Silly old men don't always know their place no more."

I felt kind of bad at that, though I don't know why.

"Actually, I'm here to attend a funeral," I explained.

He closed the paper. "Aw, hell, sonny. I'm sorry. That's what I get for sticking my beak" — he tapped that massive schnoz — "where it don't rightly fit. I do apologize."

"Forget it," I said. I pointed at a stack of papers on the coffee table in front of him. "Those for anyone?"

"For the hotel's many guests. Help yourself," he said, with a sweeping gesture.

I started to tuck a paper under my arm, then saw the date on the front page. "This is yesterday's news," I said.

The old man picked up his copy and began reading again. "So am I, sonny," he muttered. "So am I."

The room was Spartan, but my B-U-D-D-Y Mr. Sturdy was true to his peculiar word, because it was cleaner than I had any right to expect. Someone had even left a little chocolate mint atop the pillow on the queen-size bed. I reckoned it might have been there a while, though, because the chocolate had melted and rehardened, leaving a suggestive brown skid-mark on the starched white pillowcase. I threw the mint away and flipped the pillow over.

There were lots of things I *could* do now that I'd arrived; certainly a fair number of things I *should* do. But none of them felt too appealing at that moment. I didn't have much in my bag, but

I unpacked it anyway, just to waste a little time. I set my toothbrush and razor and soap out on the bathroom counter just the way I like them to be, and I had a wash. I stared at myself in the bathroom mirror for as long as I could bear the sight.

So that killed another ten seconds.

I grabbed up the newspaper and plunked myself down on the bed. It let out a hearty squeak and the headboard smacked into the wall, the way a cheap hotel bed should. Shame, really, that there were no neighbors to annoy with the noise, and no action anticipated during my stay to set the bed to any truly worthwhile squeaking. Not even a Magic Fingers.

The *Ideaville Herald* had gone from weekly tabloid to daily broadsheet, with a slick, *USA Today* look that I found hard to reconcile with the old bird-cage liner that used to report nothing more exciting than the latest bake sale, lost dog or PTA meeting. The front page even offered color photos and international news. (Well, Canada . . .) When I was a kid, the townsfolk would have regarded an out-of-state item as madly exotic, and foreign news as nothing short of commie propaganda. I was reassured, however, upon seeing that local news dominated the bulk of the paper beginning with page three. You can develop the city out of the hick town, but you can't take the hick town out of the city.

"WAR IN IDEAVILLE?" read the Metro headline. The story detailed a rumor that YellowHat Software was the target of a hostile takeover bid. It seemed that both Black X and Los Bros had their sights set on the smaller company and shares were being bought up by unknown investors. A spokesman for YellowHat denied the story, insisting that the company was determined to stay independent and would "go to war" if that's what it took. Also interviewed were the Robustos, the gaming genius siblings who are and who run Los Bros.

"We'll eat their guts for lunch," José told the paper.

"Hold the mayo," brother Francisco added.

But what really caught my attention was the photograph that accompanied the article: a good quarter of the page — almost as much space as the article itself — was taken up by a very slick picture of my ancient nemesis and the bane of my life, Ben X. Blackwell.

The Roach.

The paper didn't call him *Roach* Blackwell, of course, which was no surprise. After all, he'd come a long way from the rotten-to-the-core kid who bullied smaller children out of their lunch money, or tried to sell phony treasure maps to gullible if romantic dreamers, or who ran any other petty scam he and his halfwit pals could come up with. No, he was CEO and head of operations for Black X Software, the big boys on Ideaville's virtual block.

But he still had those beady little eyes and thin, weasel lips, and the bushy eyebrows that met in the middle. He still had the look of a reptilian predator behind that sharpened PR smile.

He still looked like a complete and utter shit.

And to me, he'd always be Roach.

I was puzzled about the prominence of Roach's picture — there was only a brief, entirely superfluous quote from him in the story — until it occurred to me to skip to the *Herald's* masthead, where I saw that the paper was a wholly owned subsidiary of Blackwell Unlimited.

Ideaville was Roach's town, through and through; the once and future king. I'd known that coming in, but now it was hitting home. *Literally* hitting home.

For a minute I thought I might be sick. In the end, I just turned the page.

And there she was: Sandy.

They trusted me.

Everyone did. Everyone knew I was the best behaved, the smartest, the most straight arrow, wouldn't-couldn't-never-tell-a-lie, reliable, god-don't-you-wish-yours-were-like-that-Christ-that'll-be-the-day kid in town.

I'd pass the bake shop on Fleet Street and Mrs. Harold would hail me to mind the counter while she dashed about running her errands. She knew she could trust me not to filch a black-and-white, much less whatever money might be in the register.

Or Mr. Muckle, the blind man, who'd trust no one but me to look after his rare tropical fish when he needed to go away for his "therapy."

Or even Principal Atelier — Atelier the Hun as he was more commonly known — who never so much as asked to see my hall pass if he saw me in the school corridors during class period. Because no way would I be out of class without permission, loafing or idling or up to no good. No way, no how, take it to the bank, make your deposit and don't forget your free Christmas calendar.

Or my dad, the Chief of Police, who took his son, from the age of ten, to crime scenes to help him solve the difficult cases. A man who trusted a kid who read encyclopedias instead of comic books, who collected FBI wanted posters instead of baseball cards, who furtively and nervously crept into the attic to sneak looks at copies of his old man's law enforcement journals instead of his *Playboys*, to find the answers to puzzles that even he — the highest legal authority for miles around — couldn't cope with.

So why shouldn't Sandy's parents have trusted me? Even at the age of fourteen, with a dick that stiffened when the wind blew and hormones pumping like the cylinders on a Formula One race car, they trusted me to be alone with their beautiful, blooming, holy-shit-she's-got-tits teenaged daughter.

Because they were quite right to do so. There was nothing at all to fear from true blue young me. Poor, poor, pitiful me.

Sandy, of course, was another story.

It was Fourth of July weekend: just the start of summer. Sandy's dad's silk-screen business was just starting to take off, and he'd used some of those newfound financial rewards to buy a small bungalow out on Blue Moon Lake. The lake was a resort spot about a hundred miles to the north: "the country" even to people like us who lived in a town that real city folk would laughingly dismiss as Hicksville, USA. The bungalow was a two-bedroom place — Sandy was an only child, so what more did they need? — but they bought a Castro convertible sofa for the "fun" room (my god, how innocent a time must that have been to foster such language!), and I'd been cordially invited to enjoy its springy comforts for the big holiday weekend.

Sandy and I had been best buddies — not to mention "business associates" in the detective game — since we were ten, and not even the perils of puberty had come between us, as it had in most every other boy-girl childhood friendship I could recall. She'd always been a bit taller than me, but Sandy was still like a kid sister more than anything else. A *good* little sister. I'd noticed her recent . . . development, sure, and maybe I even had my vague fantasies — okay, I definitely *did* have fantasies, and they weren't remotely vague — but we were still friends. *Best* friends.

My dad didn't get a lot of time off from his duties, though mom was always nagging him about it, and we certainly couldn't have afforded the luxury of Blue Moon Lake even if he did. Not on a cop's lowly salary (wink, wink, nudge, nudge, ha, ha). Spending the weekend at the lake meant missing some of the big festivities in town — the custard pie-eating contest, the jam-jamboree, the fireworks show over Mile End Creek — and I was reluctant to leave my dad on his own to deal with crime for the whole weekend, but Sandy and her mom were spending the entire summer at the lake, and who knew if I'd get another chance to see her? Her dad went up for weekends, so I could ride along with him. I was still hesitant, worrying

about potentially rampant Independence Day
hooliganism (just the year before I'd uncovered
and prevented a plot by Roach and his thuggish
pals to dump an entire crate of instant iced tea
into the park fountain), but my dad insisted he
could hold the fort.

"Go and have fun with *Sandy*," he'd said, with
a wink and just the slightest, lascivious lilt in his
voice. Then added: "Just don't do anything I
wouldn't do."

"Of course not," I'd told him. Why would I?
What could he mean?

Is it to laugh, or what?

It was on a Friday that I rode up with Sandy's
dad. He came and picked me up in the afternoon,
having left work early. He still had his suit on,
but loosened his tie and undid the top couple of
buttons on his white oxford shirt. He put my bag
in the trunk of his big, yellow Ford LTD, gave me
an avuncular slap on the back and we were off.
He was a great storyteller, Sandy's dad, and kept
up a running monologue for most of the drive. I
remember laughing and howling and feeling
about as good as you can feel; school was months
away, a holiday weekend was here, and I was off
to spend it with my best friend in the world. What
could be better? We even stopped along the way at
the Red Roost Rest for a burger and fries, his
treat (though my mom had slipped me a five dollar bill for the weekend). He gulped down a beer
with his food — cold brewed Ballantine Ale: ah,
them, rings! — even offering me a slug on the sly,
but I wouldn't have any of it. I happily slurped my
Cherry Coke through the rainbow bendy straw.

As it turned out, Sandy's mom had dinner waiting for us when we got to the lake. Her dad told her that we were famished and gave me a big wink. I went along with it, forcing down a plate of meat-loaf and instant mashed potatoes on top of my burger. Sandy's mom couldn't believe I didn't want any cherry pie for desert, but I simply couldn't find the room. Sandy looked surprised, too, but her pop gave me another, knowing wink which almost made me feel good enough to be hungry all over again.

We all took a long walk along the lakefront after dinner, then played a few hands of casino back at the bungalow. Sandy's mom announced lights out at ten thirty. There was no door on my "fun" room and only the one bathroom, so I had to change into my pajamas in there. Sandy had washed up first and was getting herself a glass of water when she saw me coming out of the bathroom. She gave me a long, funny look of a type she'd never given me before, and I felt myself flush. I glanced down to make sure everything that should be fastened was. Sandy's mom was in the kitchen, too, and I saw a worried expression pass across her face, but as she stared at me — it was *me,* for chrissakes — the concern dissolved into a maternal smile and she turned out the light.

I lay in bed, but couldn't fall asleep. Though it was cool by the lake, with a nighttime breeze that billowed the curtains and allowed slivers of bright moonlight to flicker in, I felt hot beneath the covers. Not on account of the temperature outside, but a raging hard-on that raised the Ringling Brothers big top in my pyjama bottoms. I tried not to touch myself, or even move too much, hoping it would go away on its own, fearful that Sandy's mom or dad would come back out of their room, having forgotten something essential — a pack of cards, a thermos flask, a lacrosse stick, who knew? — that they stored in the fun room. *Fun*, hah! This was goddamned torture.

What I really wanted, of course, was to spank the monkey, flog the dolphin, slam the salami and choke that chicken. God how I wanted to jerk off. Just slip into the bathroom and spurt into the toilet quick as I could (and that was pretty damn quick). I thought about it; measured the distance I'd have to cover, calculated my minimum exposure time on the run.

It beckoned to me, white whale that it was, to get in there and play with it just a little. To imagine Sandy's sweet lips and . . . CHRIST!!! What was I thinking?

I heard a door open.

You'd think the panic would have sent my balls rolling up into my abdomen. But it just made me harder.

The plip-plop of bare feet crossing the linoleum floor, getting louder as they approached, sent me scrambling for the covers which had slipped off the bed.

"Hey. You up?" Sandy whispered.

Up indeed! In my rush for the covers, my dick had popped out through the little gap that formed the casual fly of my pajama bottoms. Sandy would see my penis!

God, how exciting.

I just managed to cover my lower half as Sandy tiptoed into the room and sat down on the end of the mattress.

"Can't sleep?" she whispered.

"Umm," I said loudly, then caught myself. "No," I whispered back.

"Me, either."

It was pretty dark in there, but moonlight sifted through the billowing curtains with every zephyry puff of wind. Sandy was wearing her dad's white oxford shirt. The tails hung down to just above her knees, like a night dress, but she kept one more button open at the top than he had, so it revealed some of her milky shoulders.

And the tippy-tops of her breasts.

She must have seen me looking.

"What do you think?" she asked.

"Wha-ha," I stammered.

"It's my dad's," she said, perfectly innocently.

"What?"

"The shirt, silly. You were looking at it, weren't you?"

H-E-double hockey-sticks, I thought. "Oh. Yeah. Nice."

"I like to wear them after he does. I like the smell of him on it. It makes me feel safe in bed."

"Oh."

She grabbed at the open neck of the shirt with both hands to press it to her nose. But just as she did it, a breeze stirred the curtains, flooding the room with moonlight, and in that brief instant that the cotton fabric was away from her flesh, I saw the spherical wonder of her breasts in all their glory.

"I just love his smell," she said, the fleeting moment gone, though burned forever in my memory.

I so wanted to grab her. Reach over and kiss her and grab a fleshy mound of tit in each hand and . . .

I pulled the covers more tightly around me.

We sat in silence for a little while.

"Can't you sleep?" I finally asked.

I saw her shake her head. She slipped her nose out from inside the shirt and crossed her arms over that heavenly bosom.

"It's . . ."

She wouldn't finish the thought.

"What?" I asked.

She shook her head again.

"What?" I repeated. Still no response. Then a little too loudly, "Sandy, what?"

"Shhhh." She got up and tiptoed to the doorway to listen, then tiptoed back. "You won't laugh?"

"Of course not," I said.

"Promise?"

I crossed my heart.

Sandy stared down at the darkness of the floor. "It's them."

Roach was honest-to-god my first thought. He'd followed us here with his gang of nogoodnicks, the Aces! Followed us to . . . no, wait; that was crazy.

"Them? Them who?"

Even in silhouette I could see the girlish shrug of her shoulders, imagined Sandy rolling her eyes and twisting her lips as she always did when something — usually me — exasperated her.

"My *parents*."

"What about them?"

"They're . . . doing it."

"Doing what?" the smartest kid in town had to ask.

"You know . . . *it*."

They're solving crimes? I thought.

Then the ten-ton weight dropped.

"Oh," I said. And in the ensuing, highly charged silence between us, I could, indeed, hear a steady, rhythmic sound coming from the master bedroom. *Whump-squeak, whump-squeak, whump-squeak.*

"God, can you believe it? It's *so* embarrassing."

I'd long since learned to trust in my keenly honed senses and to believe in the evidence, however improbable, if it was undeniable in its materiality.

Whump-squeak, whump-squeak, whump-squeak.

It went on and on – how long could they do it, I wondered; how long were you *supposed* to do it, I worried – as Sandy and I sat there listening. I felt so hard, I thought my dick would burst right on through the covers like some monster from a horror flick. *Creature From the Fuzzy Pubic Region.*

Someone — I honestly couldn't say if it was her mom or dad — let out an orgasmic moan, and the *whump-squeak* finished. In the three-quarter darkness, Sandy and I exchanged a look.

And we both started to laugh.

I clamped a hand over my mouth, then bit down on my arm to stifle the noise. Sandy tried to hold it in, but had to bury her face in the mattress to drown the laughter.

The door to her parents' bedroom suddenly opened.

We weren't laughing anymore, as the sound of bare feet drew nearer. The kitchen light flicked on and Sandy did the only thing she could do: she crawled under the covers beside me.

"Hullo?" Sandy's mom called out softly. She came up to the door of the fun room and peered around inside. She wore a light cotton robe which, lit from behind, revealed the curves of her plump, naked body underneath. The fabric clung to some damp bits.

"Everything okay in there?" she asked.

"Fine," I managed to croak. "Just had a bad dream."

Sandy shifted beside me. I tried to cover the movement by flopping around on the bed, but it must have looked very odd. As I turned over, I brushed up against Sandy's bare leg. I was mortified as the snap on my fly gave way and my penis popped out, flopping across the back of Sandy's thigh. Mortified and excited beyond words. Sandy's mom took a long look in the darkness, then nodded. "It's okay, dear. Just go back to sleep. Do you want some warm milk?"

Only if it spurts from Sandy's tits, I thought.

"No thanks," I chirped.

She hesitated there another few seconds, than padded back to the kitchen and turned off the light. I listened for the sound of the bedroom door closing, but it didn't come. She must have been standing there in the kitchen, waiting and listening. Perhaps suspecting. I was breathing hard, desperate to control myself; certain — terrified — that at any second, with the slightest shift, I'd explode all over Sandy's leg. She had to know what that was rubbing up against her. I could hear her labored breaths, as well.

Finally, mercifully, Sandy's mom went back to the bedroom, and closed the door behind her. Sandy and I held our frozen pose for several minutes, until Sandy carefully slipped out from under the covers and rolled onto the floor with a muffled thud. She glanced back at me with an odd smile, but didn't say a word. I was certain she'd be so disgusted by my . . . rigidity, that she'd never want to talk to me again. I could barely look at her.

Sandy got to her feet, catlike, and tiptoed slowly out of the room. She paused in the doorway to look and listen. She took a half-step out, then whirled around and dashed back to the side of my bed. Before I knew what was happening, she bent over, kissed me hard on the lips, and ran back out. A few seconds later, I heard the click of her bedroom door closing.

I sat there in the renewed quiet, the breeze dancing with the curtain, the moonlight flickering like a silent movie across the room.

Sandy had kissed me. I had long dreamed of it, but never dared consider the possibility of it becoming real.

And her tits. I had even caught a glimpse of her tits.

Without thinking, I reached down and touched my now aching cock.

I exploded all over my pyjamas.

* * *

It was an old photograph in the paper. It had to be. She couldn't possibly still look — have looked — so young, that beautiful. There was no photo credit, but it definitely wasn't a professional shot. The framing wasn't quite right, and there was a hint of blur, as if Sandy was turning away from the camera. "Aw, shucks, don't take my picture," she used to say. She always hated it. "Least likely to be photographed, most likely to be remembered" was what it said about her in the high-school yearbook.

I know I could never forget.

The headline read: MEMORIAL FOR CRASH VICTIM. The story reported that Sandy's funeral service was scheduled for a few days hence at the Sobol & Sons Funeral Home, where the body lay for viewing. The article briefly summarized the events surrounding her death: a late-night, single-vehicle collision on the road to Wellsville. No seat belt. Catastrophic head injuries. Nothing anyone could have done. Tragic loss of a young life.

My stomach lurched just reading those awful words.

I wondered how it was that Sandy, much as I might have loved her, merited such attention in the paper. I knew that her adult life hadn't measured up to the vast promise of her youth. I may not have stuck around town, but that's not to say I didn't keep up with certain things — people and events — as best I could. The Net is great for that sort of thing. I knew that Sandy had . . . fallen. So far, in fact, that I couldn't believe that anyone would have cared about her death.

Then I saw that the eulogy was due to be delivered by none other than Mr. Benjamin X. Blackwell.

Perfect. The final kick in the teeth. He took her from me in life — along with everything else — and now the Roach would be the one to preside over her death.

There was no escaping him.

I should have known.

III. The Lady in the Lake

There are a lot of things I could have done —
should, no doubt, have done — that night:

I could have gone to visit my father; I had a
good idea where to find him.

I could have tried to look up my mother; I
knew *exactly* where she was.

I *should*, at the very least, have gone over to
the funeral home and paid my respects to Sandy.
That was, after all, what I'd come for.

But I didn't — couldn't — face a one of them.
Not even fetching my brave little car, though I
was starting to worry about it sitting alone out
there on the edge of town.

Instead, I pulled my laptop out of its case and
studied the phone situation. The Anchor not only
wasn't hardwired, it didn't even have modular
jacks. The phone cable zipped right into a hole in
the wall. I chuckled with sixties nostalgia, but
wasn't so pleased when it took me thirty minutes
to unscrew the wall plate and jerry-rig a connection for my modem. I checked my e-mail, deleted
the spam and saved the rest for later. A couple of
business opportunities, but I just wasn't in the
mood. I'd probably blow the deals by delaying
reply, but so what? There's always another hack
job coming down the virtual road.

I turned the machine off and stared at the

wall for a while. Sandy's picture looked up at me from the newspaper, her eyes seeming to follow me as I got off the bed and paced the small room. I went into the bathroom and studied myself in the mirror again. I didn't much like what I saw. I rarely do. I walked back out. I turned the newspaper over, but that felt like an offense to the dead, so I lay back on the bed and stared at her some more.

And I remembered the rest of what happened at the lake.

Independence Day — Saturday — passed like a dream. A few of the summer people on the lake threw a big Fourth of July bash, with a roast suckling pig, scads of grilled burgers and dogs and foil-wrapped corn on the cob, tubs of canned foamy A&W root beer and kegs of real Pabst Blue Ribbon, and croquet and badminton and lawn darts and games and good spirits that exist only on summer holidays recalled through the unfocused mist of times gone by. Sandy and I spent most of the day within a couple of feet of each other, but we never once touched, never so much as mentioned what had passed between us the night before. We played and laughed and stuffed our faces like fat, happy Americans celebrating our myth-laden heritage; we ooohed and ahhhed at the fireworks show on the lake and, exhausted, stumbled back to the cabin with Sandy's folks where we all went to bed and slept the sleep of the just, brave and free.

It was Sunday that changed my life forever.

Sunday was my last day at the lake. Sandy and her mom would be staying on, but I had to ride home with her dad in the evening. He needed to get back to his job for Monday morning, and I had detective work to do. My dad couldn't be expected to handle all the town's crime on his own.

We got up early and had a leisurely breakfast, along with a tug-o-war over who got dibs on the Sunday funnies. Sandy wanted to go out for a morning dip, but I wasn't in the mood. The truth is I was afraid to be alone with her out there. Sandy's new bathing suit was still damp from Saturday's fun in the sun, so she had to put on an old two-piece suit that had been left in the bungalow from the previous summer. The suit itself was a kid's suit and not all that revealing, but it was at least a size too small for her. Or rather she had grown two sizes too big for it.

Even Sandy's dad, who was nice but not the most clued-in guy on the continent, did a double-take when he saw Sandy in her old swimming costume. His eyes bulged out of his head like our pal Kenny Holt with the thyroid problems, and he actually started to choke on his English muffin. All those damned nooks and crannies. As he turned to get a drink of water from the kitchen, I saw the startled expression on his face — how rattled he really was. I can't know for certain, of course — and the man's dead now, stroked out on a commuter flight to Pittsburgh, so I couldn't ask him even if I had the nerve — but I'd bet cash money that he'd remember that as the moment when he first recognized that his little girl was no longer just his little girl.

"You're not going to let her go out wearing those postage stamps are you?" he asked his wife.

"Don't be a silly-billy. She's just a girl," she told him. He didn't look convinced. More credit to him.

Sandy tried to cajole me into coming along for the swim, stooping to the lowest form of blackmail.

"*Roach'd* do it," she teased.

It was the ultimate dare. A code we shared between us which was a polite, nice kid's way of saying: "C'mon, you fucking pussy."

I wanted to go for that swim. I wanted to get out on that lake alone with Sandy, dive under the cool, clear water and tear that tight suit from her glistening flesh with my teeth. I wanted to press myself against her, over her, *inside her*, and generate enough heat to steam the molecules of the lake around us with our fevered passion.

"Nah," I said. "Pass."

Sandy rolled her eyes, threw a towel over her shoulders and headed for the door.

"Remember, we're going over to the Appletons' for lunch," Sandy's mom called after her.

"Oh, ma, *we* don't have to go, do we?"

"I think the Appletons invited all of us to lunch," her mom chided. "They are our best neighbors here."

"But this is our last day together," Sandy moaned. I was still sitting at the kitchen table, reading the comics. Sandy came up behind me and dropped a hand on my shoulder. "We won't get to see each other again for *weeks*."

"I think the Appletons will survive without the

kids," Sandy's dad said. "I just wish I had a good excuse."

"You're awful," her mom clucked.

"Besides," her dad said, "Victor tells smutty stories."

I saw his eyes flick over his daughter's form again. I think he maybe shuddered, too. A thought must have occurred to him — a dirty thought — because his gaze shot over to me. I think in light of his recognition of his daughter's newfound . . . maturity, he considered whether I might be a Vic Appleton in waiting. I reckoned Sandy's dad would size up every male on the planet that way from here on out. I smiled my best Police Chief's son smile at him, and the hint of suspicion washed off his face. He practically shook his head at his own misplaced mistrust in me.

"Let the kids have their fun, I say." His wife still looked unsure. Sandy's mom was the type for whom a social slight was worse than a war crime. Concentration camp commanders had nothing on those who didn't use their salad forks.

"Please, please, please," Sandy whined.

"Oh, all right," her mom said. "But we'll probably be gone when you get back from your swim."

"I'll keep down . . . hold down the fort," I said.

"I won't be *too* long," Sandy promised.

And off she went.

I waited there at the kitchen table, pretending to read the paper, until Sandy's folks took off. It was weird sitting there, listening to someone else's parents' meaningless morning conversation — at least my mom and dad talked about impor-

tant stuff, like crime — but I couldn't get up for
fear that my woody would show. Even with Sandy
gone, I had a stiffy that just wouldn't quit. If
there'd been overtime for hard-ons, my dick
would have had the fattest paycheck in town.
Every time it started to ease off, I'd get a mental
flash of the way Sandy's bathing suit pinched the
top of her tanned thighs; the single strand of
pubic hair I detected poking out when she bent
over to grab her towel.

I thought about jerking off as soon as Sandy's
parents left for the Appletons, but I couldn't be
sure exactly when Sandy would get back. It
wouldn't take me very long, but I was torn
between the strain of holding back and the terror
of being caught by Sandy if she walked in.

So I read *Dondi* over and over, wishing — not
for the first time — that I was him. The kids in
the comics never have semen build-up worries.
Though these were the days before Lynda Barry.

After a while, the . . . pressure subsided.
Sandy took longer than I expected, and with her
parents gone, I could safely wander around the
bungalow. I could have gone through the stuff in
Sandy's parent's room, or flipped on the radio, or
made myself a float, or just flopped on the couch
and had a nap, or done any of the hundred things
any normal kid might have done.

I went to my overnight bag and began review-
ing my notes from a difficult case of suspected
fraud. I was up against another boy detective for
the fee, a weird little kid called Jupiter who'd just
moved to town. The only clue was a grizzled ticket
stub from a Mudhens game, which I had in my

possession. I'd been studying it all week, certain
that the answer was so obvious that I couldn't see
the forest for the trees. As I removed the ticket
from the glassine evidence envelope it was stored
in, and sat on the love seat to re-examine it, I
again became absorbed by the mystery.

I didn't even hear the squeak of the screen
door when Sandy came in. It wasn't until she
spoke that I registered her presence.

"Are they gone?"

"Huh?"

"My parents. Have they left for the Appletons'?"

Sandy's dark hair was still wet. She'd tried to
tuck it back behind her ears, but squiggly strands
sprang out like loose wires from the back of a
busted television. She kept running one hand
through her hair, to keep it from curling. A fat
drop of water dangled from the tip of her sun-
tanned nose.

"Yeah. They went a while ago."

"Thank *God*. They drive me crazy sometimes,
you know?"

The too-tight suit was wet, too, and it clung to
her form like fresh paint, revealing every supple
line and delicate, new curve. The water must
have been cold, because her nipples poked out
beneath the material like tiny rubies. And sprigs
of pubic hair graced the crease between her legs
like garlands of parsley on a steak dinner.

Between my legs something wicked definitely
wanted to come.

"Oh, gaaawwdd," she crooned, sitting down on
the love seat next to me. Her bare shoulder

rubbed against mine. "Are you still worrying about this stuff? You're supposed to be on vacation, you know? I mean, let's face it: Bobby Davis will survive even if Roach did cheat him out of seventy five cents."

She snatched the ticket out of my hand.

"Hey!" I complained. "Be careful with that." Christ, that was evidence she was handling.

Sandy rolled her eyes. She pretended to examine the ticket, then made like she was going to smush it up.

"Don't!" I cried.

"Jeez-louise. Don't you ever think about stuff besides solving cases?"

"Well, it's important. I hate to see Roach get away with anything."

I reached over to take the ticket back, but she switched it to her other hand and out of my reach. She waved it in the air, watching it flutter.

"Other things in life are important, too. Don't you think?"

I noticed then that she was breathing kind of hard, as if still out of breath from her swim. The suit gripped her a little more tightly, more revealingly with every sexy inhalation.

"Like what?" I said. I'd been looking at the swell of Sandy's chest and realized that she knew that was what I'd been doing. I felt a flush of embarrassment and she issued a little laugh.

"I can name a *couple* of things. At least."

She pretended to drop the ticket, then caught it in midair.

"Maybe you should just give me that and I'll put it away," I said.

"Why don't you just take it," she said.

And she laid the evidence across the tops of her breasts.

A black hole opened up somewhere near my duodenum. I couldn't breathe.

"Don't you *want* it?" she asked. She slunk back into the cushions, her arms at her sides. "It's a *big* case, after all . . ."

"C'mon, Sandy."

"*Come* on where? The ticket's right here." She flicked her gaze down at her chest, then up at me. "And it's yours for the taking."

I tried to swallow, but couldn't find any saliva. I think all the liquid in my body had drained into my feet. Sandy leaned back and the ticket slipped an inch farther down her chest, the edge balanced against one monstrously erect nipple.

A coldness washed over me. I breathed, opened-mouthed, but couldn't move any other muscle. I just stared at the ticket, at her breasts straining beneath the tight swim suit. There was no sound, no smell, no world beyond that couch: just me and Sandy and the ticket on her chest.

"Maybe it's too easy a challenge for the great detective," Sandy teased. "Maybe I should make it harder."

She plucked the ticket off her chest and dangled it before me. I reached for it, slowly, clumsily, like a big baby. Just as I was about to touch it, she snatched it away again, this time tucking it *under* her top. Only the very end poked out from her cleavage.

"Go for it, big boy."

I reached over, still moving oh-so slowly. I

could feel the heat wafting off her body before I touched her. My fingertips were millimeters from her breasts when she leaned forward, pressing a soft mound into my hand.

"Oh," I said. "Oh, my."

Sandy twisted back and forth, rubbing herself against my cupped palm. I felt the eraser-like nub of her stiff nipple through the thin fabric. I reached up and grabbed on for dear life with *both* hands.

"Oh, yes," she groaned.

I couldn't believe what was happening here, but neither could I dismiss the evidence of my eyes, what I clutched — and squeezed and kneaded like so much Play-Doh — in my own two sweaty palms. Sounds issued from between my lips which I couldn't identify; would not have known could be formed by human throat and tongue.

"Oh, my boy," Sandy hissed.

She reached behind her and unfastened her top. It fell away beneath my scrabbling fingers, revealing the glory of her naked breasts. Her perfect pink nipples were engorged, the brown aureole big almost as the mounds themselves.

I leaned over, my lips pursed in anticipation. Sandy smiled and lay back, closed her eyes and threw her arms over her head to provide unfettered access for my slavering tongue.

Then I noticed the ticket.

It had slipped directly between her tits, wedged on end in her cleavage, as if stuck there in partial payment for acts promised and unknown.

I leaned back, away from Sandy.

The demon's voice that raged in my head, sourced down below, was quieted as surely and swiftly as the hardness between my legs turned soft. I saw the evidence of the ticket. The evidence of what we were about to do, and the wrongness of the act. The betrayal of trust: of my father, the Chief of Police, and of my mother in whose eyes I was perfect and could do no wrong; of Sandy's parents, who left me alone with their blossoming, pubescent daughter with her brand new tits and her (I could only imagine) tight and hymenal cunt; of the teachers and storekeepers and towns-people who trusted and believed in and relied on me to be a paragon, a model, a *good* kid in a long-haired world where the mere idea of such a thing seemed an ever fading and distant possibility.

It wasn't right. It was as simple as that. If it were, the evidence of the ticket would not have affected me so.

Sandy opened her eyes.

"What's wrong?" she said.

I pointed down at the ticket.

She giggled when she saw where it had come to rest.

"*You* get it, tiger. Get it with your *teeth*."

I did get it. I reached down and grasped the edge between thumb and forefinger. As I did so, the very edge of my pinky brushed against the pliant contour of Sandy's hot breast: an ephemeral tangent of could-have-been ecstasy burned forever in my mind.

I stood up, holding the ticket.

"What are you doing?" Sandy asked.

I smoothed the ticket out and that's when it

hit me. I'd been staring at it for so long and not noticed, not realized.

"Hey!" Sandy yelled. She looked at me, then down at her exposed tits, then back at me. She cupped her tits in her hands, offering them again to me. I studied the ticket.

"This is a fake. Section C of Mudhen Park doesn't have a Row KK. It only goes up to JJ. Roach is pulling another fast one."

I held the ticket up for Sandy to see, though I couldn't meet her gaze. In that instant she saw exactly what was — and more essentially what was not — going to happen that afternoon. For a few seconds there were tears in her eyes. Tears which gave way to anger.

She stood up with enormous dignity and shook her head at me. I tried not to drop my gaze to her still-bared tits, but I couldn't help myself. She stood up straight and very deliberately allowed me to look for a moment — I was sure I'd never see them again — then she picked up her top and crossed her arms over her chest.

As she walked past me — she didn't storm, but walked slowly — she paused. In an oh-so-calm, but morgue-cold voice she said: "Roach would have done it." She took one step, then turned and pressed her lips to my ear, adding: "And maybe he will."

I was still standing there, the words bouncing around my head, when her parents came back two hours later.

I went out of the hotel to get a drink. The old dude was sitting in his spot in the lobby, though he'd swapped his newspaper for a book. Not that it much mattered, because his head was lolled back on the chair and he was snoring away. Drooling, too. Charming.

I took a wander past the pool hall, but a karaoke version of "Bad, Bad Leroy Brown" was blaring out through the open front door so I gave it the big pass. The Irish cyber-bar was too depressing even to contemplate: they were holding a Mosaic party, as part of their "Retro Web Browser Nights." I briefly considered a stroll back across the tracks into the center of town before deciding that a wine bar up the road called Dan Dunn's looked harmless enough, and might save me the torture of encountering any more old ghosts. I would have to face them sooner or later — like tomorrow — but felt I'd had my fill for a first night back in town.

I knew I'd walked into the right place when I heard Leonard Cohen crooning "I'm Your Man" on the juke box. In my current mood, what better musical card to be dealt than the Suicide King of rock and roll? The room was dark and quiet, sprinkled with couples who had the look of doomed and furtive assignation about them; the types who don't look up when anyone walks by, just slink deeper into the shadowy corners of their booths, hiding behind the umbrellas in their drinks and the shame in their hearts.

Been there, done that, taken the AIDS test afterward.

The actual bar was small, maybe half a dozen stools lined up neatly, all empty but one. The bartender was talking to his only customer, a not bad looking brunette, with big round glasses, a thin nose and fat ankles. As I grabbed a stool at the opposite end of the bar, the mixologist lifted a finger at me, and continued his conversation. I had no place to go.

On top of the bar, between the bowls of baldy Bavarian pretzels and beer nuts, was a laminated drinks list. There was a mess of imported beers and a pretty healthy looking selection of California wines, but it was the House Specials that intrigued me. They all had bizarre names and I'd never heard of a one of them: The Desert Island, The Heat Ray, The Ocean Floor, The Time Traveler, The Swamp Monster, The Bullfinch . . .

The descriptions weren't very helpful either; no mention of ingredients, just mood and atmosphere. The Voice From Space, for example, was characterized as "a solitary excursion into the depths of the unknown, with just a hint of cosmic consciousness."

But could you get it with a twist?

"Evening, partner," the bartender said. He wiped the already spotless bar top with a clean towel. "What can I do you for?"

"Interesting stuff," I said, tapping the list.

"I invented them all. That's what I do."

"Tell me, you sell a lot of Snitchers?"

"Now and again."

I read the short description aloud: "'Had Socrates no hemlock handy . . .'" I looked up at him.

"All down to your mood. What can I tell you?"

I glanced down the menu, reading out loud again: "'Everything you've lost; the life you live in dreams.'"

"Irene's Dream," he said. With a choke in his voice, I could have sworn.

"Any good?" I asked.

"I think it just might be your drink, friend."

"Bring it on, then."

I tried to make sense of what went into the drink — there was definitely some bitters; surprise, surprise — but the bartender was a whirlwind, a Dubonet dervish, and the bottles in the speed rack had no labels. In the end he put a highball glass down in front of me full of crystal clear liquid and ice, and a single drop of grenadine that floated slowly down the middle of the drink like a bloody tear.

Nick Cave took the baton from Lenny on the juke box: "People Ain't No Good." What a joint, what a town, what a night.

I took a sip of Irene's Dream. Just timing and the power of suggestion, I'm sure — Mr. Dunn should have been in advertising — but the drink's bittersweet taste set me thinking about Sandy again. I wanted to take another sip, but I pushed it away.

"Just bring me a beer."

The bartender nodded knowingly and obliged.

The woman at the other end of the bar was scribbling furiously in a small composition notebook with a green cover. Her glasses kept sliding down her nose as she wrote and she repeatedly shoved them back in place with the pinky finger of her left hand. She stopped to peer up at me a couple of times.

"What color would you say your eyes are?" she asked.

"I wouldn't. They're contacts."

She scribbled that down.

"Writing to Santa?" I asked. The Claus gambit had never worked for me before, but there's always a first time.

"Just making some notes."

I took the opportunity to sidle over a few stools, taking my beer, leaving Irene behind. "What for?"

She stopped and gave me a long hard look. "I'm a writer," she huffed, as if I'd asked what she used that hole in the middle of her face for.

Huh-boy I thought.

"So what are you writing?"

She finished her sentence and gently closed the book. "About what I see in town. Observations, moments. *People.*"

"You do this for fun or profit?"

She thought it over carefully. "Both, I suppose. Though I'm working on a piece for a magazine at the moment."

"Oh yeah?"

"About Ideaville and all that's been happening in the software business here. How it's managed to survive the bursting bubble. For *Spy* magazine."

"Huh! They still publish that?"

She sighed. "Not that anyone would know. But their money's green."

As I studied her more closely, I decided that her ankles weren't entirely fat. I could see them because she wore canvas deck shoes with no socks. And her eyes had just a bit of sparkle.

"Can I buy you a . . . ."

"Hey," a squeaky voice called. A little guy in a sweat suit stood half in-half out of the front door. "I got the motor running here. You coming or what?"

"Be right there, sport." She gave me a crooked smile and a half-shrug. She finished her drink, left a tip on the bar and was about to go when she pulled her notebook back out of her bag and made a brief entry.

"See you," she said. And was gone.

The bartender was just clearing my Irene's Dream from the end of the bar when I held up a hand. "Not so fast, Chief," I said.

He gave me another knowing nod as he slid the drink down the bar and brought it to rest on a cardboard coaster in front of me. He went and dropped a shiny quarter in the juke box and punched up John Cale's version of "Heartbreak Hotel." I sat there drinking bad memories and listening to sad songs.

Thanks a bunch, Santa.

IV. The Czar of Ideaville

I don't remember the walk back to the hotel or anything else of the night after. I slept the sleep of the dead, buried and eaten by worms courtesy of three more Irene's Dreams (the last one on the house) plus I don't know how many beer chasers. I only woke up at ten the next morning when the maid knocked, the inside of my head lagging some way behind the rest of my body as I got out of bed.

The old guy in the lobby was perched in his spot, a newspaper in his lap and a Styrofoam cup on the table in front of him. He snapped me a brisk salute as I came down the stairs. He looked all excited, like he'd been waiting all morning to talk to me — hell, the poor, lonely bastard probably didn't have much else to do — but I wasn't in the mood. I waggled my fingers at him and offered an irritated smile as I strode past. I didn't look back, but I heard a stiff, angry snap of his paper behind me. Well, I had my own damn problems.

Like an empty stomach and a Hiroshima hangover.

I was nearly out the door when I remembered I still had to do something about my car. I walked back to the front desk, contemplating my spelling, but steady Mr. Sturdy wasn't on call. When I rang the bell a dapper middle-aged

woman came out. Her name tag identified her as
V. Barr, and she had the look and manner of an
over-the-hill flight attendant who flew just one
mile too high. I explained my vehicular problem
and she agreed to find a kid to gas up and retrieve
the car for a deuce, so I left my keys and a twenty.

"A Pacer?" she asked, when I told her what
and where it was.

"It's a classic, so treat it right."

She had an it-takes-all-kinds look on her face,
but she was well-trained enough not to pass — or
more importantly, *spell* — any comment.

It was a bright, sunny day which didn't do a
thing for my headache. Grey skies are underrated,
if you ask me. I figured a walk and breakfast
would be the best cure for what ailed me, though,
and I was in no hurry to get where I knew I really
did have to go. I walked east, past the Ralph Fair-
banks Memorial Train Station — which now featured a Starbuck's and a McDonald's — and on
into the center of town. I passed a score or more
cafés and muffin shops and fast food franchises
lining both sides of bustling Geisel Road. There
was even a sushi joint called Ushi-tama, which
offered breakfast sashimi. Lovely as that sounded,
I had my heart set on one thing in particular.

If it was still there, that is.

I had my hopes because as I walked along I
realized that the shock of my initial view of the
new Ideaville had worn off some; enough bits and
pieces of the town I used to know survived to
make me feel less like an alien stranded on some
strange and distant shore, though I still couldn't
say I felt at home. But then I never do.

Sandwiched between the new chain stores and corner mini-malls, I spotted more shops from days gone by: Harold's Bakery, Radio Boys Appliances, even Alcott's Grocery. Mrs. Alcott had had a bad-war-movie eastern European accent and a penchant for cheek-pinching, and was surely dead after all these years. I couldn't imagine how the shop survived with a twenty-four hour Pathmark directly across the street, but score one for the little guys. I even saw a hoarding on the back of a passing bus advertising my old dentist, Doc Tarry. However, he too had become a franchise, with six offices and an 800 number to call for appointments; but there was a jokey caricature of Tarry on the ad — a little older and a lot balder — which I was able to connect with the young man who once filled my cavities and handed out apples.

So it was a deep breath of relief I exhaled when I turned the corner onto Centerburg Avenue and saw that Ulysses' Diner stood exactly where it should, still open for business. The neon sign in the big window was new — well, it was less than twenty years old — but in humming red letters it promised the same as the hand-lettered scroll that hung there when I was a boy: Best Eats in Town.

"Fucking-A," I whispered to myself, my hangover retreating already.

The inside hadn't changed a bit. Back in L.A., I must have eaten in a score or more "fifties cafes," all trying to out-kitsch each other to capture that *authentic* look of luncheonettes gone by.

Ulysses' was the real thing.

A long stainless-steel counter with matching
round stools bolted to the floor lined the front of
the big griddle on one side of the place; a half-
dozen cramped booths, with aluminum napkin
dispensers, paper place mats with connect-the-
dots puzzles, and wire-frame holders stuffed with
packets of pure cane sugar, were set along the
other. A big round table occupied the prime floor
space offering a voyeur's view out the front window. The smudged blackboard hanging on the
back wall listed daily specials that looked suspiciously similar to those posted a pair of decades
before. The smell of bacon and eggs, fresh coffee
and old grease — doughnut grease! — filled the
air. I spotted the old steel-and-glass automatic
doughnut machine in the corner, exactly where it
had always stood, still chugging and coughing
like an emphysemic as it spat out its tiny tori of
delight, just itching to give their all and dive into
the vats of sizzling fat and powdered sugar below.

Heart attack city, I thought, my mouth watering like Homer Simpson's. And I felt at last, for
just an instant, like I *had* really come home.

The only customers in the place were a trio of
overweight cops sitting in the front window. A
plate stacked high with doughnuts sat in the middle of the table and they were gulping them down
like nobody's business. One of them gave me a
casual once-over as I walked in, but the others
just kept popping doughnuts into their pie-holes
like the grease junkies they were. Damn, those
doughnuts smelled good!

I sat down on one of the swivel stools and
picked up a menu. Memory is, I admit, an

untrustworthy ally, but like the blackboard on the wall, I could have sworn (prices notwithstanding) that the bill of fare hadn't changed.

"Coffee?" the fellow behind the counter asked. He had already set a cup in front of me and held the steaming pot in his hand, ready to pour. He was tall and way too thin — especially for a fellow working in a doughnutery — with a scrawny, chicken neck and a receding hairline and high prominent forehead big enough to advertise on.

"Absolutely," I said.

"Know what you want?" he said, putting down the coffee and snatching a pad out of his apron with the aplomb of a master prestidigitator. Naturally he kept his pencil tucked behind one ear.

I squinted up at the blackboard in the rear.

"I tell you: I think I have to go for the Trojan Horse Special." A half-dozen mini-sausages wrapped inside an oversize buckwheat pancake.

"Hash browns?"

"Double order."

"That'll write its name in your colon. Care for a sinker or two with that?"

"A sink. . ." I broke out in a huge smile.

"What's the story, morning glory?"

"It's been a long time, a *long time*, since I've heard anyone call a doughnut a sinker."

"Well, that's what we call 'em here. That's how my uncle used to say, and what I calls 'em still. Same family recipe, too, don't you know, passed on generation to generation. None of that Dunkin' Donuts, squeezed from a tube crapola in my place."

Suddenly, I flashed back on the fat guy who used to own the diner. And I remembered the kid who'd always worked behind the counter while the old man was off playing cards and drinking ouzo with Mr. Alcott. I never did get to know the boy's name because, although he was my age, he attended the Greek Orthodox parochial school out in Sammiam Hill. Could this be that same kid? The forehead sure looked right.

"Let me have a couple of those glorious sinkers," I said. "Heavy on the powdered sugar."

"Only way we serve 'em, pal."

As he turned toward the grill, the sound of sirens blared out in the street. Three patrol cars went whizzing down Centerburg Avenue, cherry-tops flashing. I heard a blast of static and saw the trio of cops lean over to listen in on their walkie-talkies. With a half-hearted wave to the counter man, they grabbed their hats and waddled for the door. One of the three took a glance back at the table, turned around and scooped up the last of the sinkers before hurrying to catch up with his companions.

"On the cuff," the counter man grumbled. "For a change."

"Ideaville's finest," I offered. I don't believe my dad paid for a meal in town during his entire career.

"Finest my . . . why I'd spit if this wasn't a high-quality eatatorium."

Another trio of police cars went screaming past.

"Wonder what all the hubbub is," I mused.

"More shenanigans out YellowHat way, I fancy."

"How do you mean?"

The counter man glanced at me over his shoulder as he sizzled my sausages. "You in the game?"

"Pardon?"

"The business. You with one of the big boys in town? You got that YellowHat look about you, no offense."

"None taken, because I don't know what you mean. I'm just a guy passing through, come to see the sights. I hear your doll museum is something else."

"Pardon me while I don't spit again."

"So what's the story with YellowHat?" I asked.

He neatly scooped my sausages off the griddle and into the pancake and flipped it closed. He shoveled a healthy portion of hash browns onto the plate and plopped it in front of me, passing the maple syrup my way. I loaded up good and dug in right away. The griddle man seemed to take no small pleasure in my enjoyment of the greasy fare.

"Always trouble somewhere, lately," he said, looking out the window at another howling cherry-top. "Probably those Robusto Boys giving YellowHat a little hotfoot. The brothers can't stand that monkey. Then again, who can? Say, how is that?"

"Perfect," I said, through a mouthful of peppery hash browns. And it was no lie. "What do you mean, a hotfoot? What monkey?"

"Oh, those fellows been tit-for-tatting for months now, though it's mostly YellowHat's got his tit in the wringer. Pardon my parlez-vous. YellowHat planted a nasty little virus in the Los Bros mainframe, or so the gossip says. Can't believe *everything* you hear, of course, though I hears it all in here. The Robusto Boys started a little fire out the YellowHat warehouse last night. Monkey nuts fricassee."

"How do you know all this?" I asked. Monkey nuts?

"Ideaville ain't that big a town. Yet. And everybody — no matter who they're with or which side they're on — loves my sinkers."

"So if you know all this, the cops surely do."

"Pffaawww. Cops belong to Black X, lox, shmear and bagel. Ain't no secret about that. Oh, sure, they zip around town to make things look good — between eating my sinkers and not paying — but Ideaville is a Blackwell Unlimited operation. Full stop, end of the line, don't forget your personal belongings. If the Monkey Man and Los Bros want to tear each other to bits, you think Blackwell is gonna let the cops stand in their way? Get real, partner."

I mopped up the last bit of grease with the crust of my toast. The counter man topped up my coffee.

"Ready for them sinkers?"

"Bring 'em on," I said, stifling a belch.

He went and punched a button on the old doughnut machine and three perfect blobs of dough spurted out and into the grease. Even after my Trojan Horse, the sizzle and smell sent my stomach juices to flowing. I licked my chops as he fished the sinkers out of the grease and dropped them into a tray of powdered sugar. He arranged them lovingly on a plate and slid it in front of me, taking away the dirty dish.

"Urrrmmmm," I groaned, as the still-hot doughnut all but melted in my mouth. "That's a sinker."

The counterman nodded his approval. I was about to ask him some more about the "Monkey Man" when a splat and sizzle caught our attention.

"*Damn* that old bastard," he cried.

The doughnut machine started spitting out blobs unbidden. One after another, little squirts of heaven were ejaculated from the nozzle and plopped into the hot fat. The counter man started punching at the off button, but the machine wouldn't respond, just kept spurting out sinkers.

He was still cursing the thing when I finished my doughnuts, left my money on the counter, and headed out the door.

Standing in front of the faux-marble pillars of Ideaville City Hall, I felt transported through time again. However much the town might have changed — it couldn't rightly be called a town anymore — City Hall remained the same. The building was a mock version of the Capitol in Washington, one-twentieth scale to be sure, but with its own little rotunda and pot-bellied statue of liberty perched on top. (The story went that an old mayor's wife served as the model.) Two dozen stone steps led up to the front entrance, and portentously chiseled into the lintel above the door were the words:

TRVTH, JVSTICE, HVMILITY

Ah, my little town.

I don't know how many hours of my youth I spent sitting out on those steps, staring up at those magical words — the V's driving me slightly crazy as I tried to pronounce them in my head — waiting for my dad to finish work inside. The office of the Chief of Police was in the East Wing (that would be the hall to the right), one floor below the Mayor's office. Though my dad did his best work — *our* best work — at home, he had to put in his time at the office, and it was there, after school or a ball game on Saturday, that I'd go to wait for him. Everyone knew me then, of course; they all knew the smartest kid in town. The other officers would walk by and tousle my hair. The middle aged secretaries would pat my cheeks and tell me how adorable I was, how they'd love to snatch me up and take me home with them. Probably get arrested for that kind of thing today. The Mayor himself would always toss me a boiled sweet from the seemingly inexhaustible supply in his jacket pockets. And he loved to ask me questions, because I always knew the answer. The capital of Nepal. The winner of the 1934 Kentucky Derby. Mason and Dixon's Christian names. He always got a satisfied-cum-amazed chuckle out of the endless repository of crap that was my youthful brain.

Truth, justice, humility. Words to live by.

Or so I thought.

"Jesus, moron, get out of the frigging way."

I'd been standing in the middle of the steps staring up at the lintel. "Sorry," I muttered to an annoyed-looking woman wearing a yellow power suit and carrying a big briefcase.

"Christ," she spat, and walked past shaking her head.

I had to pass through a metal detector just inside the door, beneath the unhappy gaze of a uniformed officer. My loose change set off the alarm, so I had to empty my pockets and go through a second time. It held up the line and evoked a few more muttered curses from behind.

"You really have security problems here?" I asked, depositing my money back in my pockets.

"Can't be too careful," the guard said, and shrugged.

Out of ancient, ingrained habit, I started down the corridor toward the Chief's office. I was well down the hall before I realized I was heading the wrong way altogether. Or rather, I didn't know which was the right way; wasn't sure where his current office might be. I turned around to go back and ask at the information desk by the entrance, only to come face-to-face with my old pal Dink.

We froze, staring each other down like gunslingers on a dusty Tombstone street. That is, until Dink let out a bubbly fart.

"How's it hanging, Dinky-boy?" I asked through a laugh.

He stood there shaking his head, as if he couldn't believe the sight in front of him.

"E-e-e-e . . ."

"Yeah, it's me," I said. "The Banquo's ghost of . . . Ideaville."

"I'll be damned," he whispered. Dinky took a quick glance around, though there was no one watching us, before coming back to himself. He

wore a cheap polyester suit with scuffed brown
Hush Puppies. His hair had thinned almost as
much as his glasses had thickened. His skin had
such an unhealthy ashen pallor — perhaps it was
just the sight of me — that the suggestion of a
visit to the oncology clinic wouldn't have been
entirely out of order. His nose hair needed a trim,
too. "What in the world are you doing here? I
never dreamed you'd come back."

"What are dreams but expressions of uncon-
scious desire?" I asked.

He screwed up his nose in the selfsame "huh?"
look he'd always had as a kid. "Dreams are nightmares," he said. "Sometimes."

I laughed. "Good one, Dinky. You have grown
up."

"And then some. What *are* you doing here?" I
saw the lightbulb flash. "Sandy," he muttered.

"I had to come. To, you know, closure and all
that psychobabble."

Dinky shifted uncomfortably from foot to foot,
like he had to pee. He'd done that as a kid, too.

"A fellow might think an old friend wasn't
happy to see him," I said.

"Been a long time. Lots of things changed."

"It's called life, Dinkster."

"Tell me about it."

A uniformed policeman had wandered over
and stood behind my old pal who, typically, had-
n't even noticed. I nodded to point him out and
Dink spun around.

"What?" he barked.

"Sorry, Chief. Didn't mean to startle you."

Chief?

"Well, what is it McCloskey?"

"The Man from YellowHat's waiting for you in the conference room's all. You're running late again. The Man's mad as hell and that little monkey's making a goddamned mess."

"Be right there." He turned back to face me, looking something between nervous and sheepish.

"Chief?" I asked.

Dinky drew himself up to his full five and a half feet. His expression changed, too. "Didn't you know?" he asked. A bit sneeringly, I thought, as if the very question gave him some illicit pleasure.

"Know what?"

"I'm Ideaville's new Chief of Police. I've got your pop's old job."

I stood there, dumbfounded.

"You didn't know. Well, ain't that a kick in the shit-stained drawers. Times have changed, indeed, have they not?"

When I didn't answer, he started off down the hall after his officer.

"Hey Dink," I called. "You still collecting dead stuff?"

He smiled at me, and it made me very uncomfortable. "Only the stuff my boys find around town," he said. And walked away.

"Oh, Toto," I muttered to no one and everyone, "we sure as scarecrows ain't in Kansas anymore."

I had to wait my turn back at the information desk. City Hall did a brisk business these days. I'd tried looking over the building directory, but I couldn't find the listing I needed. A name plaque identified the woman behind the counter as Connie Blair, and sure enough she greeted me with a chirpy "Hi, I'm Connie. How may I help you today?" that bore all the sincerity of a burger-jerk's "have a nice day." And though she smiled, I saw a ghastly deadness in her eyes.

I told her who I was looking for. She asked me to repeat the name. When I did, she laughed so hard the specter of death momentarily fled from her countenance.

"What's the joke, sister?" I asked.

"You really want to see the Czar?"

"Beg pardon?"

"The Drug Czar. You're here to see the Drug Czar?" She failed to stifle a fresh bout of the giggles. I didn't have a clue what she was on about so I repeated my initial request.

A strict-looking security officer in a dark blue suit, clutching a walkie-talkie strolled behind the counter just then, so Connie sobered up.

"Office number 219," she said, and pointed toward the West Wing.

The security guy's head shot up. He looked at me, then at Connie. Then he burst out laughing.

"Problem, my friend?" I asked.

He literally tried to wipe the smirk off his face with his fingers, then shook his head and went back to his paperwork.

"Thanks a heap," I said.

As I walked off, I heard the two of them explode in fresh gales of hilarity.

The West Wing had always been where the town's lesser offices were housed and I saw that things hadn't changed. I walked up the stairs and past the chambers belonging to the Pothole Inspector (three doors!), the Water Purity Board,

the Bureaus of Combined Services, Essential;
Combined Services, Non-essential; and Non-
Essential Services, Combined; and at the end of
the corridor the lavish accommodation accorded
the Director of County Fair Affairs. I didn't see
the room until I noticed a little jog between the
unisex disabled toilet and the Lapsed Policy Customer Services Inquiry window. Sure enough,
there was office number 219, emblazoned with a
small bronze plaque engraved: DRUG CZAR.

And below that, handwritten on a yellow Post-
it note, my father's name.

"Christ on a crutch," I muttered.

I took a very deep breath and knocked on the
door.

"Wraaaaammmm," a voice called out. Fortunately, I speak alcoholic and opened the door.

The office must once have been a janitor's
closet. In fact, there was still a small, brown-
stained sink set into one wall which held the
residue of vomitus. A rickety student desk covered with scraps of paper and McDonald's Styrofoam fossils took up most of the floor space, empty
bottles of cheap gin the rest. A single bare bulb —
25 watt, tops — didn't do much to supplement the
yellowy light that filtered through the tiny window set high into the back wall. The room smelled
of alcohol and sweat and extreme moral decay.

But then, so did my father.

He blinked when he saw me and then dug his
knuckles into his eyes. Of course, it may just have
been the near-blinding effect of the hall light
spilling in through the open door behind me. I
shut it softly. We stared at each other for a while,

my father just shaking his head, until I gestured
at the metal folding chair which stood on my side
of the little desk.

"Can I sit down?" I asked.

"You may," he sputtered.

I knocked over a couple of bottles as I pulled
the chair out. "Sorry," I said, as I set them right.
My dad watched me as if I were some special
effect by Industrial Light & Magic.

"Quite a place you've got here," I said.

My old man sniffed, reached across the desk
and picked up a half-full glass of something clear
— gin, even a bad detective would surmise —
downing it in a gulp. He wiped his filmy lips with
the back of his dirty, frayed sleeve.

"My son's house has many rooms," he said,
and laughed uproariously.

I got the joke; it just wasn't funny.

Once upon a time, in that lost, modern fairy
tale of my childhood, my father was the most
respected, loved and envied man in town. And not
just by me. In a town like ours the Chief of Police
wasn't merely the man who wrote traffic citations
and held the keys to the jail, he was the moral pillar that sustained the entire community. My dad
was an officer of the law in the best and truest
sense. He chased down teenaged hooligans and
middle-aged thieves and petty criminals of all
manner, of course, but he also settled husband-
wife brawls with nothing more than a soft word in
a hardened ear; he kept watch over the traveling
carny that pitched its tent every August, making
sure none of the locals lost *too* much at the wheel
of fortune the gypsies ran "on the sly," or that

nothing too untoward went down behind the gaily painted trailers; he ensured that the town drunks had a place to flop in the winter, but nudged them up the road out of town when they got a little *too* ornery; he was the invisible hand of decency that kept even a quiet Midwestern burg from crossing too far over the always unsteady line of its own uncertain moral disorder.

Until, that is, he started taking kickbacks from property developers.

And blow-jobs from underage whores.

"Going a bit thin on top," he said. "Like your grandad."

"And grandma," I said, running a hand across my pate.

"Too true."

"Nice to see you back in . . . public office."

"Life's just full of little surprises. But then you know that. You know *everything*. At least, you used to."

"Drug Czar. Very impressive. Is there a big drug problem in . . ." — I cleared my throat — " . . . Ideaville."

"Only so far as the pencil-necked geeks who've flocked here for the quick bucks can't seem to get enough of the junk. Worldwide shortage, don't you know. Something to do with El Niño and the winter rains in Peru, or so I'm told. I hear the quality ain't so hot, either."

"You mean you haven't investigated? Tried it for yourself? Heavens, what's a Drug Czar for?"

The old man's face suddenly got tight. He screwed up his bloodshot eyes and pursed his chapped lips. "For shitting on and laughing at and generally playing the fool. What the hell do you think, boy?"

"So why do you do it?"

"Pork chop money," he said. "Man's gotta eat. Sometimes." He held the expression for a minute, then shrugged. I winced. My father got distracted by the meniscus of gin that coated the bottom of his dirty tumbler. He turned the glass upside down over his open mouth — he'd lost a few teeth in back — and let those last precious drops slither down onto his tongue. When he licked the rim, I saw that his tongue was black.

"What are you doing here, boy? Ain't you screwed me over enough in this life?"

"It's been more than twenty years, pop. Or hadn't you noticed?"

"Time flies when you're in the shitter. Twenty years, twenty minutes, what's the miserable difference? Don't you know that the future's the undiscovered country?"

"*Death* is the undiscovered country, dad. It's from Shakespeare."

"Well, Mr. Seen-it-knows-it-all, it just so happens I was referring to the *Star Trek* picture. The one with the whales."

Actually, he was still wrong. But I didn't correct him. "Drug Czar and cineaste. Nice to know you haven't entirely wasted the decades. Not to slight your ventures into alcoholism and sexual depravity, of course."

I thought that would rile him up, but he only offered an ugly smile.

"No offense taken," he said.

And he poured himself another drink.

On one peeling wall hung a chipped, cork bulletin board plastered with a casual collage of "JUST SAY NO" bumper stickers. Except someone — I wonder who? — had appended the letters "OKY" to the end of every one.

"Getting much these days?" I asked.

He frowned in puzzlement, then followed my gaze to the stickers. A wave of anger passed across his face, but it dived off just as quickly into the fresh glass of gin.

"Probably as much as you got in prison," he slurped. "'Cept I don't have to bend over to get mine."

"Son of a . . ."

"Didn't think I knew about that, huh? You ain't got the patent on knowing, sly boots. What was it now? Three years in a . . . medium-security facility, was it? Computer fraud, right?"

I felt a fury in my gut, tried not to let it show. "I was a hacker," I said, as calmly as I could.

"Hacker, right. We get them sorts here in town now and again. High-tech way of saying you're a sneak thief. Well, I always knew you'd come to no good. You had a mighty head start."

"*I'm no . . .*" I took a deep breath, refusing to take the bait. "I'm no thief. And it was a long time ago."

"I'm afraid it's still on your permanent record, boy. Some things don't never go away."

"That's life, isn't it. Besides, it turned out to be good training," I said. "I do security work now. For computer firms all around the country."

"Do tell. That what bring you to town? Going to work for your friend at Black X, maybe?"

"Not a chance in hell."

"What then?" My father slammed his glass so hard against the desktop that I was surprised it didn't shatter in his hand. Gin spattered the array of obscene doodles on his desk blotter. "What in the name of Jesus fucked Mary brought you back here? Haven't you injured me to your satisfaction? To your . . . haven't you done enough?"

I started to laugh, though there was nothing funny in what the old man said. "You still blame me. Unbelievable. Twenty years on and reality is still just a fantasy to you, isn't it? I was sixteen years old. Horny as a jackrabbit and broken-hearted over Sandy. You *made* me work that case. I told you I wasn't up to it, couldn't handle it, but that wasn't good enough for you. Pressure from above, you said. The boys at the State Police you were always out to impress. Had to solve this one. I pleaded with you to leave me be. Ma pleaded with you. But you made me do it. And when I did solve it, told you the evidence was weak, that the case might fail, you wouldn't listen. You took it right to the papers."

"Blackwell . . ."

"Old man Blackwell was guilty as hell, we both know it. He's a slimeball, just like his son. Proving it in court was something else again. And when you couldn't, when they all turned on you, well, that's when we saw the measure of the man. A measure that fit neatly inside some little girl's mouth."

"You got no right," he whispered.

"I've got every right. You drove Ma away. Into

Blackwell's arms, no less, you sonuvabitch. You drove us all away."

"But sometimes they come back," he muttered. He wouldn't meet my gaze.

"Like mini-skirts and wide ties and cheap Mexican meals, everything comes back sooner or later. It's the way of the world, Pop. But I've only come back for Sandy."

He looked up at mention of her name. "Sandy?"

"You do know that she's dead."

"I know," he said. He refilled his glass. "Car wreck. Pretty ugly from what I hear."

"You didn't send me the letter?"

"What's that?"

"I got an envelope with a clipping from the paper about Sandy's crash. No name on it, no return address. I thought maybe you sent it. Instead of a Christmas card."

"Don't be an ass, boy. I ain't even thought about you since . . . how would I know where you live, anyway?"

"You seem to know a lot about my life."

"Well, it wasn't me, boy. You must have yourself a secret admirer. Ha!"

"What about Sandy, then. I know how she died. I don't suppose you know anything about how she lived?"

He drained the glass. "Best not to ask," he said. "The past is a country known all too well. That ain't Shakespeare, I know, but it's god's own truth."

"I'm asking."

He reached for the gin bottle, but merely screwed on the cap. He opened a drawer and dropped the bottle inside. My father took a very deep breath before looking me square in the eye.

"I had her," he said.

My heart took a commercial break.

"I had her lots of times. And I always thought of you while I was doing her. I could afford to have her *and* treat myself to a pint bottle with the change. That should tell you all you ever need to know about your lovely girl. And me."

A tear dribbled down my cheek and I shook my head. I stood up and opened the door, squinting myself at the halls flourescent glare.

"It's Blackwell who set you up like this, isn't it? Gave you the job, the title. The office. A sick little joke for them all to laugh at. And keep on laughing each and every day that they think about you."

"Like I say, man's gotta eat."

"Ever hear of a hunger strike? Or getting a real job?"

My old man's eyes grew small and hard. "I wish I could just burn it down. Burn all of it right on down to the ground. This whole stinking, rotten-to-the-core town. That'd make me happy. For one last time that would make me *so* happy."

"Not much chance of that then, is there?" I said. I couldn't bear to look at him anymore. "See you . . . Pop."

I closed the door without looking back. I heard glass clink from back within. A passing secretary winked upon seeing me emerge from the Czar's palace, a broad smile on her too-made up face. I'd have loved to be able to share the joke.

But you can't fight City Hall.

V. Continental Ops

I fled City Hall without encountering any further blasts from the past. I don't think I could have stood much more.

The day had gone all blustery, with wrinkled aluminum foil sheets of cloud reaching over the town from the hills to the west. It felt as though my visit to the Czar's dark chamber had sucked the very sunlight out of the sky, the warmth out of the earth. Hell, I expected robins to drop dead from the trees. It's not like I thought the trip to Ideaville was going to be a laugh-riot — I'd come, after all, to face the funeral of a friend — but much as I'd geared myself up for the trauma of old homecomings, I couldn't have prepared for the raw hurt of seeing what my father had become. I'd had no delusions about him — certainly not after the humiliation of his "resignation" from the force, and the terrifying, acrimonious split-up with my mother — but twenty years out of sight is twenty years out of mind. At least, it had been for me. I'd put a lot of effort into making it that way.

Now I didn't think the image of him surrounded by cheap gin bottles and the smell of vomit in that grubby little office would ever leave me.

I'd been strolling aimlessly around town, feeling sorry for myself, which is something I'm more than passing skilled at. If I was a drinking man, or better at it, I'd have stopped in for a couple of short ones. Or maybe one very long one. I considered doing it anyway, but it would just have been a gesture. As it was, my head had barely recovered from the previous night.

Before I knew it, I'd wandered all the way over to Mile End Creek as the first drops of rain started to spill from dark skies. Bloated, cruel drops whacked me in the head, like some fat god's blubbery tears. I strolled up onto the footpath of the bridge and leaned out over the old stone wall, watching the rain make ripples in the creek.

The water was filthy, awash with detritus clearly marked with the corporate logos of the town's new businesses. Mile End Creek had become little better than an open sewer.

There came a brief lull in the shower — the eye of the storm or that fat god taking a deep breath, perhaps — in which I turned my face up toward the very bleak sky. I felt as if the clouds that had been following me for so long had tracked me all the way back to Ideaville; that they, too, were coming home. The billowing darkness seemed to take shape and gather in force as I watched, and just like that the skies opened up on me with a crack of thunder that could have passed for a mocking, cosmic laugh.

I stood there and took it. Didn't even turn up my collar against the force of the storm. In seconds I was soaked to the skin, but the cool water was a relief, a cleansing of the taint I'd felt attaching itself to me since returning to town. Again I turned my face directly to the heavens and let the cool water pound my cheeks. I opened my mouth and swallowed up all that I could, until I wanted to scream along with the sudden fury of the squall.

A horn honked behind me.

I ignored it.

It honked again. Then a third time.

I turned around, ready to unleash a banshee wail of anger at whomever had disturbed my soul-cleansing ablutions.

An extended black limousine — a Lincoln Continental — purred at me from curbside. The gleaming finish made it look like some onyx sarcophagus, the windows tinted dark, reflecting back at me my own dishevelled appearance and the menacing black clouds above.

The window rolled down, and a manicured finger beckoned me approach.

The finger was attached to a bejewelled hand, the hand to a dark-sleeved arm, the arm to a massive shoulder, a muscular body, an oblong, ugly head.

Roach Blackwell summoned me hence.

When it rains, it goddamn pours.

The Roach looked good, damn him. He'd been a chubby kid with a roll of fat hanging out over his belt, and ruddy, Scooter Pie jowls. The extra hunk of body mass that he'd carried lent him a degree of gravity and menace beyond any real strength or agility he possessed: pure bully weight. I remember how he'd turned that puppy fat flab to real muscle once we got to high school and his father finagled a place for him on the

football team. Roach's features went from bul-
bous to sharp as puberty progressed to manhood,
and his manner went from aggressive to arro-
gant. He made it as first-string quarterback, of
course, and in our junior year. The girls flocked
to him like maggots on a dead thing. (And one
girl in particular.)

Of course, I had a face full of zits from the time
I was thirteen until I was twenty one. I popped
Tetracycline like Pez, and bought a shareholder's
stake in Clearasil, all to no avail.

"Skin's cleared up nice," Roach said, grinning,
as I got in the limo.

"I guess it's true what they say about pussy
then," I said.

Roach's eyes registered some surprise — I'd
never so much as uttered a "hell" or a "damn" as
a kid — but he nodded and laughed. "Every word.
Nice that you finally got to find out for yourself,
though. I thought you never might."

Twenty years on, Roach hadn't lost his quarterback physique. He was well-packed into an
expensive-looking Italian suit which left no hiding room for love handles or a droopy gut. It
appeared that he hadn't lost a lock of his collar-
length black hair, either, though it was even
longer now, and tied back in a used-to-be-L.A.-
stylish pony tail. There was a puffiness around
his eyes, though, and just a hint of those little-boy
jowls making a comeback; but excepting a hint of
a drinker's nose, he looked as solid — and as
mean — as ever.

"Like the wheels?" he asked.

It smelled brand new — and not out of the

spray can they sell at Pep Boys. The interior was massive; you could have stuffed my Pacer inside and had plenty of room left over for a pair of Harleys and a Schwinn with training wheels. There was a mini-bar, a TV and a computer-fax-printer setup. I sat across from Roach on one of two long, leather benches.

"Not bad," I said.

"Comes with all the ops."

"Pardon?"

"All the options, and top of the line. You could live in here for a week if you had to."

"If you didn't have a home."

"Exactly. Of course, we got a nice place up on Milne. Don't think you've seen it."

"I haven't had the pleasure."

"*Ma* especially likes it," Roach said. His eyes widened a dime's worth, but I didn't rise to the bait.

"Anywhere you hang yourself is home."

"Then I guess you'd have to say I'm pretty well hung. Heh-heh."

"Still the conversational bon vivant, eh, Roach."

He leaned forward and laid his slab of a hand on my knee. "No one calls me that any more." He gave a little squeeze — just sufficient to mold anthracite into diamond — so as to emphasize the point. "Not even old friends."

"I didn't imagine you had any."

"Oh, there's still one or two around. Remember Biff? I got him heading up security at the plant. And Duke; jeezum crow, you must remember Duke K."

"Oh, I remember." Another charming member of Roach's old "club." He'd once shot Dinky with an air rifle.

"Yeah, he's still part of my posse. I got loyalty to my friends. The Duke's a sales manager now at the Blackwell New Media Place."

"Your dad's old appliance shop?"

"Times do move on. But you know that; I hear you already seen our Chief of Police."

"I never pictured the Dink as a man in uniform," I said.

"He's doing a bang-up job. Top of the line."

"From what I hear Ideaville's a bang-up town."

"You must be talking to the wrong people, then. Ideaville is the place to be right now, it's all happening. We're going to give those slick California bastards a run for their money; Seattle, too. Black X is the Microsoft of tomorrow. You can quote me on that."

"They say there's a man with a monkey who doesn't agree. And a pair of orphaned brothers with another idea still."

Roach's look got even meaner. "Those crazy bastards are staring into the abyss, my friend. And the Monkey Man's got one nut in the grave already. Only he don't even know he's on the slab."

"Hmmm."

"But enough about me. What do *you* think of me?" And he started to laugh. That same nasty, Muttley wheeze that he'd had as a kid. The laugh that launched a thousand bullying threats and penny-ante cons.

"You haven't changed one little bit, Roach," I said.

He laughed even harder. "That the truth?"

"For all your expensive tailoring and pinky rings and Continental ops. You're still exactly the same inside."

"Do tell? Of course, you'd know all about inside, wouldn't you?"

"How's that?"

"Inside. I mean, you were there. For, what was it? Three-year sentence? Of course, you only served eighteen months. But then you always were the best behaved kid in school. *And* everywhere else."

I could feel the blood rushing into my cheeks.

"But sometimes it pays to be a bad boy, doesn't it? 'Cause that's what the girls, even the good little girls — especially those really good ones — want. What they come running to."

"You scumbag."

"Who the fuck are you to talk? I know all about you, book-boy. I've kept watch and I know what a toilet your life has been. You see, the two of us are kind of linked, like on some seesaw. Those early years the tilt went your way, with your nose up high in the air while my ass dragged along the dirty ground. But you rode too high, too long and it's been a long time balancing out. And that turn around all started with Sandy. She was like a good luck charm, excepting none of it rubbed off on her. And of course what luck she had wore out a long time ago." Roach leaned over and whispered in my ear: "Same as her cunt."

"Bastard."

"Now, now: I know who my daddy is. Not to

mention my momma. And I'm speaking no disre-
spect toward the dead. Sandy was a piece in her
day, but that day was near as long ago as yours.
Can I tell you something? I'm a worldly man, and
take my worldly pleasures — I work hard and I
earn the money to do it — but would you believe
that first fuck with Sandy is one of my cherished
memories."

Roach leaned back, interlacing his fingers
behind this thick, slick hair. He narrowed his
eyes as if gazing into happy history. God, he was
an ugly piece of work.

"She wasn't my first, you gotta know that —
hell, I got more tail than Bobby Sherman — but I
was the one popped her cherry. That's not what
made it special, though. Would you believe I was
eight inches into her, riding that horny slut like
the Lone Ranger on Silver . . . and she called out
your name?"

Roach graced me with the ugliest smile I'd
ever seen.

"So I did what any reasonable fellow would
have done: I slapped her one across the chops.
And you know what?"

I couldn't respond, not even with a blink.

"She liked it. She liked it *a lot*.

"I swear I do trace things back to that very
day. Because, it's a funny thing and I can't believe
it sometimes when I think back, but do you know
in all those years when we danced around each
other as kids, can you believe I'd never heard
anyone call you by your real name? I didn't even
know what it actually was! But when Sandy
yelled it out while I was balling her. . ." — Roach
graced me with another reptile smile — ". . . it

was like some kind of magic happened. Your true name revealed, your weakness exposed. Like one of those crazy Oliver Stone Indian dreams. I knew then all I would ever need to know. About you and everything else."

"You don't know shit, Roach. You never did."

"You see: back then you were always right, or so I thought, but now you're painfully, ugly wrong. I know *everything*, and I know about knowing. The way you only ever *thought* you did, because everybody let you believe it. Because you were the Chief's precious little boy, and they all lived in fear of him."

"That's a lie."

"Is it now? You don't think your old man just turned bad one day? That . . . oh my god. No, this is too good to be true. You still think it was you, don't you? That when your father went after my old man for those grey market appliances, that it was you who screwed up the investigation."

"I did screw up."

"You were *set* up, loser!"

"What are you saying?"

"Who told you about that deal? Where did you get your, as it turned out, very bad information from?"

I hadn't thought about any of this in years. I didn't like to think about it. But I cast my mind back to the details of that final, awful case and . . .

"Sandy," I gasped.

"And whose pink popsicle was tickling her tonsils in those glory-filled days?"

"No. No way. Even after . . . we were still friends. She told me that. Even though she was . . . seeing you. She wouldn't have."

Roach folded his hands over his chest and looked up at the roof of the limo. "Oh, thank you God for bestowing such gifts upon your humble and unworthy servant."

"Sandy," I repeated.

"She sold you *and* your old man up the river on a slow boat while I spanked her tight little ass with the paddle. But your old man had been dirty for years, so what difference did it make? He'd have taken a fall one way or another, sooner or later. The times they were a changing."

The car eased to a stop, but my head continued to spin.

"Seesaw, Marjorie Daw. What did she see? Your mommy!" The liveried chauffer — who was, I realized, another ex-member of Roach's old gang — had opened the door and Roach was half out of the car. Looking over his shoulder, I saw that we'd arrived at the Blackwell family manse. "Care to come in, say hey?" Roach asked.

I could only shake my head.

"Shame. I'll send your regards to *Mom*." He turned then to the driver. "Take him back to the Anchor. Room 214."

I glanced up at my ancient and eternal nemesis.

"Unlike *some* people, I really do know everything," Roach said. "At least about what happens in town. *My* town." And he slammed the door.

It barely made a sound. Nothing like a Continental.

Knowledge is meant to be power, I know, but ignorance is surely bliss.

Lying on my bed, staring at the blurry hotel flower print on the wall, I felt sick to my stomach. It wasn't anything I ate — though those greasy coffee shop sinkers had well and truly sunk — but rather something I was struggling to digest.

I used to get stomach aches all the time when I was a kid, sometimes so bad that my mom would keep me out of school. Not that the teachers minded; as far as they were concerned I was so far ahead of the other kids that the odd missed day didn't matter a whit. And what with my reputation, I didn't even need to bring in a sick note the next day. They all knew that if I was absent it had to be for a damn good reason. Hell, they were always trying to skip me forward a grade or two anyway. Create more of a challenge for my abilities, they said. My dad had been all for it — he revelled in my reputation — but Mom wouldn't let them do it. She thought it might affect my socialization.

Nice call, Ma.

It wasn't until years later that I considered that all those stomach aches and so-called twenty four hour bugs — I threw-up a hell of a lot as a kid — might have been a result of something other than a delicate GI-tract or too many Mr. Goodbars. It was while I was doing time in California that I agreed to try some one-on-one therapy (lying on a couch beats stamping out personalised license plates for fifty cents an hour in the prison shop; and the screws counted therapy sessions double toward good-behaviour time). The prissy shrink was convinced that my nefarious life as a penny-ante hacker was a delayed response to my father's position of authority at home and in the community. *Real deep, Doc* I thought at the time. But if you pissed him off he chucked you out of the program and it was back to the prison shop and (literally) watch your ass, so I nodded thoughtfully, as if this idea had never occurred to me unbidden. I'd grown used to playing dumb by then.

"And did you suffer from stomach ailments as a child?" the doctor asked.

The question caught me by surprise. "Yeah, I did."

"And why do you think that was?"

"My mother always said I had a susceptibility to viruses."

"And do you believe that to be true?"

"Sure. Most kids are like that."

"Are they now. Do you remember your other little friends suffering from similar afflictions?"

Sandy never missed a day of school in her life. Dinky lived with a grandma who smelled like mothballs and lilac. He would have crawled to school with two busted legs to get out of the house every morning. And Roach, well, what manner of bug could possibly have infected him?

"No," I whispered.

"Yet, you suffered from stomach aches as a matter of course. And over a period of some years."

"You're saying it was all in my head?"

"No, the ache was definitely in your stomach. But maybe there was something in your head. Perhaps far *too* much for your own good."

I continued to see that doctor for almost a year after I got out of the slam. He helped me a lot —

a lot more than I ever would have expected. At
least until he tried to convince me that I was a
repressed homosexual and that he should be the
one to free me from the cage of my own repres-
sion. He prescribed a dirty weekend in Santa Bar-
bara for the two of us. I passed. I also gouged a
two-foot tear in his leather couch with his Scrooge
McDuck letter opener.

He was right about the stomach aches,
though. And about there being too damn much in
my head.

I always ask people I meet about their child-
hoods. Not because the sissy shrink turned me
into a raving Freudian (though I did feel com-
pelled to read the collected Freud when I started
therapy, if only to comprehend before rejecting his
essential tenets), but even though you *can* go
beyond the limiting forces that shape your
upbringing, I don't believe you can ever
unshackle yourself from the brutal truth of their
existence. These days you can dye your hair,
change the color of your eyes, firm your chin and
extend your dick if that's your fancy. But you can't
unring the bells of history. And to me that's the
fundamental flaw in therapy: understanding why
you are what you are can be interesting in an all-
consuming, self-indulgent way, but it doesn't
make changing yourself into something better or
different one iota easier.

And that's why even Uncle Sigmund never
could give up his smelly, phallic cigars, and died a
painful, mouth cancer death.

Which is not to say that I'm not an introspec-
tive person — quite the opposite (in case you
hadn't noticed). Sometimes, I fear, I'm so intro-

spective that I'm in danger of disappearing up my own too-tight asshole. I spend a lot of time thinking about myself — not that I've ever met anyone who didn't — and about all the things that went wrong.

My conclusion, after much soul-searching, is that it's a matter of information. Like everything else.

The Ideaville of my youth may have been a small place, but it maintained its place in what was still a very big world. The Ideaville I'd wandered back into — been drawn back into by Sandy's death — is not yet a really big place, but it exists in what is undeniably a much smaller world, a world *made* smaller by the profusion and ubiquity of endless, if too often useless, information.

I'd always thought that information was my friend; it is how, after all, even to this day I earn my living. When I was ten years old and renowned as the smartest kid in town, it wasn't because I was literally "smarter" than the many college and life-educated, not to mention emotionally mature adults; it was because I had a command of information that far exceeded even Principal Atelier, who was the only person in town with a Ph.D. It had nothing to do with genius or intellect or even cunning.

I'm just a freak: I was born with a near-eidetic memory. I remember just about everything.

People often mistake knowledge of facts for insight — it's why most kids are so in awe of what their teachers appear to know. (Or used to be; I don't imagine kids who pack Glocks along with

cookies and apples in their Flintstones lunch
boxes are overly awed by anything. Then again,
maybe that's why they pack the Glocks to begin
with.) I never shared that awe, because I always
knew the facts better than my teachers. From the
time I learned to read — and that was at an
admittedly precocious two-and-a-half — and discovered that everything that went into my head
stayed there, I committed myself to absorb every
fact I could digest. While other kids were learning
their ABC's and 1-2-3's by brute rote force, I was
memorizing page after page of Encyclopedia Bri-
tannica. (Our home copy was actually police property, confiscated by my dad in a raid on a local
bunco artist, and conveniently "stored" in our living room bookcase for years thereafter. Corrupt to
the core.) It's not hard to impress old ladies who
do crossword puzzles when the answer to any fac-
tual question is imprinted in your brain as readily as the image of your mother's face. Teachers
ate it up, too, and a talent for memory gets you
very far on those pathetic standardized tests we
use to gauge and guide people's lives.

Sandy used to think I was the bee's knees. Her
exact words. Kids still talked like that only a few
decades ago. Today, when kids all talk and dress
(and *shoot*) like Samuel L. Jackson, she'd probably have called me a righteous motherfucker. We
spent countless hours in my parent's leaky garage
— our detective "office" — just talking. Sandy
liked to sit on a pile of shipping crates in the corner while I shuffled would-be important papers
on my desk: a wooden door scavenged from the
junk yard, laid across a pair of paint-spattered

saw-horses. At least I had a real chair to sit on. It was a huge old rattan horror that my mom was about to throw away. It was three times as big as I was and more suited to Sidney Greenstreet than a ten-year-old, but I thought it lent the place a certain exotic atmosphere — very Blue Parrot. Sandy would sit on her stack of boxes, the *Information Please Almanac* propped open on her lap, and ask me questions. Who won the Preakness in 1942? What is the major crash crop in Papua-New Guinea? When did Hannibal kiss his first elephant?

I knew it all. And I thrilled in that knowledge of my knowledge. Sometimes the other kids would come by, even if they didn't have a case and a dime to fork up for the retainer, just to watch and listen as I rattled off answers to unknowable questions with impossible ease. Never a moment's hesitation. Always correct.

Of course, the other kids were mostly freaks, too, though I didn't realize it at the time. Goofball Dinky and his collections, cockeyed Pete with his mania for the Civil War, Pinky the paper-thin albino, the just-slightly retarded Bobsies . . .

Christ, what a crew! No wonder Roach and his buddies were always bullying us, beating us up. I'm not saying it was right, but looking back on things from a position of (relative) normality, I can see that we all had "victim" stamped in gold leaf on our foreheads. As we all find out, that's just the way of the world.

The thing is: facts only get you so far. That was the hardest lesson that I learned. Facts can take you a long way, especially if you can apply them laterally, which was the not very deep secret

of my detecting career. Most people — even intelligent adults — can't think laterally at all. To the
extent that I really was smart, not just fact-
smart, I relied on this talent of seeing ever so
slightly around the corners of a situation when
everyone else had the narrowest of tunnel vision.

But facts only get you so far. At some point you
must develop a deeper understanding; that's the
true nature of childhood's end. Ironically, it's the
Roaches of the world who seem to achieve that
satori first. Because achieving that level of
understanding depends on a comprehension of
power and its uses. And who knows about power
better than a bully?

I can recall still the day that I felt the tides of
our lives begin to change. It was our first semester of high school, in ninth-grade American History class. It was the only class that Sandy, Roach
and I were all in together. Roach wasn't in any of
the Honors classes, but for some reason, a clerical
error most likely, he'd been placed into Honors
History. He never knew the answers to any of the
questions and showed little interest in anything
other than copping feels off the mousy Honors
girls when the teacher, Mr. Verral, wasn't looking.
Roach was always a bit precocious in matters
relating to sex. He'd even stick his arm out in the
aisle, as if stretching, when a well-developed girl
walked past, just to try and graze her chest.
"Elbow tit" he called it. He didn't figure to be with
us in second semester Honors.

"To what in particular can we attribute the
North's great victory in the Civil War?" Mr Verral
asked. It was the day before the Thanksgiving
break and the heads of even the Honors students

were filled with thoughts of turkey and stuffing and two days off school. There was no response.

My hand went straight up.

Mr. Verral looked all around the room, in visible despair, waiting — praying, maybe — that someone else might, for once, volunteer an answer. He waited and waited. His eyebrows arched when I lowered my hand, but it was only to switch arms. I'd learned the hard way never to put them *both* up at the same time. Eventually, Mr. Verral surrendered to the inevitable and nodded at me.

"The North's great strength was the moral rectitude of it's cause," I said. It was a direct quote from our textbook, *America: History and Destiny*.

"Yes, of course," Mr. Verral said with a sigh. "But right doesn't always make for might, now does it?"

I held in my head the precise figures for blue and grey troop reserves and casualties, but as they hadn't been gleaned from the textbook, I was reluctant to recite them. In the moment of hesitation in which my hand stayed down, Mr. Verral again cast his gaze around the room.

"Benjamin. What do you think?" the teacher asked.

Several of the other kids looked puzzled. No one ever called Roach by his given name. Even he didn't respond to it at first.

"Huh?" he said, after Mr. Verral had been staring at him for some time.

"The Civil War. Why did the North win? Simple question."

Roach sat catacorner from me, one aisle to my

right. I saw that he'd been gouging a picture of a big spurting penis into his desktop. He covered it over with his notebook.

Roach just shrugged at the teacher. Honors History was the only place in Ideaville where Roach wasn't in charge. I loved it.

My hand shot back up, but Mr. Verral ignored me.

"Why did the North win?" he asked again. He locked his eyes on a squirming Roach. "Tell me what you think, Benjamin?"

Roach think? I had to stifle a laugh.

Roach mumbled something, still not able to even look up.

"Say that again?" Verral prompted.

"They kicked ass," Roach said.

A buzz went across the room. *No one* spoke like that in class; especially not in Honors History. But a flicker of a smile danced across the teacher's face. "Can you expand on that?"

Now Roach did look up, and as he did, the teacher offered him a nod and an encouraging smile.

"Like, they were way tougher," Roach said. "They did shi . . . stuff that the South didn't do. That burning Atlanta stuff and Sherman's March and all. They just had, like, more will. They had the ba . . . guts to do what had to be done."

"*Exactly*," Mr. Verral exclaimed.

I felt the world stop on its axis as the stars fell out of the sky. How could Roach even have heard of Sherman's March, much less have gotten the right answer? The *exact* answer?

"Yes?" Mr. Verral asked, looking my way.

"What?" I said. Then I realized my hand was still up. I quickly yanked it down. "Nothing," I said. "I mean, I don't know."

A titter of laughter went up behind me. I'd probably never spoken those three words aloud in my life. Roach turned around and grinned at me.

When the bell rang and we filed out of the room, I noticed Sandy give Roach an appraising look. It was nothing like lascivious, but she happened to run her tongue over her lips as she looked at him, just as you do. Or so I thought.

Roach actually nodded back at her. She didn't respond, but she didn't quite ignore him, either.

As Roach walked past the teacher's desk, I heard Mr. Verral say: "Very good, Benjamin. I hope to hear more from you in the future."

As always I stopped at the desk to talk to the teacher, But Mr. Verral was already on his way out the door.

A so-small thing, an insignificant event in a long and intricate life.

Everything ends with the bang of such whimpers.

It sounds crazy, I know, but I felt everything begin to shift from that moment. That day marked the point where my *see* began to plummet and Roach's *saw* started to rise. It wasn't just that class, of course, it was lots of things: Roach Senior's suddenly booming discount appliance business and his rise from scuzzy salesman to Chamber of Commerce charmer; Roach's discovery that he could channel his bullying nature into stunning success on the high school football field;

Sandy's radical transformation from Girl Detective to boy-crazy teenager; my parent's slowly brewing, ever-worsening domestic crises.

And, of course — if I'm going to be at all honest — the changes that were happening in me.

Much of it was the run-of-the-mill, Beverly Hills 90210 trauma: pizza face, hair in funny places, boners at the breakfast table with a life of their own. The stuff every boy encounters when adult hormones start to bubble and flow. No big deal in hindsight, however hideous it is to live through at the time.

But there was something else.

I had never realized it while it was happening, but my whole identity leading up to those teenaged terror years was bound up in my role of boy detective/smartest kid in town. It wasn't just the public accolades — the old ladies in the street patting my head or the Mayor handing me the key to the city for solving yet another case — it was my *own* notion of who and what I was. I'd always been the smartest kid, from my first day in nursery school through to making the valedictory speech in junior high. And everyone knew it. I always scored the highest grades, knew the right answer, was the one held up as the role model for all the other kids. Looking back, I realize how awful a figure I must have cut, how intensely the other kids must have loathed me, seen me as some lickspittle icon of fulsome goody-twoshoeness.

But what's cute in a ten-year old — what brings old lady head pats and mayoral smiles — isn't half so adorable in a crackly voiced adolescent. A ten-year-old with a dangling shirttail and chocolate milk moustache who knows more than his elders can be seen as *advanced*, or simply precocious; a teenager with real facial hair, an armadillo in his trousers and a leering eye on your daughter is never more than a wiseass hooligan.

Had puberty merely signalled the end of life as the Boy Detective — and admittedly by ninth grade the old ten cents-a-throw agency had long since passed Chapter XI status, even without splitting profits with Sandy — I probably could have handled it. I was still helping my dad out with cases, albeit on the sly, and found the challenge of that more satisfying than scampering around town looking for lost roller-skate keys or catching out Roach's ever more ambitious scams. Even I had to recognize that the agency — the very idea of the agency — was an essentially childish thing, however much I missed sitting in the garage, shooting the breeze with Sandy. I could live with that.

I could not so readily live with Tommy Fitzgerald.

The Fitzgeralds moved to town from Utah during Christmas vacation of ninth grade. Tommy turned up at school first day back after New Year. I didn't think much of it, nor did anyone else. Tommy was small for his age — small for most any age. He was at least six inches shorter than Kay Tracy, who'd always been the littlest girl in school, and he looked as though he'd curl up like a bug if you so much as breathed his way. Tommy had one of those bowl haircuts, with

bangs that only added to his girlish looks, and he
dressed in clothes that weren't scruffy or thread-
bare, but so utterly out of fashion — out of any
idea of fashion — as to appear practically alien in
design. It hadn't occurred to me, but talking to
Sandy after we laid eyes on him in Miss Hinton's
English class, we agreed that his clothes must
have been made at home, and his haircut too. He
had to have been more or less our age to have
been placed in the class, but whereas telltale
signs of puberty were visible all around — hairy
pits, budding tits — Tommy Fitzgerald, with his
little-boy voice and peach fuzz face, seemed to
have missed the hormonal boat altogether. In
short, he was USDA grade-A prime bully-bait, so
it came as no surprise when he showed for school
the second day with a big black eye and a scared-
to-death look. I probably felt sorry for him in the
same way I did for all victims of Roach and his
ilk, but it was a survival of the fittest, every man
for himself and Roach against all kind of world.
And I had my own troubles.

Little did I know.

The truth of the situation began to out the day
we got back our first trigonometry exam. I had
been in a panic when we took the test the week
before — it was the first school exam I'd ever
taken where I wasn't sure I knew every answer.
Trigonometry, you see, is one of those subjects
that isn't just fact and rote memorization, but
that requires a specific and exact application of
reasoning and logic. I'd always thought I was the
master of those disciplines, too, but lateral thinking doesn't get you where you want to go in the

world of mathematical proofs. I came out of that
exam shaking, barely comforted by the fact that
the other kids were shaking even worse. When
Mr. Wyatt handed back the papers and I saw that
I got a 57, I nearly passed out.

It was the lowest grade I'd ever received in my
life. I'd only once, ever, scored below 90, and that
was in French class, which I hated. How could I
ever tell my mom — my dad! — that I'd failed?

But then I glanced over at Sandy's paper and
saw *she'd* scored a 42. And Sandy was always
right up there with me when it came to tests. People started comparing grades and I heard gasps
about 23s and 31s and even a 17. I started to
cackle with a mixture of relief and delight. Even
with a grade of 57 out of 100, I'd still come out top
of the pack. Let's hear it for the kid. Sandy stuck
her tongue out at me, as she always did when I
beat her at anything.

Then Mr Wyatt went up to the blackboard and
made a list of the range of grades for the class. He
started the chart with the lowest scores — someone had actually scored less than ten! — and
recorded the number of grades in each band of
ten. When he got to 50-60 and scored a single
tally mark, everyone looked at me with their
usual envy and hatred.

But Mr. Wyatt kept on writing.

60-70, no tally marks.

70-80, no tally marks.

80-90, no tally marks.

He's a bit of a completist, I remember thinking.
Why bother to write out the rest of the list when
no one could have scored that high?

Then: 90-100.

One tally mark.

The class, which had been positively abuzz with excitement — no one in an Honors class was used to getting grades like this — suddenly went silent. I felt my heart skip a beat, as I forgot to breathe. I had already shown off my impressive 57, so who could have scored higher? Everyone looked around at everybody else, but there was just a collective shaking of heads and shrugging of shoulders. I turned around in my chair and glanced at Tommy Fitzgerald, sitting at the last desk in the back corner. He was curled into his usual ball, but his face had gone Coke-can red and his eyes zipped back and forth in their sockets like tumbling dice. He had his hands folded on the desk on top of his exam paper, thumbs twiddling nervously. As Sandy, and some of the others, followed my gaze and began to stare at him, Tommy's blush took on the hue of overripe plums.

I stood up and walked down the row until I stood in front of his desk. I'd never before gotten up from my chair without asking permission of the teacher. I reached down and took the corner of the exam paper between my fingers. Tommy stopped twiddling for a moment so he could hold the paper down on the desk, but as we locked eyes — and I saw him swallow — he surrendered his grip. He really had no will of his own. I turned the paper over and saw the grade.

Ninety-four was circled in red. Next to it, triple underlined in red, Mr. Wyatt had written: Superb!

He'd only written "good" next to my 57.

A furor exploded around me with the realization that Tommy Fitzgerald had not only gotten a higher grade than me, but had *trounced* me by almost forty points. I turned to Sandy for comfort, but she studied me as if she'd never seen me before, her mouth a gaping oval of puzzlement and — to this day, I swear — disappointment.

"Take your seat, please," Mr. Wyatt said. He had to say it three more times before I realized he was talking to me. I did sit down, but I don't remember anything else that happened in that class or for the rest of that day.

The king is dead; long live the king.

It was, of course, a fundamental lesson I learned that day; a lesson that everyone learns sooner or later, and one which, had I grown-up as anything other than the son of the Chief of Police in a town as parochial as Ideaville, I'd have taken on board years earlier. As most people do. The lesson is a simple, if painful one:

No matter how smart you think you are — no matter how smart you *really* are — there is always, but always, someone smarter than you.

It's so incredibly obvious, isn't it? You probably learned it when you were three or four, took it for granted by the time you got to kindergarten, didn't even think about it after you were five or six.

Learning that lesson in Mr. Wyatt's trigonometry class from wimpy, preternaturally prepubescent Tommy Fitzgerald — facing up to the humiliation of the most elemental fact of life (of course, as we know, I wasn't too good at any of the truly important facts of life) — just destroyed me.

I sometimes think I haven't got over it yet.

I'd laid on the bed so long that my nausea had turned back to hunger. A glance at my watch revealed that two-and-a-half hours had drifted by, and I'd barely even noticed. Ever since my stint in the joint, time passes differently for me. Nothing like doing time to readjust your attitude to justice, boredom threshold, and feelings about sodomy.

But enough rehashing good times. The day was getting old and so was I. My time in Ideaville was limited, and the time inevitably comes when a man has to do what a man has to do.

I went to visit Sandy's corpse.

VI. Farewell My Lovely

A man of grit and determination, a man sure of himself and his purpose, would have gone straight to the funeral home where the love of his life lay waiting and said his goodbyes; said all the things that he wanted to, needed to say in order to get on with the tatters of his life. He would have done that, got in his car and made his way straight out of town without once looking back.

I got as far as the hotel lobby before deciding I should stop first for lunch.

The old man — whom the hotel staff referred to as Mr. Ricky — was in his chair, reading his newspaper. I offered him a wave, but he pretended not to see me. Probably pissed off because I'd blown past him last time through. Well, fuck him *and* his hemorrhoids — no skin off my apple.

My Pacer had been gassed-up and retrieved, and was parked in the hotel garage, but the storm clouds of morning had passed, so I decided to walk into town again. I needed the fresh air if nothing else. And as soon as I stepped foot outside the hotel, my hunger pangs returned. Along with that even more painful need to put off the inevitable.

Walking past the railroad station, I saw a sandwich board advertising lunch specials at a place called The Boxcar, a restaurant built in an old, converted red railway car sitting on a disused

114

and rusty spur jutting out into the packed station parking lot. I think there's a restaurant like it in every town — can't be long before some strapping entrepreneur turns them into a franchise — and though I normally disdain such cutesy (and typically overpriced) places, the lunch deal sounded good. And I was intrigued by a note on the bottom of the sign mentioning "the best in home-cooked fare for a quarter of a century." I had no recollection of the place from my childhood, and felt sure that I would have remembered a restaurant in a railroad car. My dad was a keen model-rail enthusiast, and just corny enough to have dragged us out to dinner in such a place had it existed.

(Of course, I've been in enough places promising "home-cooked" or "just like mom used to make" to be more than wary. For one thing, my mom was a terrible cook who couldn't cut the crusts off a slice of Wonder bread; for another, what in the world is the point of going out to eat if it does taste like something you could have at home? But then maybe I'm just another cynical product of a shattered American family. I know: take a number . . .)

Steps leading up to the front door had been carved out of an enormous tree stump which had been varnished to match the red of the boxcar. It was a little past peak lunch hour, but the place was still about half-full. It looked as though the restaurant had been constructed out of a genuine boxcar, but the back had been opened up and extended to make room for the kitchen and a small luncheonette counter. I was taken aback, because the restaurant really did smell warm and homey inside, a rich mixture of food and woody odors. All the tables and chairs, even the lunch counter itself had been carved out of thick redwood. It felt like sitting in the middle of a friendly forest. A long shelf was affixed to the wall by the kitchen, with little ornaments — a pink teacup, a big kettle, an ancient white water pitcher cracked from base to spout — illuminated and highlighted by hidden spotlights as if they were academy award statuettes or Olympic gold medals. The objects were prosaic and pathetic — there was nothing special about them at all — yet . . . somehow they lent the place a coziness that I couldn't quite fathom. I felt like I'd stepped out of the world and into some hidden grove in a magical wood. Weird.

"Hello. How are you today?"

The woman who greeted me, menus in hand, offered such a genuine and friendly smile that I found myself responding to it without volition.

"Just fine, thank you."

"My name is Vi. Welcome to The Boxcar."

"Uhhh . . . . nice to be here."

"Yes it is, isn't it. It's so nice. So very nice."

She reached up and pulled on a string which dangled just behind my left shoulder. A dinner bell, fashioned out of a large, dented tin can, rang out with a tone as true as the finest Stradivari.

"All aboard!" she called out and everyone in the place looked our way. Each and every diner had a big smile plastered on his face. A few even nodded at me. I looked around for Rod Serling, but couldn't spot him.

"I'll just sit at the counter, if that's all right."

"Whatever makes you happy," Vi said. "We want everyone to be happy in The Boxcar."

She led me over to the counter and gently guided me by the elbow as I sat down. She placed a napkin in my lap and handed me the menu.

Stay away from the brownies, I told myself.

A very short busboy came along and put a big glass of ice water with a slice of lemon down in front of me. I always get thrown by busboys when I'm not in California, because I forget that they don't *have* to be Mexican, but I did a double take anyway, because gender notwithstanding, he was a dead ringer for happy Vi. When he saw me looking, he stopped and held out his hand.

"Hello. I am Bennie."

I shook his hand without really thinking — out of simple shock, I suppose — and even half-stood up. I'd likely have doffed my cap if I wore one.

"Welcome to The Boxcar. If I can do anything to make your meal more enjoyable, won't you please tell me?"

"I will," I vowed.

He smiled broadly and scurried off.

A waitress in a pink uniform emerged from the kitchen with an order pad in her hand. Her name tag identified her as Jess, but one look at her face told me she was kissing kin to Bennie and Vi; more haggard and drawn, but not quite old enough to be their mother. Brother and sisters, I decided, and tried to recall if I might have known them in the old days.

"Decided?" she asked.

The big dopey smile that had been plastered to

my puss since walking in drooped at last. I had been getting into the happy treatment and sort of wanted to shake her hand, too. I swallowed my disappointment and made a quick scan of the menu — it all sounded so wholesome! No fried or greasy spoon dishes to be found — and settled on Grandpa's pot roast with a slice of Mrs. Moore's cherry pie for desert. Whoever Grandpa was he knew his way around a brisket of beef, and if Mrs. Moore had been out in the kitchen I might just have had to propose. I mentioned this to my pal Bennie when he came to clear away the dishes.

"Oh, no," he said. He tittered — it wasn't pretty, but there's just no other way to describe the sound that emerged from his thick red lips — and covered his mouth with his fingers. "My big brother Henry does all the cooking. Henry looks after us. Henry looks after everything."

I'd noticed a sweaty man in a white T-shirt and chef's hat stick his head out of the kitchen a few times to chat with Jess the waitress, and this must have been Henry because the siblings all bore an uncanny resemblance to one another. What with it being old home week and all, I couldn't resist the temptation to ask about them when Jess returned to top up my coffee.

"This is a family operation right?" I asked. She nodded at me. "You always been at this location?"

Her eyes went a little glassy; part wistful, part thousand-yard-stare. "We have always lived in The Boxcar," she said.

"I see," I muttered. I felt certain I caught a glimpse of Rod in my coffee just then. "Check please."

As I got up to pay, I spotted the thick-ankled-yet-attractive reporter I'd met in the bar the previous night at a corner table with a man wearing mirror shades. She had her little notebook open in front of her and was madly scribbling away as her companion talked. I thought about going over and saying hey, but something about the look of them didn't invite company. Vi took my money.

"Did you enjoy your meal?"

"Very nice," I said. "Hell of a pot roast."

"Oh, that is very good. I am so happy. Please do come again. We would so love to see you."

Her brother the smiling busboy had come up behind her. "Yes, we really would. You are always welcome at The Boxcar."

As I opened the door, she reached up and rang the bell again.

"One getting off," she called out.

Not a minute too soon, I thought.

Sobol & Sons Funeral Home had always stood out. It sat on a huge parcel of land at the opposite end of Main Street from City Hall, marking what used to be the edge of town. The two buildings had served as bookends for the tiny business district, both being constructed of gleaming white marble. But where City Hall was all ancient Roman glory, Sobol & Sons was outlandish antebellum plantation. Mr. Sobol had a reputation for eccentricity — it was said he didn't even need the money from his business; that he worked as a mortician because he *liked* it — and building the monstrosity that was his funeral home provided proof positive. With its three-story stone pillars and immense front portico complete with wicker swing chairs, all that was missing were the rhythmic darkey servants and tall mint juleps in sweating tumblers. Hell of a place to hold a funeral, but for years Sobol had no competition so he got all the business. One of the most disturbing memories from my youth was the sight of the local ambulance screaming around town on the odd emergency call. Nothing unusual, you might think, except that the volunteer service was sponsored by none other than Sobol & Sons, and the name of the funeral home was plastered across the side of the ambulance. Talk about conflict of interest!

If the funeral parlor had looked ridiculous in the best of times — Christ, could I really still believe that's what those days were? Is the human mind a funny thing, or what? — the sight of it now crossed the line into the deeply bizarre. It wasn't so much the tacky series of cascading fountains that had been added to the immense front lawn (bizarrely, the frolicking figures in the water weren't nymphs or angels or seraphs, but tiny former presidents of the United States), or even the 24-hour ATM that had been installed on the portico, but the fact that the town had so grown up around the place. Sobol & Sons no longer stood at the town limit; the place was now abutted by a huge CompUSA store. Convenient, admittedly, if your loved one's departing legacy was a PC with insufficient RAM, but jarring nevertheless. Excellent parking, though.

Walking past the gurgling fountains on the

front lawn made me want to pee. Or maybe it was the Boxcar coffee perforating holes in my large intestine.

Or maybe I was as shit-scared nervous as a man on his way to view the earthly remains of the lost, one-and-only true love of his life could be.

Nah, probably just the coffee.

Soft violin music greeted me as I set foot on the portico. Something slow but not too turgid or mawkish, semi-classical I thought until I recognized it as an unusual arrangement of "Mandy" by Barry Manilow. Surprisingly tasteful, actually, and though it might just have been the coincidental rhyme — Sandy/Mandy — I had to swallow back a choke as the line "and I sent you away" rang around my head. Christ, this wasn't going to be easy.

I'd only been inside the mortuary once before, to accompany my parents to the service of the one-and-only member of the town's finest ever to die in the line of duty during my father's reign as Chief. The sad sack was a young deputy named Barthes on jaywalk patrol who, as he was chasing after a miscreant with his citation book, got distracted by the sight of a buxom young woman in hot pants — okay, so the old days weren't entirely without redeeming value — only to be flattened by a milkman's truck. Practically the whole town showed up for the funeral, even the milkman, though eventually he had to change his line of work due to post-traumatic stress. I seem to recall that the slattern who sparked the event, branded the local Jane Fonda, was shamed into leaving town.

For no good reason, I expected Mr. Sobol himself to be there at the door, and he was, though not looking quite as I expected. Of course, he was a pretty old geezer when I was a kid, so I shouldn't have been surprised that he'd long since found need of his own services. He hadn't entirely quit the business, though, for just inside the front door stood a marble pedestal with a golden urn on top, and a tastefully flickering eternal flame suspended just above it. A plaque on the urn offered Sobol's name and the inscription: Our Father . . . Who Art (Is) in Heaven.

Just below the plaque, leaning against the urn, was a tasteful display offering full color illustrated Sobol & Sons brochures. From what I remembered of him, I think the old guy would have approved.

There was no one at the staid reception desk, just lots of flowers and a big box of tissues. It didn't matter because there was a display board with the names of all the current occupants of the premises, and a corresponding list of the rooms in which they lay. There was only one dearly departed other than Sandy: a Lyman Baum, who was on view in the Emerald Room. Sandy had been laid out in the Tulip Suite.

Two corridors led off in different directions from the lobby, neither one marked. With a mental eenie-meenie-miney-mo, I took the one on the right. And that has made all the difference.

Actually, it didn't make any difference at all, but it wasn't the right choice. It led me to the Emerald Room, which was indeed as green as a capitalist's heart. It was also empty, Mr. Baum apparently having already departed for the flame or the grave.

I wandered back down the hall to the lobby, where I was greeted by an appropriately sober young man in a dull, black suit. He raised a quizzical eyebrow at me and tapped at his clean-shaven chin with the tip of his index finger. Something about him seemed familiar to me, but I couldn't quite place it.

"You're tall," he said.

"Only for my height."

"You're very tall for a Baum mourner."

"Actually, I'm looking for the Tulip Suite," I told him.

"Ahhh," he intoned, and a sorrowful look took hold of his face with all the subtlety and natural-ness of the animatronic Abe Lincoln at Disney-land. "A tragic loss of young life. And I once knew the fair lady. Truly tragic. Please follow me."

As he led the way up the hall, past the Lilac Chamber and Hyacinth Hall, I continued to rack my brain over where I knew this guy from. Sadly, like innocence and good skin, my flawless memory proved yet another casualty of the end of my youth.

The funeral guy stopped near the end of the corridor and opened a set of double doors, taking a step back to usher me in.

"With an end to life, comes an end to strife," he told me, nodding.

It was the kind of banal, insulting sentiment that you'd expect in such a place, and the words were uttered with the same reflex vacuousness that suggested he said it ten times a day. But the silly rhyme rang the bell in my head.

"Farny?" I asked.

His eyes widened with surprise, and his lips unpuckered for the first time.

"Francis, actually."

"Farny the poet. Sandy beat the crap out of you when you were fourteen."

The blood, such as there was, ran out of his face. If the embalmer had happened by at the moment, he might have carted old Francis off to be drained and stuffed.

Farny was a couple of years older than me and had fancied himself a teenaged aesthete. He was the only kid in school who wore a jacket and tie on days when they weren't taking class pictures. He tried wearing an ascot once, but Roach played the Isadora Duncan game with him and he never made that mistake again. Farny was always spouting poetry, some real, most of it self-written and genuinely dreadful, to impress the girls. It worked, too, up to a point, and he'd tried to woo Sandy with some of his home-brewed doggerel. She was sufficiently flattered by the attention of an older boy to go for it. Sandy never told me the full story, but I think one of his rhymes must have been too blue, because she broke his nose with a flurry of punches when they finally went out on a date. It proved to be an important event in his life, because by the time he graduated he was voted "most likely to pursue an alternative lifestyle."

Farny continued to study me, until ancient recognition set in: "You!" he snarled.

I'd bought Sandy a big ice cream sundae to celebrate her first-round knockout of the bargain basement Byron.

"Poetry thing didn't pan out, huh?"

Farny sniffed at me. "I still dabble. I've provided any number of comforting verses for the bereaved and the departed. A few well chosen words can make all the difference at a difficult time."

"It's a wonder T.S. Eliot didn't choose your line. Roses are red, violets are blue, J. Alfred Prufrock's dead, At least he wasn't a Jew."

A blank look.

"Good seeing you again, Farny. Sorry . . . Francis."

Shaking my head, I entered the Tulip Suite.

The sight of the coffin at the far end of the long narrow room hit me like a January wind. I gasped out loud, as any and all of my wise guy-itis froze and shattered in an instant. Even Farny must have sensed it, because in spite of everything, he offered a comforting pat on the shoulder, and gently closed the doors behind me.

I was alone in there with Sandy.

Again.

For the last possible time.

A dozen rows of empty chairs, lined up on either side of the narrow aisle, stood between us along with twenty-odd years and the impenetrable curtain of mortality.

No music played in the Tulip Suite. I didn't even know what Sandy might have wanted; the last time I'd seen her she was into the Monkees and the Turtles. But under the circumstances, "Daydream Believer" wouldn't have been any more appropriate than "Happy Together."

I walked up the aisle, slowly. Real slowly. Zim-

mer frame with training wheels slowly. Some
places you just don't want to get to.

The coffin was a plain one, cheap looking. No
fancy brass knobs or handles, not even much of a
gleam in the wood. It reminded me of a worn pair
of shoes, too scuffed even to take a good buff and
polish. That made me more depressed.

The lid was closed. I guess I should have
expected it. Sandy had, after all, been killed in a
car crash described in the paper as "cataclysmic."
Even allowing for a little tabloid purple prose,
you had to figure that her body took a bruising.
But somehow — foolishly, desperately — I had
assumed that I would be able to take one last
look at her. I'd been carrying around the image of
her perfect young face in my head for days, felt
that I'd never be able to get it out of my mind if I
couldn't look at her one last time.

That prison shrink was a big fan of closure.

With each slow step I took toward the coffin,
another mental snapshot of Sandy flashed in the
photo album of my memory. (Just my luck, I go all
eidetic when I least want to.) The stunned look on
her face that afternoon when we first met and I
bested her in our introductory "battle of the
brains." The pride in her eyes the day her dad
was named president of the local Kiwanis Lodge.
I stifled back a sob at the memory of her long legs,
glistening in the summer sun as we lay on the
beach at Blue Moon Lake.

I saw the broken-hearted darkness of her hurt
and fury the day I rejected her loving advances.

And then I was there: standing in front of the
dull box in which she'd be laid forever in the cold,
cold ground.

Just then a door opened at the side of the room, and an elderly woman in a stained grey smock came in. She stopped short when she saw me standing by the coffin.

"Oh, dear. I'm sorry, I didn't know anyone was here."

"That's all right," I said.

The woman reeked of chemicals, and I suspected that she worked in the embalming room. I didn't like to guess what those stains on her garment might have been. A small shudder went through me.

"I'll just get on out," she said, and headed back toward the door.

"Wait!"

She half-turned back to me, looking apprehensive.

"It's closed coffin," I said, pointing at Sandy.

The woman offered a twitchy blink of her eyes, then nodded.

"Does it have to be?" I asked.

"It's for the best."

"Have you . . . are you . . ." I felt uncomfortable asking the woman if she was the resident embalmer. It felt like prying into her sexual proclivities. "Did *you* see her?"

The woman blinked hard and nodded again. "Not very nice," she said. "Through the windshield. And then some."

Another gasp-cum-sob escaped me. It emerged of its own accord. The woman started blinking hard. Definitely backroom staff.

"Okay," I muttered, finding some composure. "Thanks."

The woman let out a big sigh and all but ran

for the door, like a fox who'd finally chewed that leg off and was free from the trap. I wished I could escape so easily.

I turned back to the coffin and stared at it some more. "And then some" the woman had said. I fought the image, but a picture formed in my head anyway. *Mechanized Death* and all those awful road safety scare films they used to show in high school came back to me, with images of people who'd been gored by steering wheels and had their heads sliced in half by broken glass. I tried to imagine the projectile force that sent Sandy hurling through the windshield, the sight of her sweet face slashed to ribbons, her head lolling off her tender neck.

I sobbed again; I couldn't hold it back. I reached out, gently, to brush my fingers against the lid of the coffin. A last, long goodbye. A touch, a kiss, a tear and I'd go. For good. Forever.

Someone coughed behind me.

I spun around, didn't see anyone at first. The lighting was dim, after all, *subdued*. I was sure no one had been in the room when I came in, hadn't heard anyone enter since. But sure enough, a tall, lean figure stood in the back corner of the room. I couldn't quite make out his features, but he looked pale and unwell: ghostly. The hairs on my neck stood on end and I felt as if the deathly cold from Sandy's coffin had spilled out into the room and rushed through me. The figure took something out of his pocket and put it to his lips. A cigarette? No. I heard a crinkle.

A chocolate bar.

I took a couple of steps down the aisle, and the

man sat down in the last folding chair in the last row. His legs were so long that his knees banged up against the seat in front of him. Though he was largely bald, he had the gangly look of a puppy or a young teenager who hasn't quite grown into his body. He continued to eat his candy bar. Three Musketeers. His face, like his frame, was long and lean, his pasty complexion pockmarked with deep acne scars. He had a bent, once-broken nose and as I got closer I could hear the labored breaths he took through it. Everything about him was awkward and off scale. Big hands dangled from too-short sleeves, thin neck lost in too-wide collar. As I neared the end of the row in which he sat, I could see how sheerly unwell he looked. Like a cancer patient, all drawn and hollowed out, holding on to life by a thread. If I looked like that I wouldn't hang out in a funeral home — not with a working-on-commission embalming lady floating around.

I was about to ask him who he was when the doors to the Tulip Room flew open and I once again found myself face to face with Roach Blackwell. As ever I remembered, a coterie of thick-necked, hard-eyed lackeys trailed a pace behind him, shuffling uncomfortably and looking nasty as old meat.

"Paid your respects then?" Roach said.

"Much as you can."

"Come to do the same. Figure I owe it to her. For old time's sake, if you know what I mean." Roach reached down and performed a minor adjustment on his balls. I dearly wanted to help him, and it must have showed, because his thugs stepped up closer behind him.

"You'll be heading out of town now," Roach said. There was definitely no question mark at the end of the sentence.

"Something like that," I said.

"Well, let's be sure and do this again in a few decades. If you're not back in the joint, that is."

I was still conjuring a worthy reply, but Roach had entirely dismissed me. He glanced over at the sickly fellow in the corner and offered him a pitying half-nod.

"Den," he said. "How's that dying thing coming along?"

The thin man finished his Three Musketeers with a big bite and noisily stuffed the wrapper in his pocket. He held up his hand and flexed his wrist in an unmistakable jerk-off gesture. His eyes were glued to me the whole time.

"I think you'll find that comes in handy now that she's gone," Roach said with a cruel chuckle. Then he walked up the aisle toward the coffin, his entourage in tow. I looked again at the man in the corner, wondering exactly who he was, what he was doing here. Though there was nothing like a family resemblance, it had occurred to me that he might be a relative. Sandy didn't have any brothers, but I had met some of her cousins once upon a time at Blue Moon Lake. For all I knew, her parents could have divorced and remarried, with the thin man being a step-brother.

Or an ex-husband, for that matter. Though the newspaper obituary hadn't mentioned the names of any survivors. And, foolishly if predictably, I didn't like the thought.

I still felt horribly disappointed that I hadn't

been able to look at Sandy one last time — it was really what my whole trip back was about. It felt incomplete, unfinished without that gesture. Damn that shrink!

Roach had reached the front of the room and was evaluating Sandy's coffin. I could tell he didn't think much of the workmanship. He called out to the thin man: "Aw, hell, Den. If this is the best you could afford, you should have come to me. This just ain't right. I wouldn't bury a broke-dick dog in a box like this."

The thin man — Den — took the words like a blow to his concave chest. I swear I heard an exhalation of air as they hit him. Fucking Roach.

Roach took a step back from the coffin, pointed at one his lackeys who I didn't know. "Open her up," he said. "Let's take a hasty bananas look, then get out of here and back to work."

"No!" Den and I screamed at the same time. I don't know about the thin man, but I wasn't about to let Roach see Sandy's body when I hadn't. It was too obscene to contemplate.

Roach's minions reached inside their jackets as the two of us made a move toward the front. They didn't quite pull anything out, but it was enough to stop the both of us in our tracks.

Roach smiled, fat and ugly. "You heard me, Wilmer," he told the first lackey, "crack her on open."

Just then the doors crashed open again and two men in floor-length dusters burst into the room. The pair looked very much alike, with long, greasy black hair tied back in ragged pony tails. They both were wild-eyed crazy and emanated

waves of psychopathic energy like B.O. This time
Roach's boys pulled the pieces out from inside
their jackets and levelled them at the pair. They
seemed not at all bothered by the fact that the
thin man and I stood directly in-between.

As soon as Roach's crew flashed their iron, the
two crazy men pulled matching shotguns out
from somewhere beneath their dusters. They covered Roach and his crew, and didn't seem too concerned by us monkeys in the middle either.

"We come to pay our respects," the taller of the
two said. In a jaw-dropping, Alphonso Bedoya
accent.

"Pendejo," the smaller man added. And spat
on the Tulip Room carpet. "Cucaracha."

These, I realized, could only be Los Bros: the
legendary Robusto Boys.

Roach just smiled his viper's smile at them.
"Got four guns up here, fellahs, only two down
there. You really want to start a ruckus, José?"

"Francisco," the taller one said. He nodded at
his brother.

Francisco lowered his left hand from the barrel of the shotgun, still keeping it perfectly level
and aimed at Roach's gut. He slowly reached back
under his duster and came out with a pineapple
grenade in his hand. He pulled the pin with his
teeth, grinning as he spat it across the room.

"Jesus Christ," I said.

"Easy now, boys," Den pleaded.

"C'mon, cabron," José called, "let's play it out.
You think we're not ready to die? Los Robustos
always ready to die. We *born* ready to die, maricón."

Roach was cool, I give him that. "For the love

of Mike, you boys ain't even Hispanic. Why do you insist on talking like that?"

I took another look at the Robustos, and realized that black hair notwithstanding, they were the palest, most white-bread looking pair of low-riding bad boys I'd ever seen. Spanish-American is an ethnic identity and not a skin tone, I know, but I met my share of Chicanos in the joint, and none were as pale as this pair.

"We're Latino, not Hispanic! You racist bastard. I bet you still say 'black' and not 'African-American.' We take you down now, I think. Let's do it, Francisco."

"Fuck," I yelled, ducking.

"Viva Zapata!" Francisco screamed.

At that instant, the door behind the Robustos opened up again and Farny sashayed on in. He took a look at the two armed camps and threw his hands on his hips.

"Oh my stars and garters," he exclaimed. "What in the world do you scoundrels think you're doing?"

Everyone froze, Francisco with his grenade arm cocked over his head, ready to release.

"*This* is a funeral home," Farny chided. "*This* is a place of respect and dignity. If you want to fight, you take it outside into the parking lot like all the other families. This simply will not do."

Roach actually blushed, and I swear, his boys all looked sheepish. Even Francisco glanced at his grenade with a gee-how-did-that-get-there look, before stuffing it back in the pocket of his filthy duster. Den took the opportunity to grab the pin off the floor and politely hand it back to him.

"Next time, cabron," José called out.

"Chinga su madre," Francisco hissed.

Roach nodded, and Los Bros slipped back out the door and ran down the hall. Roach's crew stowed their guns back inside their jackets. Roach jerked his head at the back door and the group of them followed him out.

I was still breathing hard, wondering how I hadn't been blasted into Swiss cheese or blown to kingdom como esta. Den was back in his corner chair, unwrapping another candy bar. Snickers.

"That was pretty slick, Farny," I said.

"Pshaw," he spat, "try orchestrating a Greek Orthodox funeral. *That's* trouble, my friend."

And he went back out the door.

I glanced at Den eating his chocolate. I took a long, soulful look at my beloved's coffin.

Shaking my head, I walked on out.

I started to head back toward the Anchor. There was nothing left for me to do but pack my bag, check out and put a heap of miles between me and Ideaville as quick as my trusty Pacer would take me.

Couldn't. Couldn't do it.

It wasn't that I didn't want to go; the visit had been a disaster from the moment I ran out of gas at the edge of town, and the sooner that Ideaville — and Roach and my father and everything it dredged up for me — could be slotted back into the recesses of unpleasant memory, the better.

But I couldn't do it.

I may not be the smartest kid in town anymore, and my powers of observation and detection are manifestly but a shadow of what they once were (or what I'd always thought they were), but something smelled rotten in the town of Ideaville. There was nothing I could put my finger on exactly, though clearly any place built in Roach Blackwell's image could be nothing other than corrupt to the core, but I had a nagging feeling that there was more to it; that something simply wasn't right.

Something to do with Sandy.

For one thing, I still felt a burning urge to have one last look at her. If Roach could walk on up there and pry open the coffin, why couldn't I? However awful the sight, I felt I could take it. I had to do it.

But there was more.

I suppose it was possible that even a vile specimen like Roach could be sentimental enough to pay his final respects to Sandy, but from what I'd heard about her — from what my father and the newspaper had told me — it didn't add up. If Sandy had fallen so low, what would Roach still want with her? Even in Ideaville, a town he ran, the most prominent citizen and leading businessman wouldn't want it to be known that he fraternized with hookers. And from the evidence, however much it pained me to admit it, that is what Sandy had become. I could easily imagine the joy Roach must have taken in Sandy's degradation and humiliation, getting even — and then some — for all the times she and I had foiled his juvenile capers in days gone by.

Must have been almost as good as seeing my mother every day in that big house of theirs. Calling her "mom," himself.

But even if I could fathom Roach's presence at
the funeral home, chalk it up to some sliver of
sentimentality, what in the world were the
Robustos doing there? I'd heard a little about
them, and from that encounter they seemed twice
as crazy as folks made them out to be. I tried to
convince myself that the grenade in the younger
brother's hand couldn't have been for real, but the
looks on the faces of Roach and his men suggested
otherwise. And those shotguns definitely weren't
just for show. What could a pair of crazy coders
like the Robustos have had to do with Sandy? It
was a bit rich to think that they should coinci-
dently show up just at the same time as Roach.

And then there was Den.

He was a sad looking creature, with his ghost-
white skin and shaky hands, but he showed surprising mettle in the middle of that free-for-all.
Roach's comments suggested that he had some
kind of romantic, or at least sexual link with
Sandy. Was he a john? Her pimp? Another lost
love come to say good-bye? What the fuck was
going on my big little town?

I knew I couldn't bring myself to leave until I
knew. Because this time when I did leave, I vowed
that it was going to be forever.

The funeral home closed at six, but the Comp
USA store was open until nine. I went in and
browsed for a while, keeping an eye on the front
door of Sobol & Sons, killing time playing games
on the demo machines until the staff started giving me dirty looks, and the security guard tapped
me on the shoulder. No more than half-a-dozen

visitors came and went from the mortuary the whole afternoon, and it was precisely at six that I saw Den shuffle out the front door. He walked with a wicked slouch and was slightly bowlegged — he looked like a bent-out-of-shape coat hanger. He didn't appear happy to be leaving the funeral home, and Farny had to practically shove him out the door. Even then he stood staring at it a while, before shambling on up the road toward the center of town.

I snuck around to the back of the property and ducked down behind a pissing Millard Fillmore fountain. I was hunched down there for half-an-hour before Farny came out the back door, accompanied by a young woman, also outfitted in conservative black. Farny locked the rear door and chatted with the woman for a few minutes, then they waved at each other and got into their separate cars. I waited another thirty minutes until the woman in the smock came out, and again locked the door behind her. She departed on a gleaming Harley, which probably offers some moral about stereotyping people, but at that particular moment I couldn't be bothered to draw out precisely what it might be.

Forty-five minutes later it was fully dark and, careful to keep out of the view of any late night shoppers in the computer store parking lot, I snuck up on Sobol & Sons.

I once owned a set of professional lock picks, but I didn't have them now and had never mastered the art of using them. It looks easy on TV, but then so does heart surgery. I don't have the knack for that either. What I had noticed while

hiding on the grounds, was a small open window
on the second floor. The glass was frosted over, so
I suspected it was a bathroom window. Someone
had opened it while I watched, and I'd prayed
that they'd done a smelly enough dump not to
close it again. Sure enough, it was still open, with
a rose-laden trellis leading almost to the spot.
The trellis wobbled as I started to climb, and I
was ruining the flowers, but it just did hold my
weight. The balancing act at the top was tricky,
but with a small (if courageous) leap, and with
the sound of snapping wood beneath me, I managed to grab hold of the window ledge and pull
myself up. I pried open the window and just managed to wriggle my fat ass inside, no worse for
wear than a tiny wood splinter in my palm.

I'd just have to tough it out.

Sure enough, I found myself in a toilet, though
it smelled of chemicals like the embalming
woman. There was still enough twilight for me
not to need to flick on the ceiling lights, and as I
gently eased open the door to the hall, I saw that
there was sufficient illumination to work my way
down to the Tulip Suite. It did occur to me that
there might be someone on duty at all times —
death waits for no man, and all that jazz — so I
proceeded as cautiously as I could up the hall and
down the stairs. I prayed that there was no alarm
system, reckoned from the fact of the open window that there couldn't be. If there was, no doubt
I'd have another encounter with Chief Dinky to
look forward to.

As I approached the Tulip Suite, I saw a book
of remembrance just outside the door. I hadn't

noticed it before, and certainly didn't sign it. I was tempted to do so now, though I resisted the impulse. Glancing at the pages, I saw only two signatures. One was Roach's, and the other was a blotchy scrawl I couldn't decipher: Den, perhaps. The pathetic quality of it brought all the sadness of Sandy's death — and life — back to me in a rush. Who, I wondered, was the book even for? Who was there to keep it and to remember?

Taking a very deep breath, I entered the Tulip Suite. Most of the lights were off, but a pair of flickering electric candle-bulbs at the front saw me up the aisle. There were no windows in the room, so I felt safe flicking on the ceiling lights. Even at full strength, the lighting was ever-so-tastefully subdued.

I walked up beside Sandy's coffin, rested my fingers on top and stroked the rough wood. I felt a sudden flash of paranoia and spun around to look in the corner of the room, but of course Den wasn't there.

It was just the two of us. Alone again at last.

And at the last.

"I'm sorry, Sandy," I said to her. I laid my cheek down atop the coffin, felt the tears welling in my eyes. "I'm sorry for everything. For failing you. And for failing myself. I'm sorry for my father and for what they did to you. I'm sorry for the life you had and for the life you should have had. For the life you deserved and that I should have given you.

"I'm sorry . . . for being me."

I stood up and though my hands were shaking, I found the latches that secured the lid of the coffin. Summoning what will I had left, I twisted open the catches, and closing my eyes, I opened the lid.

I opened my eyes and I looked at her.

Her hands were folded across her chest, the stem of a withered lily woven between her interlaced fingers. She was clothed in a simple grey dress that reached from her neck to her ankles. She wore scuffed black shoes on her small feet.

Her head was wrapped in a black shroud.

How awful were her injuries, I wondered, that even in a closed coffin her features had to be secreted from view? I was reduced to loud, choking sobs at the thought of how her life had ended, the pain she must have felt.

I wanted to crawl into that box beside her and be lowered into the forever darkness with her. It was, I felt, the very least that I deserved for my sins.

I started to unwrap the shroud. Whether to see her, or merely to punish myself to the maximum, I can't honestly say. I touched my fingers to the coarse cloth beneath her chin and unwrapped the first fold.

I saw her pretty face, bathed in golden sunlight, her perfect plum lips stretched in a wide smile, her eyes alive with the joy and ignorance and unfettered splendor of raw youth.

I tucked the shroud back around her throat. I saw, if only in the painful wonder of memory, what I'd really come to see.

I bent down and kissed her cold fingers. For the last time, I said good-bye.

I stood up to close the lid, had it halfway to

shut when the jolt ran through me and I threw it open again.

Careful not to disturb the placement, I pushed the lily aside and examined the fingers of her left hand. I rubbed my eyes and looked again at her flawless skin, then went over to see if there were any other lights I could turn on. There weren't.

I went back to the coffin and studied her hands, right and left, for a good ten minutes. My breathing had become ragged and labored, and a sheen of sweat dappled my brow. I was shaking like a plate of jelly on its wedding night.

"Fucking hell," I said to the empty room. My voice cracked.

I gently shut the lid of the coffin and resecured the latches.

I fled Sobol & Sons as quickly, if cautiously, as I could. Outside, I kept a worried lookout behind me for spying eyes.

I must have walked for hours, but I had no sense of the passing time. I think I traversed every street in Ideaville. Not a one registered in my consciousness. I know it was dark, surely I must have been cold, but none of that made any difference. I do remember stopping at one point to throw up in an alley near the corner of Prince Street and Exupéry Boulevard. Otherwise, I just walked and wondered.

And considered.

I only came back to myself sometime in the wee hours. Without volition, but clearly with some measure of subconscious desire, I once again found myself on Shortall Street, staring at

Sandy's old house. It was dark, of course; good people everywhere — are there good people anywhere? — were long since abed, dreaming dreams of fat-free ice cream, magic impotence pills, and all the myriad wonders of this third-millennium world. Nary a house light on the street was lit, and even the street lamps seemed dim. A soft breeze whistled across the manicured lawns and through the evenly spaced trees, carrying with it that late night-early morning scent that holds, in equal measure, death and promise: the hour of the wolf. A rail-thin fox dashed across the street, not even giving me a sideways glance, so still did I stand. No dogs barked; no night birds fluttered; not even the rumble of a truck on the highway, though a lonesome railroad whistle wouldn't have gone amiss.

Just me and the night and the unavoidable truth of what I knew. And as I stood there, staring at Sandy's old house, allowing myself yet again to be washed over by the seductive tides of nostalgia and self-pity, I knew, too, exactly what I needed to do; where I had to go. It was as clear as spring rain and as plain as a soda cracker.

Knowledge isn't power at all, you know; it is, pure and simply, unadulterated poison.

I went back to get my car and started to drive. I took off in the wrong direction at first. I was two miles west of town at Miller's Crossing before I remembered that I should be heading east.

My thinking wasn't all that it should be.

I hung a U-turn in the middle of the road; it didn't matter — there was no one else about. I cruised back through town at an even thirty, gunning it as soon as I hit the city line again. As the Blackwell Unlimited sign thanking me for visiting Ideaville faded in the rearview, I felt the sense of dread begin to lift from my shoulders. I knew what I expected to find at the end of the road — there was no logic to it, but I was as sure of it as you can be sure of anything in this life — and I was anxious as a virgin schoolboy copping his first feel. But just being out of the physical environs of Ideaville made me feel better.

Just as it had that day decades before when I hitched my way out of the old town, determined never to return.

I flicked the radio on, but there was nothing but country music. Why is that? Must have something to do the character of those who drive by night. The cassette deck hasn't worked for years and I could never bring myself to install a CD player in my Pacer. It violated the natural order of things.

So I drove in silence, with only my staticky thoughts to keep me company on the three-hour drive. In a way it formed a country-and-western soundtrack of its own.

The exit for Blue Moon Lake came on me so fast, or I reacted so slowly, that I had to jam on the brakes in order not to miss it. As it was I had to reverse down the highway ten yards in order to make the turn-off. The area didn't seem to have changed much over the years, but it had been so damned long, and the road was so dark, that I couldn't tell for sure. I couldn't even remember if I was heading in the right direction, but then I saw a battered sign promising three miles to the lake, and my heart began to race.

Blue Moon Lake had been an upscale resort when I was a kid, at least by boring, Midwestern standards. Of course, no one used the word "upscale" back then. And as I approached the road that circled the lake, I realized that not too many people would use it now.

Even in the dim glow of my headlights, I could see that the resort had come down in the world. The lakeside houses looked shabby and decayed, and more than a few were obviously abandoned. One or two were totally burned out. The little shopping district at the bottom end of the lake looked like a rust belt main street, with just a mangy general store and gas station still in business, surrounded by a row of vacant storefronts. A sign of changing times, I reckoned. Where once upon a time summer at the lake, in "the country," would have gone down a treat, today people'd just as soon go to Disney World. Probably doesn't cost a whole lot more and you get Universal Studios to boot. I was tempted to stop and go down to the lake itself, stick my fingers in just to reassure myself that it still was full of cold, clear water.

But I had someplace to be.

I continued counterclockwise around the lake, slowing as I got close to four o'clock. It had been a long time, and I couldn't remember clearly.

That's another lie. I knew exactly which bungalow it was, but was scared shitless to see it again.

Accepting the fate I'd decreed for myself, I stopped the car in front of Sandy's parents' old summer house as the first predawn glimmer lightened the eastern sky. Their house, too, was looking decrepit. The once-gleaming white paint peeled from the wooden timbers in queen-sized sheets. The screen door had come off its hinges and was propped against the porch rail, which itself had come detached from the wall, rotting away. The front door stood shut, but one pane of glass was missing from the window and another had a crack in the shape of a crescent moon. I cocked my head, wondering what was missing, then I realized it was the squeaky cry of the rocking chair. It no longer filled the front porch, but you could see the spot where it had stood, because the wood that had lain shadowed beneath it remained a shade lighter than the rest of the porch floor. That floor creaked, though, as I strode up the steps, the wood mushy beneath my feet. There was bird shit everywhere, and a collection of cat turds in a window box which was now filled with filthy sand.

I bent down to peer through the broken pane of glass in the door, but the inside of the house was as dark as out. It looked messy in there, but not abandoned. I turned the knob — it wasn't locked — and pushed open the door. I stepped inside and was greeted by a chorus from the past.

"You're not going to let her wear those postage stamps," Sandy's father said.

"She's just a girl."

"They're . . . doing it."

"It's yours for the taking."

"Go for it, big boy."

"Oh, baby."

"Roach'd do it. Roach'd do it. Roach'd do it. Roach'd do it . . ."

"STOP!" I yelled. I heard some creature scuttle out from under the house and run into the woods.

"Please stop," I whispered.

Why does life hurt so much?

I walked over to the kitchen table and picked up a dirty coffee cup. I sniffed at the dregs and put it back down. I went over to the refrigerator and opened it. The light didn't come on, but it was cold inside and there were eggs and milk. I touched my fingers to the drain in the sink; they came away wet and a little bit slimy.

I walked back out to the front porch. An old barrel lay on its side. I remembered how Sandy's parents used it as a card table on summer nights, and would sit across from each other playing cribbage and sipping martinis. I'd thought it was the most sophisticated thing in the whole damn world and prayed that I'd grow up to be just like them. I righted the barrel — it still felt pretty solid — brushed it off and sat down on it. It wobbled a little, but it held my weight. I stared out into trees and across the lake which reflected the first shimmering rays of a bright morning sun. I waited and listened, but there wasn't a sound. I waited some more before I called her name.

I called it again. And a third time.

"Come out, Sandy. Please," I said.

There was only silence, and for the briefest of moments I considered that I was entirely wrong in my deductions. Again.

But then there came a rustling from the

brush. A swish of leaves, a twig snapping. A sigh full of the sadness of ages.

Sandy emerged from a dirt trail leading off into the woods, and walked up onto the overgrown bungalow lawn. She was older, sadder, heavier. And so broken.

She was also more beautiful than I remembered, than I could bear. Tears rolled down her cheeks, but a wisp of a smile played at her perfect lips.

"How did you know?" she asked.

VII. Playback

Sandy walked across my field of vision, from right to left, until she stood with her back to the lake, the rising sun a halo of fire behind her head. For that moment, I forgot everything that had happened; I was in the presence of some angel of heaven returned to earth, and I literally slumped to my knees in wonder. The years, the decades, melted away like cheap candle wax before the savage heat of that vision and I was once again a boy, sure of myself, untroubled by the woes and weariness of a life gone inexorably wrong. The delicate morning breeze carried with it a freshness, a scent of something rediscovered, a palpable taste of a better past, long since forgotten, or consigned to musty boxes of memory stashed away in the attic of bitter experience. Rekindled inside me was a sense of opportunity, a feeling that anything and everything remained possible to a young man in a wide and wonderful world. I felt an explosion in my chest, a detonating firework of joy in my heart, warming me from within as the golden rays of morning sunlight bathed my skin from without. I felt a surge of passion as an eruption of energy flooded through my veins and pumped through my organs, into my brain and out, I'd swear, through my eyes and fingers and thinning blades of hair. I felt — beyond expectation, beyond hope — *young* again.

Then Sandy stepped out of the penumbra of light, and I saw her — and everything — for what it truly was.

She'd gone puffy with the years, bloated as from too many cream-filled pastries, too many shots of Boodles, beer back. As a girl Sandy'd always had chipmunk cheeks and been partial to sweets and treats — many's the time we shared Knickerbocker Glories at Looie's Sweet Shoppe (I always gave her my maraschino cherry — does the symbolism just kill you?), and many was the time I accompanied a nervous Sandy to the dentist. As a luscious teen, she'd learned to curb her sweet tooth and took to playing tennis and volleyball to tone her fine body. But those athletic days were clearly behind her, and the taut muscular lines of her teenaged years had given way to the slack curves of impending middle age. She wore her hair too long, and tied back in a pony tail — no woman over the age of seventeen can get away with a pony tail without looking like they're trying too hard to be young. Her chin sagged with excess flesh, and the golden complexion I remembered from that summer long ago had faded into a mottle of pockmarks and emerging liver spots. She wore a baggy Addidas running suit, but I detected beneath it the first distending dome of a pot belly. Her breasts were as full as ever, but had dropped like the stock market on a black Monday and her white ankles, visible between the cuffs of her sweats and her dirty ankle socks, were unshaved. And though she had trouble meeting my gaze, I saw a blankness in her teary brown eyes. The vitality and intelligence that had resided there had dulled to a stupor of sadness and loss.

Yet still she looked utterly, heart-stoppingly beautiful to me. Just because the impossible had happened and she was alive.

Because she was, and would ever be, my Sandy.

"How did you know?" she asked again. She strode up to the single step at the edge of the porch. Her hair had gone darker with the years and split-ends stringy.

"Maybe I just know you too well," I said. With an insouciance I didn't really feel. I was sure Sandy could hear it in my voice.

"You don't know me at all," she said, and she laughed. It wasn't a happy sound, though. She pulled a pack of Camels from the pocket of her sweatshirt and lit up with a cheap, disposable lighter. "What in the world are you doing here, anyway?"

"I came for your . . . for the funeral. I wasn't actually planning to go to the funeral itself, but I came to say good-bye. To see your . . . to see you."

"No shit?"

"I felt like I owed it to you. Good one, huh?"

"You don't owe me shit. And that works two ways, boy-o."

I shrugged. "Maybe I thought I owed it to myself. Or maybe I'm just a sentimental jerk."

"You said you'd never come back," she said, and coughed a smoker's phlegmy morning hack

"People talk. People lie. Life goes on. Oo-bla-dee-bla-da."

"You *swore* it. Vowed. Like I've never seen any-

one swear before or since. And I've seen and
heard some swearing in my time, believe me."

"There's a county coroner who'd probably
swear on a stack of bibles that you're dead. Or is
he in on the gag, too?"

"No gag," Sandy said.

"You're a fine looking piece of stiff, Sandy."

"Nice of you to say. I see you're still a pretty
fair liar."

"No lie. You're still beautiful, Sandy. You
always were to me. You always will be."

She took a final drag on her cigarette, shot the
butt into the dry grass without putting it out. She
ran a hand through her oily hair in a self-con-
scious way. She stepped up onto the porch and
stood right in front of me. She smelled a little
funky — two or three days without a bath — and
the closer she got, the clearer the sadness of the
current state of her became.

"You lie like the chickenshit asshole you are,"
she said. "But then I've always liked that in a
man. Want to come inside?"

She'd already walked past me to the door
when I nodded my assent. There was nothing in
the world I wanted more than to follow where she
led. She pushed open the door and ushered me in
with an exaggerated sweep of her hand. I paused
at the threshold and looked her in the eye. She
wouldn't meet my gaze for more than a flash, but
as I went through the doorway, she lurched back
at me like a cobra and planted the most fleeting
of kisses on my passing cheek.

"Welcome home," she whispered, and dashed
into the old bungalow.

The summer house didn't look any better in the
daylight. The once-happy wallpaper — Sandy and
I'd "helped" her folks paste it up long ago —
curled away from the cracked plaster walls, and
brown Rorschach patterns of mold and damp dotted the ceilings. Rusted springs poked through
the worn fabric of the broken-legged sofa, and a
rainbow coalition of insects were holding their
very own Olympic games at various sites around
the living room carpet. Where once the bungalow
had been a place of summery brightness and
warmth, it now reeked of mustiness and dark and
cold. I tried to connect it back with gayer times,
but it felt like a different house altogether.

I trailed Sandy into the kitchen. There was an
empty space where the stove used to stand,
though an old refrigerator hummed away in the
corner. Sandy gestured for me to sit down at the
rickety breakfast table, while she put on some coffee. She had to boil the water in a dented pot atop
a single-ring hot plate. There's something inher-
ently depressing about hot plates: only people
who live alone — who can cook their meals in a
single pot — have them. Hot plates always make
me think of my grandfather, long since dead, who
used one after my grandmother died, despite having a big kitchen to cook in. People who *choose* to
cook on hot plates are people who have given up
on life.

Of course, in Sandy's case that was the literal
— at least the legal — truth of the situation.

Sandy poured instant coffee straight from the
jar into mugs and added the water. She took a
half-pint container of skim milk out of the fridge,

made a face as she sniffed it, and held it out toward me.

"You a gambling man?"

"Black's okey-doke with me."

"Smart boy."

She put the sour milk back in the fridge — I don't know why — grabbed the mugs and plunked them down on the table. She dragged a three-legged stool from in front of the sink and sat down across from me.

"So how did you know I wasn't dead?" she asked.

I took a sip of coffee. It was half-past stale. A bunch of packets of restaurant sugar — from The Boxcar, I noted — sat on the counter. I grabbed a couple and spilled them into my mug. I looked for something to stir with, but didn't see anything at hand. Sandy watched me, but didn't offer to get a spoon.

"Well?"

I put down my coffee, reached out and took her right hand between both of mine. She tried to snatch it away, but I tightened my grip.

"The answer's right here," I said. I rubbed the skin of her knuckles beneath my thumb. A thick, if ancient, scar cut across the second and third knuckle, faded almost — *almost* — to the point of invisibility.

She stopped resisting and stared down at her hand in mine. She shook her head and issued a little laugh.

"Jesus Christ. Who else would remember?"

"No one. No one in the world but me. Not even Roach, I wouldn't think."

"Though if anyone shouldn't forget . . . "

"Do you remember how it happened?" I asked her.

"God! That stupid baseball game."

"The coin toss."

"I *remember*," Sandy said. She let me continue to stroke the back of her hand. "We challenged Roach and his cronies to a put-up or shut-up game to determine who was the best in town. I was pitching. Like always."

"You had that wicked curveball. I never did learn how to throw it."

"I tried to teach you so many times, remember? I *could* have taught you, if you'd only let me."

"You could have taught me a lot of things. If I'd only let you."

"But for a smart kid, you were a slow learner."

"I was an idiot."

She flicked a look into my eyes, then turned her gaze back on our hands. I kept on rubbing at her calloused skin. Her fingernails looked like they'd been gnawed by a grizzly bear.

"Roach insisted we flip a coin for home side and visitors."

"Visitors were always skins," I said.

"I think I still would have done it, you know," Sandy said. "I really would. Just to shut him up. I would have taken the fifty-fifty gamble, and if I'd lost, pitched bare tits to the world. And I still would have struck him out with the slow curve. But Roach insisted on using that stupid trick coin of his for the toss."

"The same one he used to con that fancy Swiss army knife off of Alvin what's-his-name."

"I heard from his mom that Alvy got killed in the Gulf," Sandy said.

"I really nailed Roach on that knife scam . . . "

"*We* nailed him, you mean."

"We nailed him, and he thought we wouldn't notice it was the same stupid coin."

"He flipped it anyway," Sandy said, "and when it came up heads, he demanded that I take my shirt off, 'cause 'fair's fair.' What a jerk. I told him no way."

"And he smiled that nasty Roach smile and called you a cunt. The others were so shocked they gasped, but I didn't even know what it meant. I'd never so much as heard the word before. Typical or what?"

"I'd heard it," Sandy said. Her lips formed a sad smile. "Who would have known he was so prescient."

"He turned to look at his buddies and laugh."

"He never should have taken his eyes off of me."

"You hauled off and slugged him with everything you had. You wound-up just like you would have done to throw the big curve. You caught him square in his fat laughing mouth."

"Man, did that hurt."

"But it hurt him more. The sucker went down like a building in one of those controlled demolition jobs. Crumbled, just like in slow motion."

"Blood gushing out of his mouth, pouring out of the cut on my hand. I was bawling like a baby. I had to have stitches in the end."

"Roach needed two false teeth."

"I got grounded a month for each tooth."

"And you got a scar." I held her hand up between us. "This scar. This scar that isn't on the hand of the corpse of the girl in the Tulip Suite at Sobol & Sons Funeral Home."

She pulled her hand away and hid it under the table.

"Once a detective, always a detective, huh?" she said.

"No one else would remember," I said again. "No one in this world."

"It's ironic, really."

"How do you mean?"

"That day. I sometimes think about how it maybe shaped everything that came afterward."

"I don't follow."

"Roach just wanted to see my tits, didn't he? That's what the whole stupid challenge game was really about. I didn't even have any tits then, that's the laugh. And he sure got to see all he wanted in the end."

Now I pulled back, crossing my hands over my chest defensively.

"He likes to do it Spanish, you know. Far and away his favorite."

"Spanish?" I asked. My voice squeaked.

"Still the little virgin ears, huh?" Sandy shook her head sadly. "Spanish, you know? Roach liked to titty-fuck me. Just crazy for it. I think mostly it was because when he shot off that way he could spurt over my face. Boy, how that made him laugh. I did wonder sometimes if it didn't all start that day on the diamond, though. What if he'd got his gander way back when? Maybe he'd have been satisfied. Probably not."

I had no response to that. Sandy saw my discomfort, which seemed to harden her look.

"Sometimes I just imagined it was you."

"What?"

"When Roach was doing it to me. Fucking my tits, coming all over my face."

Sandy got up to boil some more water. I sat there, hung my head, and wished I had died. A long, long time ago.

We moved back out to the porch. The house was just too dank, too depressing. And a sunny day, crisp as a new dollar bill, had settled in. A lone rowboat appeared out in the middle of the lake, a couple of early morning fishermen trying their luck. I swear I could hear the sweet "choosh" of their beer cans opening all the way across the water. Sandy and I sat side by side on the concrete step. As we'd done for so many hours, so many years before. Her skin looked sallow in the bright sunlight, so much so I wondered if she maybe had hepatitis. Or something worse.

"So who's the girl?" I asked.

"What?"

"In the coffin. The dead girl with no face and no scar and your name. The girl they'll be burying in your grave?"

"Burning. It'll be a cremation."

"Of course, much more convenient. But who is she?"

"Does her name really matter?" Sandy said. She whirled the remains of her coffee around in her mug than splashed it out into the dead grass. "She won't be missed, believe me."

"Everybody has a mother," I said. "I should know."

Sandy shot me a look. "You being queer?"

"No more so than usual."

"I forgot," Sandy said, nodding. "It has been a long time."

"You haven't answered the question."

"What are you going to do if I tell you?"

I started to reply, then stopped and took a deep breath. I didn't have the faintest idea, actually. I wasn't running to any plan here, just moving by instinct. Which is what landed me back in Ideaville to begin with.

"I don't know," I admitted. "For Christ's sake, Sandy, what *could* I do?"

"Wow," Sandy said, "ain't that a kick in the teeth. The three little words I thought I'd never hear you say: 'I don't know.' The Boy Detective's all grown up now, isn't he?"

"It happens to the worst of us," I said.

Sandy studied me and nodded. I saw something different in her eyes.

"Her name was Georgina and she was a working girl," Sandy told me. She got up and started pacing back and forth in front of the porch. "Like me."

Sandy checked for some reaction, but I don't think I offered one. After the conversation with my father, I wasn't surprised to hear what she'd been doing, how she survived, but in any case I hoped I was enough in control of myself not to let any disapproval show.

Not that I was in any position to disapprove of somebody else's life.

"It's not who — where — I expected to be," she said.

"I think we can all say that."

"Really? Even Roach?"

I had no answer to that.

"Me and Roach, we sure were an item. I suppose you remember that much."

"I'm not likely to forget."

"You sent me running to him. Shot me out of a cannon practically. That day, here. The Fourth of July weekend."

"I know what I did. Or failed to do. I don't suppose it matters that I didn't mean to hurt you. Didn't want to."

"Not a whit," Sandy said. But there wasn't rancor in her voice so much as resignation. I'd have preferred rancor, I think.

"It was fun for a while, in that teenaged way. Roach had become everyone's hero and I was his girl. We were the star couple, the ones all the other kids envied and despised and wished they could be. It was so amazing after all those years of being an outsider, of being the freak because I was so smart."

"So what are you saying? You suddenly got stupid?"

"I played stupid," Sandy said, and sighed. "I was the Meryl Streep of stupid, right down to the hokey accent. I wore short skirts and tight tops and fluttered my eyes whenever Roach and his pals passed by. I played all the petty, girly high school games, and gossiped and bitched and smoked cigarettes in the toilet. And of course I gave hand jobs under the football stands."

"You smoked?" I asked. It drew a withering glance.

"But mostly I put out for Roach."

Sandy turned her back to me and stared out at the lake. One of the fishermen in the boat was standing in the prow, pissing out over the side in an extravagant arc of yellow. It reminded me of the fountain at the funeral home.

"Roach had his appetites, even then. He still does, of course. At first it was like he couldn't believe I would even agree to go near him — he always thought of me as your girl. I suppose everyone did. Except maybe you."

I cleared my throat.

"He treated me like a princess for a while," she continued, "like something too precious to touch. But he got over that fast enough."

"You don't have to do this," I said. For a second, god help me, I almost echoed my father. "The past is . . . "

Sandy looked back over her shoulder at me. "Don't you want to know? Would you rather not know? Who are you worried about? Me or you?"

"Go on," I croaked.

"It was just raging hormones that sent me running to him. And spite for you, of course. That first time I actually had to grab his hand and shove it between my legs. Tell him that I wanted him. *Where* I wanted him."

"I didn't have to tell *him* twice."

She turned around and sat back down beside me on the step, lighting up another cigarette.

"It was pretty wonderful for a while. Roach gave me the physical satisfaction that I wanted and needed. That you wouldn't provide. And I gave him a kind of . . . "

"Legitimacy?" I suggested.

"Yeah. Respectability. At least at first. Kids — teachers, even — who'd always dismissed Roach as a thug and a bully started looking at him differently. If a smart, nice girl like me could go out with him, then maybe he was all right. Of course, I never considered how being with him might reflect on me."

"Your parents . . . "

Sandy laughed. "Right. You wouldn't even know. My mom got ill right after you took off. Liver cancer. She was in and out the hospital for months. My dad became totally preoccupied with her, barely noticed if I came or went. Or who with."

"Sorry."

She shrugged. "It was rough, but it kind of suited me. Hell, the empty house just made it that much easier for me and Roach to have a place to screw. And man alive did we ever screw."

"You like saying that to me, don't you? You like the effect the words have on me, the power in your mouth."

"Honey, the power in my mouth has kept me in Milk Duds and DVD's for a lot of years now. So don't knock it. And, yeah, maybe I do like the way it feels, and the look it draws out of your face. Why shouldn't I like that?"

There was no good answer to that.

"So what went wrong?" I asked.

"Roach was still Roach, wasn't he? He could throw a football, and he could talk up a storm; sell the hell out of those hi-fis and fridges in his dad's appliance shops. But in the darkness of his tiny heart, he was still the Roach."

Sandy stood up again, shook her legs in a little dance. "Gone to sleep," she explained. She draped herself around the peeling pillar that supported the roof of the porch. It was a very girlish gesture, one I remembered from long ago. It made my heart hurt even more.

"We were supposed to be the homecoming king and queen senior year. Can you believe that?"

"No," I said. "I can't."

"Just shows to go you. I'd gone from being the little Miss Marple of the freak brigade to the belle of the ball in the space of a few short months. And all it took was leaving you behind. Well . . . "

"Well?"

"Well," she went on, "that and sucking Roach's cock on demand."

My veneer of non-judgmentalness must have cracked at that point. Sandy nodded her agreement at my sour expression.

"I didn't mind. Truth be told, Roach gave good as he got in those days. Until he started moving up in the world, he knew a thing or two about going down. But that wasn't good enough for our old pal."

"I'm not surprised."

"I was. I guess I was still pretty naive. I hadn't reckoned on Roach's . . . generosity."

"What?"

"Roach didn't believe in keeping a good thing to himself, no sirree. Share and share alike was Roach's philosophy. And share he did."

"Sandy . . . "

She ignored me. "Week before the homecoming dance, Roach told me he had a special surprise for me. He told me it was waiting for me back at that goofy old clubhouse his gang used to keep by the junkyard. Remember?"

I nodded.

"God, I was so excited. I was sure he was taking me there to pin me. Hard to imagine kids doing that today, or even caring about something so dumb. But I was just certain that was the night we were going to officially be 'going steady.' Roach had a flask of hooch with him and we drank from it as we walked. Or I did. I didn't realize at the time that he never took a sip. I'm afraid the powers of observation you had so carefully honed in me had slipped a little by that point."

"I take it there was something more than booze in the flask."

"Oh, yeah," Sandy said. "Roach was years ahead of his time when it came to date rape techniques. A real innovator. Amazing what a little bit of Benzedrine will do to a slightly drunk waif of a teenaged girl."

"And at the clubhouse?"

"Oh, I got pinned, all right. Pinned and pricked and stuffed and . . . The gang was all there. And apparently the gang that bangs together, hangs together. Or so Roach must have believed."

"Jesus, Sandy . . . "

"Especially when you get pictures of them all in the act."

The fishermen had drifted out of sight, but I

saw a car driving along the lakefront road. It was on the far shore, but other than the rowboat, it was the first sign of life I'd seen.

"Needless to say, I didn't make it to the homecoming dance. I barely left my room for weeks. In the end, it was only because my mom died that I came out at all. When people saw how awful I looked, they figured it was from the shock of her dying. Them that didn't already know the truth, that is."

"How do you mean?"

Sandy clucked her tongue, offering me a disgusted look that said *grow up*.

"Roach couldn't keep those pictures to himself. Quelle surprise. Everyone in school saw them. I got obscene phone calls for months. Jizz-filled rubbers dropped through the letterbox in our front door. I couldn't walk through the park without some asshole waving his dick at me or coming up and grabbing my ass. In broad daylight! It was open season on the senior slut."

"You should have reported them," I said. I tried to swallow back the words even as they sounded in my ears.

Sandy laughed hysterically.

"Shall we talk about your dad, the esteemed Chief of Police?" she asked. "And about his involvement in Ideaville's small but highly profitable prostitution racket? Perhaps you're already aware of his fondness for buggering young girls."

The car had now driven all the way around the lake and was slowing as it approached the cabin. Sandy finally took note of it. I shot her a questioning look, but she didn't seem concerned. As it came up the crumbly ruins of the driveway,

I saw that it was a lime green Dodge Dart, near as old as my Pacer and possibly worth even less. The brakes screeched to a halt and a tall, lean, sickly-looking figure emerged carrying two paper bags filled with groceries. The driver shut the car door with his foot and approached us on the porch.

"Hey," he said to Sandy. He eyed me with evident suspicion and dislike.

"I take it you've already met Den," Sandy said.

I nodded, but wasn't at all sure that I understood.

Sandy was boiling more water on the hot plate. She made Den a cup of instant hot chocolate and more coffee for the two of us. Den had brought back some fresh milk, so I lightened mine up. Sandy drank hers black as night. Den snatched up his mug, dug a big package of fun-sized Milky Way bars out of the grocery bag and retreated into one of the bedrooms. I heard him flick on a TV, followed by the squeaks and squawks and repetitive chirpy melody of a video game. The little light bulb went off.

"Den's a gamer, isn't he?" I said.

Sandy shrugged, half-nodded.

"How bad?"

"You see how he looks," she said, matter-of-factly.

"Terminal?"

"Probably. We don't talk about it. We're pretty much a day-at-a-time kind of family. Suits us both."

"Jesus. What are you doing with a guy like that, Sandy?"

She laughed in my face. "Well, George Michael is gay, and Matt Damon is spoken for, and George Clooney simply won't return my calls, the rat bastard. So what's a girl to do? And who are you to ask me that question?"

"I just meant . . . "

"Fuck you. Den takes good care of me and I look after him. Much as I can, at least. He doesn't care what I am or what I've done. Or who's done me. He's a gamer, yeah, but so what? I'm a whore. Den doesn't care. He worked for YellowHat once, high up, too, but they cut him loose when the gaming got too bad; when he got heavy into the VR. He still finds the odd coding job around town — pirate work pretty much, off the books. Sometimes they stiff him, just 'cause they can. But he does it for me." She gestured around her at the shabby bungalow. "Keeps us in the style to which we've grown accustomed."

"And the dead girl, the *other* whore? Did Den do that for you, too?"

Sandy's anger faded again into sadness.

"No," she said, "that was the Robustos."

"Caramba," I muttered.

"Like Roach, those boys have got their appetites. You must have heard about how they killed their parents. Shot-gunned both of 'em in the back and walked away from the trial clean as driven snow. The things money can buy."

"What a fucking town."

"I thought you'd grown up, Boy Detective. Maybe you're not such a man of the world after all."

"Maybe I never thought that world could come here," I said.

"Maybe it's always been. Ask your dad, if you've any doubts."

I dropped my head in my hands. Sandy just clucked at me.

"You're either on top or you're on bottom in this life," she told me. "And I'm not talking bedroom positions here. There's them that's got and them that's not, and god bless the child that's got his own, like the junkie sang. I've been down so long the bottom of a well'd look like up to me. I've been whoring around this town for twenty-odd years, seen and done things that you still can't imagine. I've been had by everyone who'd have me, and done half the rest for kicks. I spent a weekend not too long ago with that Man from YellowHat. You seen his little monkey? People think it's so damn cute. Goes everywhere with him. Does everything he does. *Everything*. Do you understand what I'm saying? What do you do, where do you go after something like that?"

"I don't know," I whispered, still staring at my shoes.

"You go to the grave. Or you get put there."

I looked up at her.

"Why didn't you just leave, Sandy. Like . . . "

"Like you did?"

I nodded.

"Roach wouldn't let me. You think there's anything in this town out of his control? He still likes to have me sometimes, you know. Hell, my knees have probably made a permanent impression in his office carpet by now."

"That can't be it. I mean . . . "

"No, I know what you mean. I know a thing or
two about playing the skin flute, but it's not just
that. Roach can get pussy up the wazoo if he
wants it. No, I think he holds onto me because of
what I represent to him: a triumph over his past.
I'm his memento, his trophy. You cut out long ago.
He didn't get the chance to stuff your head and
mount it on his wall, much as he would have liked
to. So he stuffs mine, and mounts me wherever he
can. I'm the symbol of his triumph over you. And
everything you stood for: the town, the life that
was, the past that he hated."

"Oh, Sandy . . . " For a second a thought I was
going to be sick and fell to my knees. Sandy mis-
understood.

"No," she said. "Get up. I don't blame you. At
least, not any more. C'mon big boy, it's okay now.
I live with who I am. I don't mind it."

As I looked up she held out her hands. Tenta-
tively I reached out and grasped them in my own.
With deceptive strength she hauled me up off the
floor. We stood there, face to face for a moment.

Then I took her in my arms.

I squeezed her tight, burying my face in her
neck. Her earthy, unwashed scent smelled like a
blast from a florist's open door. I felt her arms slip
around my back and I gripped her even tighter. In
spite of everything — the squalor of the bungalow,
the pain and guilt of all the memories — the years
suddenly washed away like hopscotch chalk off a
sidewalk in a hard rain. Tears flowed and my nose
started to run. I turned my head to the side and
opened my eyes, catching a glimpse of the pair of
us in the grimy reflection of an old hall mirror.

There was me: draped over my childhood love, sobbing, shattered, broken.

There was Sandy: standing stiffly, mechanically patting my back, staring off into space with a whore's bored and calculating gaze.

As I shoved her away, her eyes widened and went — I thought — just a little sad as she saw that I recognized her for what she'd truly and utterly become.

"This is me," she said. And her voice cracked. It didn't sound at all rehearsed or rote, but who the hell knows? "This is me."

I ran out of the house.

Den was sitting with Sandy at the kitchen table when I got back. He was slurping a fresh mug of hot chocolate with a big swirl of whipped cream on top, and tucking into a hunk of chocolate fudge cake the size of a baby's head. Sandy held an empty coffee cup in her hand and stared at the floor. It looked like she'd been crying.

"Hey," I called through the ripped screen door. "Can I come in?"

Den ignored me. Sandy almost shrugged. I opened the door.

"I'm sorry," I said.

Sandy offered another semi-shrug.

"Running away didn't work all those years ago; I don't know how I thought it would help now."

"You here to help?" Den asked through a cocoa mustache.

"Yeah, I am." I grabbed a McDonald's napkin from a stack on the counter and tossed it to him. As if to prove it.

"How you gonna do that?" Sandy whispered. She still hadn't looked up.

"I don't know yet. I'm not sure. But I've got to do something. This is . . . sick."

Now Sandy looked up.

"Not you," I said. "Not you. I'm in no position to pass judgment on anyone; not you, not my dad, hell, maybe not even Roach. But as I was walking along the lake, thinking about what I could and should do, where I might go, I realized it's time I confronted what I've done to myself. What I've made of my life."

"Heavy," Den said. Then he cut himself another slice of cake and walked out.

"I told you I came back to Ideaville to say good-bye. To you. And I thought that's what I was doing, convinced myself that's what the trip was all about."

"Wasn't it?" Sandy asked.

"In part, sure. But there was more to it, things I didn't want to admit. I always swore I'd never go home again because I told myself that there was nothing there for me; as long as you were here, with Roach, hating me, laughing at me, there was nothing but the bitterness I'd run away from to begin with."

"But it hasn't been like that."

"I know that now. I see the reality of the situation and not my childish illusions. But that reality in some ways is even worse than what I had imagined.

"Sandy, for all that happened, Ideaville —our *old* town — remained some kind of bright and shiny beacon in my mind. A Shangri-La or

Brigadoon that heart and soul ache for because it can only ever be out of reach. Did you ever see that movie *Local Hero*? I have the tape, must have seen it fifty times, and I still cry, feel my heart break a little every time at the end when the guy has to leave that magical little town. That's my Ideaville. *That's* what I always dreamed might still exist here in some shape, some form. Even knowing that you were with Roach. Even knowing what had happened to my parents. Somewhere in the last vestige of my romantic imagination I held out the hope that if I wanted to, if I had the nerve, that I *could* come back here and find everything that I'd lost."

Sandy shook her head, but a smile played on her lips. "You're not even smart anymore," she said.

I laughed out loud. "No, I'm not. The bitterest pill, the toughest lesson was learning that being the smartest kid in a dull Midwestern town ain't worth the proverbial bucket of warm spit. I hadn't been out of town two days when that message started to sink in."

"Must have been tough."

"Brutal. But all the important life lessons are."

"So what have you decided?"

"That depends on you," I said.

Sandy suddenly looked wary. "What do you mean?"

"All this," I said, waving my hands about. "Everything that's happened, that you — you and Den — have arranged. Do you really want out of here? Tell me true."

Sandy looked so fragile, so pained, that it broke my heart all over again She could barely bring herself to nod her head.

"It'll take more determination than that," I said. I had to force a hardness that I didn't truly feel.

"I do want it," she pleaded, "I do want out."

"Okay," I said. "But there are some things I have to know. First of all, the dead girl. You said the Robustos were involved. You mean that they killed her, right?"

"Oh, yeah."

"And they know that you know? How could they let you live?"

Sandy turned away again. "I do things for them. All kinds of things."

"So they've helped you set all this up?"

"Yes. They use me in their fight against Roach and Blackwell."

"Good. That'll work for us."

"How? What do you want to do? What *can* you do?"

Den stumbled back out from the bedroom just then, glassy-eyed and pale as any corpse.

"More cake?" he asked.

I pointed at the woeful gamer. "We'll start with him," I said.

VIII. Woman in the Dark

I left Sandy with Den at the cabin on the lake, and spent the next two days engaged in a furious data-gathering exercise. Most of that time was spent alone in my room, just me and my modem trawling the endless threads that weave the Web, locating and pressing contacts where I had them, forcing my way through firewalls and corporate security where I didn't. Den, as it turned out, had worked for all of the big boys in town (and most of the small ones) and for all his pathetic gaming ways, had taken care to learn a thing or two about the systems everywhere he worked. Following his leads and developing a few of my own, I managed to get a pretty fair sense of what was going down at and between Black X, Los Bros and YellowHat. The software war among the three powerhouses had more-or-less been a cold one for eighteen months or so, with Black X slowly using their hefty market share to drive the Robustos and the Man from YellowHat ever closer to the edge. Los Bros had the best and most violent games, and YellowHat the cleverest designers and coders, but through sheer force of money and resources Roach was the 800-pound gorilla in the Ideaville bar, and he damn well sat where he pleased. For all his might, however, I saw that the ongoing cold war could be heated up fast, if only a few small fires were lit beneath any

173

of my sordid town's many combustible tinder
boxes.

Just call me blowtorch.

The place to start, loathe as I was to admit it,
was with José and Francisco Robusto. As I'd
already seen, the brothers were highly excitable
— hell, downright insane — in their most lucid
moments. I didn't relish the idea of riling the
lunatics, but I couldn't come up with any better or
quicker way to set my schemes into motion. Just
going to see them was a risky play, but I had to
hope they would hear me out before they reached
for their sawed-offs. Or fired them, at any rate. I
couldn't contemplate taking them on, however,
until I faced up to one other unpleasant chore. I'd
been putting it off since I'd arrived in town; even
more so than my visits to the Czar or to the mortuary. One last piece of painful, unfinished business from the past. One last person to see.

Once upon a time, I called her mommy.

I drove across town, to where once had stood
an expanse of wildflowered meadow that now
comprised Ideaville's most exclusive neighborhood, and turned up Milne Lane: Roach's street. I
drove slowly past the gated entrance to Chez
Roach, didn't see the big Continental parked in
the circular drive. I spotted a couple of security
cameras mounted along the high fence and up in
the trees, guessed there were others I couldn't
see, and made a mental note of the locations.
Then I continued on around the corner and
parked. I knew that sneaking up on Chez Roach
probably wasn't the cleverest thing to do in the

middle of a sunny day, but then no time would ever be the right time if I stopped and thought about it too hard. This was just something that I needed to do.

I walked all around the enormous block. The big, manicured lawns rolled right up to the edge of the black tar macadam, leaving no room for sidewalks and a very clear message to the likes of those who might be inclined to use them. The houses that had been built here — Elsevier Estates, they called it — were all immense; bigger than any I could remember from when I was a kid, except for the old Keene mansion up on Drew Hill, and that had been vacant for years. I couldn't imagine what the people who lived here did with all that space. Elsevier didn't have the feel of a family neighborhood, and besides, the kind of people who could afford these places weren't likely to be saddled with gaggles of little kids. The houses were just big for the sake of bigness, I reckoned; yet another particularly salient sign of conspicuous consumption.

I felt yet another pang for the lost town of my dreams.

Sizing up the distances as best I could, and taking a cautious look around for spying camera eyes and big-jawed dogs, I nonchalantly walked up the freeway-sized driveway of a white colonial monstrosity. Looking as innocuous as I could — which mostly meant plastering a politically incorrect, retarded-do-not-disturb smile on my puss — I strolled around the side of the house, moving faster once I was out of line of sight of the street. The backyard was impeccably landscaped, with a

Zen rock garden in the middle that was large
enough to bring calm to the better part of rush-
hour Tokyo. I could have used some of that tran-
quillity myself, but was afraid to stop and smell
the chrysanthemums. With a look back at the
house for anyone staring out of the Xanadu-sized
bay windows, I cut across the lawn and made for
the line of trees at the very rear.

A small copse of oaks with a single, out of place,
weeping willow separated the property from the
ones behind it. I saw that my calculations were
ever-so-slightly off: Chez Roach was catacorner to
the yard I'd entered, set off by a six-foot-high stone
fence. Shards of broken glass were fixed into the
top of the fence to deter burglars, but the effort was
somewhat half-hearted; with the help of a few
thick, overhanging branches, I hoisted myself up
and over without incurring so much as a scratch.

I moved even more cautiously on the Blackwell side of the fence. I scanned the trees and
fence-top for more cameras, but couldn't spot any.
I did note a motion detector and some spotlights,
guessed they weren't likely to be left on during
the day. The LED on the motion detector flashed
as I scooted by, but no lights came on and I didn't
hear any alarms. I was trusting too much to luck,
but then what else did I really have?

Crouched low, I passed through the trees and
into a plot of thick shrubs planted along the back
of the rear garden. I crawled along on hands and
knees, cursing as I ripped my pants on a busted
mosaic tile sticking out of the moist soil. I could
hear voices drifting across the expanse of lawn
and as delicately as I could, opened a hole in the

wall of green that separated me from the sight of Chez Roach.

A two-story redwood deck was built along a substantial section of the back of the house. A man in a dark green smock was attending to a hot tub built into the upper level — a hot tub! In Ideaville? — his back to me. A gently sloped ramp spiralled down the breadth of the deck from the upper level, to a concrete paved patio below. Part of the patio sat in the shade of the deck, but a section of it, including an ornate koi pond, extended out into the yard and the bright sunlight. A very young woman in a skimpy French maid's outfit and black stilettos — I kid you not — fussed over a small flower bed, either collecting or simply mutilating a vase-worth of blue roses. She was a little wobbly on those heels, and you could pretty well see Paris (not to mention the whole Eiffel Tower) when she bent over in that get-up. I reckoned that Sandy's estimation of Roach's . . . appetites remained smack dab on-target.

I hunkered down, prepared to wait until the hired help completed their appointed rounds and the coast was clear — though the hot tub guy had the slow motion look of man who earned his money on a by-the-hour basis.

Then the sliding glass doors that led out to the patio from the ground floor slid open.

The nurse, dressed like my friend Cherry in starched whites, was neither young nor pretty, so I knew that Roach hadn't hired her and guessed she must be damn terrific at her job. She jerked her head at the maid, whose permanent pout stretched the depths of its collagen-enhanced

swell as she skedaddled into the house with her
flowers. I thought I caught a glimpse of the Arc de
Triomphe before she vanished, but it might have
been a trick of the light. The nurse walked out to
the edge of the lawn and took a good, long look
around. It was too late to slip back into the shrubbery, so I held my breath and froze. As the nurse's
beady, falcon eyes passed right over me, I
breathed a sigh of relief. I must have been better
hidden than I'd feared. I kept my position as she
turned around and went back into the house
without closing the doors.

Ten seconds later she returned, pushing an old
woman in a wheelchair in front of her. The nurse
wheeled her charge to the edge of the shadows,
but the woman in the chair held up her hand just
before it emerged from under the upper deck and
out into the sunlight. The nurse shook her head
and gave a theatrical look to the heavens (or perhaps just the pool man up above), then set the
brake on the chair and waddled back into the
house. She emerged yet again carrying a tray
with a sweating pitcher of clear liquid, which she
set on a table beside the wheelchair. She poured
the woman a drink, balancing the glass on the
arm of the chair.

The old woman waved the nurse away, and
she vanished into the house, sliding the doors
shut behind her. The nurse paused to watch the
old woman through the glass and stuck her fat
tongue out at her charge's back. Hard to get good
help, I reckon.

After a minute, in which she didn't move a
muscle or blink or change a hint of the deathly

expression on her deeply lined face, my mother picked up the glass and drained it in one impressive swallow.

Vodka and tonic, I wagered. Always her favorite.

At least, from the day she started drinking. The day that . . .

The past washed over me like a summer thunder shower. Two memories abided above all others; the yin and yang opposites and extremes of my childhood memories of her.

Yang: from grade school days, even before the establishment of the garage Detective Agency, before Sandy's family moved to town.

I was a bit of an odd child (as you might well imagine), not bullied or entirely excluded by my peers, but set apart from them by my so-called intelligence. I had friends, I wasn't shunned or despised, but I wasn't loved. Not by the other kids, certainly. Lunch times were the worst. I could sit with them, eat with them, even joke with them once in a while. But I was never seen as "one of the gang."

Most kids ate in the school cafeteria; either the hot swill the pallid lunch ladies ladled out over the counter, or metal lunch boxes and brown bags full of baloney sandwiches, warm tuna, apples, cookies, juice. But you could go home for lunch if you wanted — if you lived close by. I went home most of the time. Ma was always there anyway, with hot soup or a bowl of Chef Boyardee's finest Italian recipe. Milk cold from the fridge, not lukewarm in sweaty little cardboard cartons from the lunch ladies.

And every Wednesday, like clockwork, Ma would be waiting for me just outside the school gates. Sitting in our old, blue Chevy Belair, engine running, head ducked as she looked out the window to see me running down the path. Into the car and back to town for lunch at Vito's Pizzeria, the best pizza in town. Every Wednesday, me and Ma, two slices of pizza, extra cheese. A Dr. Pepper for me, large black coffee for Ma (iced, when the weather was warm — Vito was the only restaurateur who'd even heard of iced coffee back then). The two of us sitting there, eating our pizza, drinking our drinks and talking. God knows what an eight-year-old had to say, how much interest it could have had for an intelligent young woman. But, God, how I loved those Wednesdays. I don't think I've ever been happier at any time in my life. Not even with Sandy. Just me and Ma and Vito's pizza and nothing else in the world that mattered. What I wouldn't give to be able to have just five minutes of one of those lunches to live over again. Just thirty seconds of that happiness.

Yin: the day it all, finally and utterly, fell apart.

The storm had been brewing for weeks. I'd uncovered the details of Blackwell Senior's grey market escapades in the appliance trade and passed them on to my father. I warned him that the facts were straight but the evidence circumstantial and unlikely to stand up in court. Dad said he didn't care, that justice was the main thing. I believed him, of course. It was much later that I discovered that the true source of the enmity between the patriarchs dated back to a notorious Kiwanis "meeting" when my father refused to take sloppy seconds from Mr. Blackwell

on a line-'em-up hooker. My father's pride
brought him down in the end — like father, like
son — as he came to believe that he literally *was*
the law: the omnipotent Judge Dredd of the
dreary Midwest. It never occurred to him that
men like Blackwell might be out there keeping
score. Keeping photographs.

I think my mother would have forgiven the old
man a lot of things. I think she could have lived
with the charges, with the disgrace of losing his
office and the respect (and fear) that went with it.
She was disappointed, hurt, distressed. But not
broken-hearted.

It took the pictures of Dad and the little girl at
the Elk's Lodge to do that.

"YOU MONSTER," she shrieked at him. It was
a voice I'd never, ever heard come out of her mouth.
My mom didn't yell (and certainly not at me). But
these words were gouged from a throat filled with
broken glass, winded by lungs seared with acid.

"Now, honey," the old man said.

"ANIMAL. Is nothing good enough for you.
Weren't the degradations you put me through
enough to satisfy your awful lust."

I tried, then, to slink out of the living room,
but my mother ran and blocked my way. I cried
out as she pulled me by the hair and flung me
down to the couch.

"Babycakes," my father tried.

"He should know! The boy should know what
you are, what you do!"

She threw the photographs at me. My dad and
a girl from my school. Two years younger than
me. He'd had her every which way, including a
few I was then unfamiliar with and didn't under-

stand the physics of. I turned the pictures over, spotted the "Blackwell Processing" stamp on the backs of them.

"What's wrong with these?" my mother screamed, and tore her blouse open. She cupped her cross-your-heart-bra-braced tits in her hands and held them up to my father. Then she raised her skirt up over her hips and bent over, showing her big-panty-swaddled ass. "And this? You poodled up my pooper! I let you do it up my pooper. I hated it, god how I hated it, but I did it for you. I let you. And it still wasn't enough for you."

My mother began to shake her ass, like some insane hoochie-coochie girl. "My pooper! My pooper!" she shrieked. She suddenly stood upright and ran over to me where I sat crouched in shock on the couch. One tit had jumped out of her worn bra and I could see half of her nipple.

"HE POODLED UP MY POOPER," my mother yelled at me over and over. At that moment her face had become one that I couldn't have picked out in a line-up.

I screamed.

My dad ran over and slugged her as hard as he could. Ma spun around in a full three-sixty, like some cartoon character, but stayed on her feet.

So he hit her again.

And again.

I remember her blood on the couch, on my clothes and in my hair. I remember the screams and the terror.

I pissed my pants and passed out.

The yin and the yang, exploding in my head like a lightning bolt from that summer storm.

I stood up and stepped out of the shrubbery, taking one step onto Roach's big back lawn. Ma hadn't aged well. Dad had put her in the chair, so that wasn't news, but the lines and sags and sallow skin were. Her hair had gone thin and grey, her cheeks hollow, her lips thin and pale, so that she looked twenty years older even than she was.

She looked up and I saw that she still had bright, brown eyes.

We were locked in place there, the two of us. Even the thin afternoon breeze died in that moment of recognition.

She raised her hand off the arm of the chair, and I prepared to acknowledge her wave. She knocked the empty glass off the armrest; it took forever to fall. The fine crystal chimed even as it gave its last and shattered on the concrete path. The sliding doors whizzed open and the nurse was at her side in a thrice. She saw me standing across the lawn and took two steps toward me, anger filling her face. I saw my mother's lips move, but I couldn't hear what she said. The nurse stopped. My mother spoke again and the nurse turned to her. She looked back at me and issued a snarl, but retreated to the patio. She released the brake on my mother's wheelchair and pushed her back inside the house. Back within the safe confines of Chez Roach.

My mother never looked back at me.

I stood there, alone, staring.

Eventually, when the tears stopped, I climbed back over the wall.

* * *

Los Bros had set up shop in an old meat-packing plant on the same side of town as the Anchor. The place was ringed with ten-foot-high, barbed wire fences and running tracks for guard dogs. There were all kinds of warning signs promising death and worse to "trespassers, gringos and pains-in-the-butt," and though the guard at the drive-in gate wore a floor-length duster and needed a shave, he was just as polite as could be. He plastered a Visitor sticker to the inside of my windshield and directed me to a small parking lot just off the main entrance. There weren't many other cars around, and I couldn't call it surprising to learn that the brothers didn't get a lot of people dropping by.

Los Bros were one of the computer game industry's great success stories, a classic garage start-up gone public. They made their name (in more ways than one) with their very first attempt at commercial software, the dizzyingly violent Teddy Bear Massacre. A campaign to have the game banned created a tidal wave of publicity that made it a must-have for every kid with a PlayStation, and made millionaires out of Francisco and José. The brothers were smart enough to rush out a second title, Slaughter House Party, which cemented their reputation for ultraviolence and controversy, and their fortune. They stumbled some with their next effort, DisMember, but landed on the front cover of *Forbes* when Garottic earned more money in its first weekend of release than *Variety's* top ten movies combined. The brothers seemed to be on top of the world when the story broke that they'd been accused of the cold-blooded, shotgun murder of their parents. I must have read that they'd gotten off for it, but never paid attention to the details. It didn't surprise me to hear Sandy say that they'd bought their way out of a guilty verdict.

My father was the only object lesson I ever needed regarding the processes of American justice.

The brothers hadn't done a lot to the inside of the sausage factory. Maybe it was just knowing what the building had been, or the graphic posters plastered over every wall advertising Los Bros' violent wares, or simply the effect of the boys' reputation, but I'd have sworn I could smell blood as soon as I walked in the door. The place was cavernous, with what little private space there was carved into cubicles by those portable, semi-carpeted room dividers. The high interior walls of the building were metallic, eerily reflecting the flickering lights from the workstation monitors that dotted every desk. Electronic pings and two-bar bursts of music occasionally echoed around the place like gunshots. The few workers I could pick out in the murky light all looked mean and weary, like extras from some AIP biker flick. I nearly jumped out of my penny loafers when I heard a nasty grinding noise followed by a loud squeal — a pig meeting its maker, I thought — but it was just a secretary freeing a paper jam in a photocopier.

The receptionist was a tight-cropped brunette in an even tighter-cropped tube top, chewing grape Bubble-Yum (I could smell it) to beat the band, and reading a dog-eared copy of *Piercing*

Monthly. I thought she was just browsing until she put the magazine down and leaned back, at which point I saw the death's-head stud rammed through her navel. Damned if the grinning skull didn't look like José. Or maybe I was just projecting. She was none too interested when I said hello, but perked up when I told her I wanted to see the brothers.

"José and Francisco?" she asked. The wad of gum plopped out of her open mouth, landing on the space bar — largely unused, I suspect — of her keyboard.

"I don't mean John and Joey Travolta."

"You want to *see* Los Bros?"

As she said their names, her accent mysteriously migrated from Jersey to Juarez.

"Yes, please."

"Nobody sees Los Bros, gringo."

Gringo? She was Waspier than me by several shades of pale. I played it cool.

"I think they'll see me," I said. I grabbed a pink Post-it pad off her desk and the pen that was tucked behind her ear. I scrawled two words on the pad — her pen wrote in purple ink; I resisted the temptation to dot my "i's" with little hearts — tore off the top sheet and stuck it to her chest, just above the pierced, bleeding heart tattooed over her real one. "Just show 'em that," I added.

The girl got out of her chair — she wore an electric green micro-skirt; Christ, how did they get any business done here? — and staggered backwards across the floor, keeping a nervous eye on me the whole way. I saw her nod at someone, and glanced behind me. One of the duster-cloaked security guards had taken up a position in front of the exit. Both hands were lost inside the folds of his dirty garment and I could make out something long and stiff underneath. I felt pretty sure that he *wasn't* just happy to see me. His name badge identified him as Chet.

The receptionist went back to a small, caged lift in the corner, of the type you might see in some old New York tenement. More like a glorified dumbwaiter than an honest-to-god Otis elevator. I watched the contraption slowly rise along its exposed shaft and disappear though a hole in the ceiling. I glanced upward and saw that it led to a tinted glassed-in loft area that looked out over the entire work floor. At regular intervals there were tiny rectangles cut into the wall of glass, like little mail slots. I couldn't make head or tail of it until it struck me that they could only be gun ports.

The place had gone quiet as the girl rode up in the elevator, everyone seeming to track her with their eyes. Several of the other secretaries crossed themselves as she passed up into the loft. There was then a long, nervous silence after the sound of the elevator ceased during which I could hear the sweat oozing out of my pores.

The silence was broken by a stream of cursing from above. I saw one of the secretaries finger a rosary she pulled from her drawer, and two of the coders dove for cover. I glanced at Chet, but he merely eyed me coolly, hands beneath his duster. The hum of the elevator started up again, and I heard a collective exhalation of breath. When the receptionist appeared in the cage — seemingly unharmed — there was a palpable sense of relief, and some scattered applause of the type you hear on airplanes when the pilot's made a smooth landing after an especially turbulent flight. She walked back to the desk shakily — it had nothing to do with her high heels — acknowledging the blown kisses from her co-workers with an I-can't-believe-I-won-the-lottery smile. The Post-it, I noted as she sat back down, had been removed from her chest.

"Los Bros will see you now, señor."

She waved in the direction of the elevator, then put her head down on the desk and started to sob. I thanked her quickly and walked on.

Heading for the elevator, I felt like a prisoner on The Last Mile at San Quentin. I half expected to hear the coders in their cubicles cry out "dead man walking" as I passed. As I stepped into the cage and closed the mesh door in front of me, I thought again that I caught a whiff of freshly spilled blood, and feeling like a sow on the sausage run, briefly vowed never to eat meat again. I had to resist the urge to cross myself.

I pushed the button, and the elevator started its slow ascent. Gaining altitude, I saw that there were more coders and techs on the floor than I had realized. Most of them were watching me (a few saluted), but some remained glued to their monitors. One team in the corner wore head-to-toe VR suits, dangling from suspension rigs and running hither and yon on trackball treadmills. Los Bros might be cold and cruel, but they were also cutting edge.

The elevator passed through the hole in the

ceiling and on into darkness. I felt a jolt of vertigo
as the blackness took hold and the cage continued
to rise. It soon jerked to a stop though, and the
only illumination came from the little LED blinking on the up-down control panel. That, too, went
out and I was left completely in the dark.

"Hello?" I called out.

No response. Thinking about those gun ports
in the glass, and about the big gaps in the mesh
of the elevator's cage, I felt very vulnerable
indeed. Nevertheless, I fumbled around in the
dark until I could feel the handle that opened the
door to the lift. I drew it across my body, opening
the elevator door. Feeling first with tippy-toes
and mercifully finding solid floor beneath me, I
took a tentative step out of the elevator.

A blinding floodlight caught me full in the
face. I flinched, throwing an arm up in front of my
eyes. I heard a very loud click in my right ear. A
cold hand grabbed a goosefleshed flap of skin at
the back of my neck.

"Jew move, jew die," a gritty voice exclaimed.

I held my tongue. And every other muscle.
Including, miraculously, my sphincter.

A shape stepped in between me and the bright
light. A tall silhouette, with long stringy hair and
a hard, jagged profile.

"I kill heem? I blow his brains out? I take the
leettle bones and grey stuff and I . . ."

The silhouette held up a palm. I saw the head
cock: right, then left. Then right again. It nodded.
Slowly.

"I know you," the shadow said. "I seen you
before."

The lights suddenly came on and the flood-light blinked out. José Robusto stood ten feet in front of me. A big, pearl-handled Colt dangled from one hand, the other hand pointed, dirty fingernail first, right at me. I risked a glance to my right, caught sight of Francisco, six inches shorter than me, a half-step behind, the barrel of his very clean Smith & Wesson pressed to a point just behind my ear.

"I want to see the grey stuff," Francisco whined. "I never get to have no fun."

José waved his brother off. I felt the gun slip away from my head, though Francisco kept it levelled at my heart as he stepped around me, and stood beside José. The taller brother gestured for me to step into the room, raised his hand when he wanted me to stop. I wasn't about to take so much as a baby-step without a "mother may I." José held up the little Post-it note at me.

"What you mean by this?"

I had prepared my spiel in advance, suspecting I might not manage to get too many words in with these boys, and determined to catch their attention fast. I swallowed, found my voice had vanished somewhere between my throat and lips.

"You must be loco," José said.

Francisco's finger tightened on the trigger of the S&W. *This is it*, I thought, *good-bye, Sandy. I've failed you again.*

José shook his head. "You write in purple ink on pink paper?" He waved the Post-it, then crumpled it up in his hairy fist. "I almost couldn't read it. You take chances, my friend."

I exhaled a hot-air balloon's worth of relief.

"Sorry," I said.

"You should be, hombre. And what you mean writing this name on this paper." He waved his fist at me and Francisco nearly fired. "What you know about this puta."

"I thought it might attract your attention," I said. I nodded at a chair in front of the desk and raised an eyebrow. José reluctantly nodded back, so I sat down. It was either that or *fall* down. José plopped himself in the big leather chair behind his desk, Francisco on the desk's edge, the gun balanced on his thigh still pointing my way.

"We got lots of interests. Murder, mayhem, though we looking to cultivate some new demographics, too. Bloodbath Barbie. What you think?"

"A real winner," I quickly said. "I'd buy it for my little girl."

"We're working on the licensing issues," José said. "There's some reluctance being shown as regards to corporate image."

"I theenk we get it," Francisco piped in. He raised the barrel of his gun. "I got a knack for negotiation."

We all laughed, but José quickly held the Post-it up to me again. "The name," he said.

It had been a gamble to be sure, but I suspected it was the one thing that could get me in to see Los Bros. I'd written down the name of the dead prostitute who lay in Sandy's coffin. Killed, so Sandy had told me, by the brothers themselves.

"What's in a name?" I said, with an insouciance I pulled like a rabbit out of some magician's hat.

"Todo el mundo," Francisco said. With an

intensity that melted any leftover insouciance that might be sitting in my pocket.

"Name means a lot to Los Bros," José said. "Our name is all we got."

"And our guns," Francisco added.

"Our name and our guns," José agreed.

"And stock options. We each got options for five hundred thousand shares of common and . . ."

"¡*Hermano!*"

Francisco shut his mouth and went back to looking like the poster child for butchery.

"So you see, name's a very important thing to Los Bros. You come in writing a name in purple ink on pink paper, a name like this, you got to mean something by it. Where you get this name?"

"A little birdy sang it to me."

"Don't like no singing birds," Francisco said. "Mi madre" — the brothers crossed themselves, then spat simultaneously — "she had un canario amarillo. It liked to sing. It sang all the fucking time. I say, 'Shut up jew fucking bird. Shut up or I kill jew.' But it never shut up. So I kill it. And then I kill . . ."

"¡Basta!" José yelled.

I stared, mouth agape, at Francisco, who'd worked himself up into a quality dandruff shampoo's worth of lather.

"I know theese leetle bird who sang to jew. Leetle bird might get some birdshot in her big mouth. Jew get shot in the mouth, jew don't sing no more. Or jew do sing, jew got a funny whistle where the hole is."

"You think this name means something to us?" José asked me.

"Come on, José, give it a rest. Coy is *not* your brand."

José stood up, Colt back in his hand, and I thought I'd pushed it too far. He came around and sat on the edge of the desk, next to his brother.

"You don't know nothing about my brands," José said.

"He likes Aqua-Fresh," Francisco told me. He smiled a big, white smile. "I like Crest."

José silenced his brother with another look.

"You want to put your cards on the table? Okay, we put all the cards on the table. 'Cause we holding the aces, gringo. You got . . ." — he thought for a second — "eight words. Then I let Francisco play with your grey stuff."

Francisco smiled broadly. I thought carefully. Then, counting on fingers, I said: "Roach Blackwell's balls. In your hands." I leaned back, smiled and added: "Or not."

"You just bought yourself some more words, amigo," José said. He put his gun back down.

Francisco had been looking very puzzled throughout this exchange. Now he turned to his brother and asked: "Why jew like Aqua-Fresh anyway? I hate those damn stripes."

Son of a gun: I was still alive.

I had to sit in my car in the Los Bros parking lot and collect myself for a while. God knows, I felt like I'd shattered into a zillion pieces. The Robustos weren't just hard work, they were a thirty-year career. Someone should have handed me a gold watch inscribed "a job well done" for getting out of their office alive. One of the big duster boys was still watching me from outside the front door, but after José and Francisco, he was nothing but a pesky gnat. Though I wanted to wait for my hands to stop shaking before I attempted to drive back to the hotel.

"La Cucaracha's cojones?"

"Right between your fingers," I had said. I held an imaginary sphere between thumb and forefinger, then pinched them together. You could almost hear the plop.

Francisco made a face. "I'd want to wear gloves," he said.

"How you gonna make this happen?" José asked.

Slowly, I reached a hand inside my jacket. But not slowly enough. My fingers had barely brushed my lapel when I felt the barrel of Francisco's gun pressed under my chin. He might not be the brightest light west of the Mighty Miss, but the crazy son-of-a-gun was lightning-fast. I froze.

"It's just a disk," I said.

José gestured at his brother, who reached in for me and pulled a DVD out of my pocket. He looked at both sides, sniffed it — I can't imagine what for — bit it, as if checking for gold, then tossed it onto the desk. "It's clean," he said.

I ignored him.

José picked up the disk and held it up to me, eyebrows arching.

"A sign of good faith," I told him. "Go ahead and boot it up."

José went over to a workstation in the corner and sat down. Francisco prodded me with the gun, and the two of us followed him, to watch over

his shoulder. He was about to stuff the disk into a
drive when he froze.

"Better not be no virus on here. There a virus
on here, you get a bullet up your asshole, asshole."

Francisco whispered in my ear: "Jew get a bullet in jew ass, it don't come out. It's like that leetle battery bunny: it just keeps going and going.
Comprende?"

"The disk is clean," I said. "Just take a look."

Francisco slotted the disk into the drive, then
flicked at his mouse.

"Click on *cojones.exe*," I said. I had a feeling
about how these boys might think.

It took a minute for the huge file to load. José
squinted at it for a while, but to my surprise it
was Francisco — smarter than I had credited;
I'd have to remember that — who cottoned on
first.

"Madre de dios," he whispered. He put his gun
down and grabbed the mouse away from his
brother. The two of them jabbered exclamations
of shock and wonder at each other as they scrolled
through the file.

"I take it you boys understand what that is."

They both shot me a dirty look, and Francisco
glanced at his gun, but didn't pick it up.

"That code is the heart of the engine for Blackwell's latest development project."

"We can see that, cabron."

"You can see, but do you know what it's called?
It's not in that file."

I let the silence linger, until I had their undi-
vided attention.

"Blackwell calls the beta version *Dead Mexicans*."

"Andale, andale," Francisco screamed, and ran straight toward a shotgun rack mounted on the far wall. He had something akin to an elephant gun in his hands, a box of shells tucked into his belt, before I could even react. "Vamanos!" he screamed.

José kept to his chair, but I could see the fury in his eyes. "Easy, hermano. No rapidamente."

I let out a deep breath which had gone sour in my lungs. I had to bear in mind just how excitable these boys were. José turned back to the monitor, but it blinked out as soon as he touched the mouse.

"Qué paso?"

"It's gone," I informed him. Behind me I heard the ker-chunk of a shell being jacked into Francisco's considerable breach. "For now," I added.

"What kind of game you playing here, gringo? Who you think you're fucking with?"

I affected a coolness I didn't feel, hoped that my true fear didn't show. Or didn't show too much. "The game is yours," I said.

My voice only cracked a little as I heard Francisco's footsteps coming up behind me. "But the game — all the games — are going to belong to Roach Blackwell if he gets this out on the market. This is the killer game app. Pun intended."

"What's the pun?" Francisco asked. He stood right behind me now. I could see the shadow formed by the shotgun barrel on the floor in front of me, and imagined that my last sight might be the shadow of my brain case exploding outward if I wasn't careful here.

"We got games of our own," José said. "We know a thing or two about killer apps."

"But you're not the only ones."

"What jew mean?"

Slowly, slowly, slowly, I leaned forward and pointed at the computer. José nodded to indicate I should go ahead. I typed a series of commands on the keyboard, then flicked at the mouse. It brought back the initial menu screen. I highlighted the second file on the disk, *muerte.com*, and indicated to José that he should execute the file. He was still wary, but he right-clicked the mouse.

A new file appeared on the screen. The brothers recognized it immediately.

"Dios," José whispered.

"Puta!" Francisco screamed. And rammed the barrel of the gun into my neck. "I kill heem now," he shouted.

"NO!" José yelled, and every bit as quick as his little brother, swiped at the barrel a fraction of a second before Francisco pulled the trigger.

It was the loudest thing I'd ever heard: a meteor strike played through a stack of Marshalls that went to "11." I felt the shot tear out some of my hair. I wondered how much of my scalp went with it. As I fell to the floor, I thought: dead isn't so bad; just like being alive, but with an empty bladder and no hearing. After a minute or two on the floor, staring up at the ceiling — it was riddled with bullet holes — I decided I was still alive. For what it was worth.

José had taken the shotgun away from his brother, who looked a little abashed. No less

crazy, just a little abashed. The ringing in my
ears had reduced from Notre Dame on Christmas
Eve to the little church on the corner at noon on a
Thursday. I ran my fingers along my scalp, was
pleased and astonished not to come away with
anything red or wet. My bald spot did seem a little bigger, though.

José hauled me up off the floor and set me
back down in the chair. He gestured at his
brother, who pulled a Corona out of a big fridge
and handed it to me. I saw José say something to
Francisco, but the words were just a buzz amid
the ringing. Francisco took the beer out of my
hand, went back to the fridge and jammed a pre-
cut quarter of lime into the neck of the bottle. He
handed it back to me, and I took a big swig.

Muerte.com had been nothing less than several thousand lines of code from Los Bros' current
hot project. With some help from Den, who'd
worked for Blackwell *and* Los Bros, I'd managed
to hack the code for both games from their systems. In fact, I'd managed to score only a small
piece of the Los Bros game, but as the evidence of
my ears proved, it was more than enough to convince them that their security was in doubt.
Black X Software was even easier to hack — Den
knew almost all the passwords or how to get them
— which was how I managed to steal the heart of
their new engine.

José and Francisco had scurried off to a corner
to confer in private — not that I could have heard
them anyway. I alternately sipped from my beer
and pressed the cold bottle to my forehead. By the
time the bottle was drained, the ringing in my

head had almost stopped. The brothers approached me again, though mercifully neither was holding a gun at the moment. José asked me a question.

"Yeah, right," I said. "Like I'm going to tell you how to fuck my sister."

He repeated the question and I felt silly.

"Oh. Your system. It wasn't that hard, believe me. And if I could do it, no reason to believe Roach can't. Or the Monkey Man."

"What you want with us?" José asked. "What you doing here? Why you bring this to us?"

"Like-minded interests, boys." I grabbed the crumpled Post-it with the dead whore's name off the desk. "The little birdy who gave me this is on your side. You must believe that or she wouldn't still be singing."

"Yeah, so?"

"There's an old saying: The enemy of my enemy is my friend."

I saw Francisco trying to work this out in his head. José elbowed him hard in the side. "So?" he said.

"So maybe we have some mutuality of interest here. The Blackwell gaming engine you saw — the rest of it's on the disk, but you'll need a password to access it. Try to fiddle with it and the disk wipes. Believe me, I'm better at this than you are. You know shotguns, I know computer security."

"Keep talking, gringo."

"You want the rest of the code for the engine? Help me take Blackwell down."

"Why for you want to do that?"

"That's my business. But since it helps your

business, it seems like a good proposition from where I'm sitting."

"Jew sitting in our chair."

"For the moment," I said. "But remember: I've got your code, too. And anything . . . untoward happens to me — like, say, a shotgun blast to the back of the head — and all of that code gets delivered to Blackwell and to YellowHat, just as neat as you please."

José hissed out a breath between his teeth. "Dangerous game you playing, amigo."

"The game is on, José. The question is, are you boys really players?"

I held my breath, half-expecting another explosion. It didn't come. A good sign, I thought.

"What's in it for jew?"

Francisco was studying me, and once again he didn't look so dumb. I also thought I saw a hint of respect in his eyes, like maybe he was glad he hadn't blown my head to bits just to play with the grey stuff. For the moment.

"That's my business. Let's just say that we both have a bone to pick with Señor Roach Blackwell. And maybe, if we work together, we can help each other pick his ugly bones dry."

José smiled at me and nodded his head. "Maybe, amigo. Maybe."

The brothers and I came to an understanding after that: they'd do what they could to . . . interfere with Roach's operations around town, and I promised that when I saw results, I'd give them the password that would hand them the rest of the software code they desired. I fed them a little more as a good faith gesture, and somewhat to my surprise, they handed me some inside dope on Roach they'd gathered through their own dirty dealings. I couldn't be sure that they'd live up to their side of the bargain, but I had a feeling that they didn't need a lot of arm-twisting to go out and do crazy things. As I sat there in my car, marvelling over my continued ability to breathe and my general good luck, that feeling was confirmed when I saw a half-dozen of Los Bros' duster-wearing security guards run out the door and pile into a Ford Bronco, which tore out of the parking lot, the group of them screaming like marauding Visigoths on Sack Rome Day.

I started the engine and pulled out of the lot.

The games were seriously afoot.

IX. The House Dick

"Mr. Collinson. Excuse me, Mr. Collinson!"

I was so preoccupied with my schemes that I forgot the name I'd registered under. It was only when my pal D. Sturdy started to spell it out, that I caught on and went back over to the Anchor's front desk.

"This just came for you. Y-O-U. Special delivery. U-P-S."

I puzzled over that for a while until the penny dropped. Sooner or later somebody was going to make this jerk cry U-N-C-L-E; and I don't mean Napoleon Solo. I studied the envelope, which had no return address, but could only be from Sandy. I walked out of the desk jockey's line of sight before tearing it open. A disk fell out into my hand, no label. A brief note was attached:

> Here's more code from Den. He says it might give you some leverage with or against YellowHat. He says don't ask how he got it. He has his ways. Suddenly seems quiet out here. Didn't feel that way before. Funny. Be careful. — S.

My heart did a brief cha-cha-cha in my chest at the bit about things feeling different for her, and I especially liked the "be careful." I would have preferred if she'd signed it "love," but I was probably just being foolish. I should have torn the note up and thrown it away, but I carefully folded it and stuck it in a compartment in my wallet. What a jerk.

"Computer stuff you got there?"

The old man, Mr. Ricky, was in his seemingly reserved chair in the lobby, the obligatory pile of newspapers spread out around him. His pants had ridden up the one thin leg resting on the coffee table and I could see the bulge of massive varicose veins, like cords of hemp, through the thin fabric of his support-hose. A pair of filthy blue slippers sat on the floor by his side. He looked so damn pathetic, so lonely, that tired as I felt, I had to go over and talk to him. I spotted a coffee machine in the corner and asked if I could get him a cup.

"Nah. Love the stuff, but at my age the mocha java plays the devil's own tiddledywinks with my innards. Sends me straight to the shitter, don't you know. But I'll take some of that hot chocolate if you're buying, though it ain't all that hot and far as I can tell's never been within shooting distance of a cocoa bean much less a Hershey bar."

"You got it," I said, and thought: *Christ, no good deed . . . .*

His nose was back inside the paper as I deposited the Styrofoam cup on the arm of his chair. He was right, it wasn't very hot. Neither was my coffee.

"Reading yesterday's news again?"

He lowered the paper. "If you want to find your way around the future, make certain that you understand the past."

I burst out laughing — I couldn't help it.

"I say something funny?"

"I'm sorry," I said, "but for the last few days I've been exploring my past in minute, even excruciating detail, and it's not a very happy study. If the future is bound up in it, I think I'll just shoot myself now and get the whole mess over with."

Mr. Ricky wrinkled his already wrinkled nose at me. "That's no way for a young feller to talk."

"I ain't that young, pardner. Not anymore."

"Piffle. Why looking at you I'd say you're . . ."

He gave me a good looking-over and guessed my age nail on the head.

"That's a pretty good trick," I said, impressed. "You used to work at a sideshow or something? Want to guess my weight, too?"

"No tricks involved, sonny. Nothing more than keen powers of observation." He tapped a finger just under his right eye. "Went with the territory."

"Yeah? What kind of work you do?"

"Oh, some of this, some of that. Little bit of law, once upon a time."

"Lawyer?"

"Law *man*."

I leaned forward and studied Mr. Ricky a little closer. I knew I'd never seen him before — good memory, remember? — but there was something about him that wasn't entirely unfamiliar. Could he have known my dad in the old days, been on the force?

"Here in town?" I asked him. "You a policeman in Ideaville?"

"No, no. We're talking years and years ago, and I was strictly big city. Up Chicago way, a plainclothes man most of my years. Didn't settle here till long after my law days was done. After my Tessie passed."

However much I detested my father, I found I still couldn't help but be interested by cops and their lives. It's simply how I was brought up. The reason that so many policemen's sons become cops is that it really does get absorbed in the blood. Some particularly twisted combination of proteins in that weird double-helix that Chubby Checkers inside us all.

"You ever miss it?" I asked. "Law, I mean."

Ricky stared down at his paper, flattened a sloppy fold. "'Course I do. You can take the man out of the force, but you can't take the force out of the man. Had some good friends in law — the best there is. Pat and Sam and Liz. Had me a hel-luva Chief, too. They don't draw 'em like that anymore, believe you me."

"I think I know exactly what you mean."

"Begging your pardon son, but you don't look like you spent no time in blue."

"Not exactly," I admitted. "Though there is a . . . family connection. I know some cops. Or I used to."

"Good people. The best."

"I don't know," I said. "They run to about the same mix of good and bad as the rest of the world, I reckon. I do know that there's nothing worse than a cop gone bad. 'Cause when they go, man, they go as far as they can fall."

"But don't you know, son? That's what makes 'em put the uniform on to begin with. If they didn't have that in 'em to start, they'd never sit behind the badge. Who else could do the job, take the life?"

I couldn't agree, but I didn't want to argue the point with him. If Mr. Ricky really was a cop and had been out of it for as long as he said, he probably couldn't imagine what the job and the streets had turned into. I felt certain he was the kind of man who couldn't imagine that there were cops like my father. But then again, maybe cops had always banged little girls on the beat. If so, I didn't want to know.

"Way you watch the place, you could practically be the house dick here," I said, changing the direction of conversation. "If they still have them."

"Oh, I keep an eye out. These legs may not take me too far no more, but I can still see just fine. Can still add up one and one and make it come out two."

"I'm sure you can."

"Like that disk you're fondling there." He pointed at the floppy which I'd been fiddling with. "Must be something important."

"Just some business," I told him.

"Maybe. Or that note that come with it; the one you tucked away in your wallet. Maybe that come from your sweetie?"

I frowned at him. "How did you know that?"

"Way you folded it. Most people get a note they read it and crumple it up. Stuff it in their pocket or toss it away if it ain't important. If it's business, maybe they fold it back in three just like it come from the envelope. They don't hold it like some precious flower, fold it neatly in half with a delicate touch like they're going to treasure it forever. Like you just did."

"Nothing wrong with your eyes at all, is there? I'll have to remember that."

"Aww, don't take it the wrong way, son. I ain't being nosy or nothing. Just an old man sitting in a hotel lobby with nothing better to do with his time than stick his big bazoo everywhere it don't belong. Don't mean nothing at all."

"It's all right," I said. "I got to get up to my room though. Business waits for no man."

"Business is business, and you got to do what you got to do. Can't be monkeying around with the likes of me, that's for sure. Thanks for the cocoa, son. Much obliged."

I smiled at him and said good-bye. But I decided I'd better start being a little more circumspect given the game I was playing, the events I'd set into motion. After all, my dad probably looked like a harmless old man to those who didn't know better, too.

Appearances are always deceiving.

As far as I could tell, me and old Mr. Ricky were the Anchor's only guests. I'd not so much as passed anyone in the hall during the course of my stay or heard the thunkety-thunkety-thunk of the ice machine spitting out its watery jewels in the still of the night. You'd think that the least you might expect from a stay in a cheap hotel is the second-hand enjoyment of rumpy-pumpy creaky bedsprings and the headboard-against-the-wall pounding of illicit sex from the next room, but the only fevered groans and squeals of passion to be

found came courtesy of the pay-as-you-go adult
movie channels on the TV.

So I wasn't spooked by walking the Anchor's
dimly lit halls all alone, without sight nor sound
of human activity.

What did spook me, though, was seeing the
door to my room ajar, a healthy pie slice of light
cutting into the gloom of the hotel corridor.

There was a time, when I smoked a little dope,
did a lot of hacking, and was vastly more para-
noid, that I carried a stun gun around with me.
They're illegal almost everywhere, but easier to
order by mail than a bouquet of FTD roses on
Valentine's Day. I was never brave enough to
walk around with a real gun, and liked the idea of
a non-lethal deterrent in my pocket. That was
until I accidentally zapped myself with it one
time, meaning to turn off my car alarm.

Now my only weapon is my endearing person-
ality. *Concealed* weapon.

So I was extra careful.

As I approached the door, I caught a whiff of
something I couldn't place. It was a slightly
damp, very musky odor; animalistic, yet overlaid
with just a hint of medicine. The scent grew
stronger outside my room. I tried to peer in
through the slightly open door, but couldn't see
beyond the closet just inside. Steeling myself, the
funky animal smell heavy in the air, I pushed the
door open and stepped inside.

Everything was in its place. No one was in the
room.

I took a good look around. I assumed I'd been
robbed, but nothing appeared to be missing. My

notebook computer sat where I'd left it on the desk, undisturbed, the modem cable still snaking out the back and into the phone line. My bags were as I left them, with nothing taken, nothing moved. The musky smell was thick in the air, though, so I opened the window as wide as it would go. I walked into the bathroom, saw that nothing looked out of place there, either.

Almost nothing.

Just before I left the coast for Ideaville, I'd stopped into a drug store and bought a brand new bottle of mouthwash. I had taken it out of my toiletries case and set it on the counter, but I'd yet to even break the plastic seal.

The bottle stood on the shelf, half-empty.

Who in the name of halitosis would break into my room to use my Listerine? Truly, a mystery worthy of a Boy Detective.

Still scratching my head, I went back out into the bedroom and took another long look around. I don't know how I missed it the first time — obviously I'm not the eagle-eyed observer I used to be — but there it was sitting on my pillow where I should have found my chocolate mint. The blanket had been neatly turned down, though I didn't imagine that housekeeping had left it that way. I sat on the bed and picked it up.

A banana peel. Fresh and still reeking of its contents, just a hint of oxidation where a trace of fleshy fruit clung to the thick skin. Chiquita label (the old song started to play in the jukebox of my mind: *I am Chiquita banana and I'm here to say, I am the top banana in the world today . . .*). Whoever had left it hadn't been gone long — it was still warm. I turned it over in my hand, saw a message scrawled in black ink on the inside of the peel. A time, a place.

I put two and two and two and two together — the smell in the room, the medium of the message, the people I'd been to see earlier in the day — and knew whose calling card it had to be. The Man from YellowHat would be waiting for me.

Though I was in a hurry — the message in the banana didn't leave me a lot of time to get across town — I stopped to ask Mr. Ricky a question. True to form, he hadn't stirred from his place in the lobby.

"You see anyone suspicious loitering around here earlier this evening? Before I came in?"

The old man offered me a crooked smile: a badly drawn line across the bottom of his face. His teeth were nicotine-stained. "Any monkey business, you mean?"

I remembered his previous comment about 'monkeying' around, and realized that he'd been offering me a clue. I hadn't been looking for one, though.

"Why didn't you just tell me?" I asked him.

"Tell you what, sonny? Who listens to crazy old men?"

"Thanks for nothing," I said, and made for the door. The old bird called to me to wait, but I dismissed him with a vaguely profane hand gesture.

The streets were unnaturally quiet. Quiet for Ideaville, at any rate, but much more like the little town it used to be, where the sidewalks got rolled up promptly at five thirty. (Eight o'clock on Thursdays. Whatever happened to Thursdays being the night stores stayed open late?) I could hear the odd police siren in the distance, but didn't run into any of Dink's troops as I drove. Were the escalating software wars keeping the good folk of Ideaville tucked safely in their houses? At least it made it easy to park.

I'd looked in the phone book for the address of the place, but there was no listing in the Yellow Pages under either Restaurants, Bars, or Night-clubs & Discotheques. (And surely the Ideaville Yellow Pages was the last official source in America still employing the word "Discotheque" in anything other than a post-ironic context.) There was no telephone book in the room, so I tried calling information. The place either didn't have a phone or was too exclusive to be listed, because it was no soap there either. However, if the people who edit the Yellow Pages are terminally unhip, the folks who answer the phones at directory assistance are way more in touch. While there was no official listing, the operator I spoke with happened to know where the club was and gave me directions, along with a peculiar chuckle. I still managed to walk past the entrance twice before spotting it. There were no other commercial venues on the street and only a tiny, hand-lettered sign above the buzzer provided the name of the club.

Tesseracts clearly was not interested in having John and Jane Q. Public wander in.

After staring up into a tiny video camera for a while, I was buzzed inside. I walked up a dingy and steep flight of stairs, only to wait while

another camera inspected me and I was allowed
to pass a second, iron-plated door.

The assault started the instant I stepped
inside.

The walls were blanketed floor to ceiling with
sizzling red neon letters curled into lines of the
same repeating words. WHATSIT, WHO and
WHICH strobed at me from all around in different variations, the IT of WHATSIT flashing in
every combination. One entire wall consisted of
nothing but ITs in epilepsy-inducing, blinking
patterns. Somebody had a serious thing for information technology. Or so I supposed.

Music — if that's what they call it — seemed
to rise up out of the floor. Low bass throbs, that
settled into your bones like cancer, punctuated by
an occasional Theremin wow, all pulsing in coun-
terpoint to the twinkling words on the walls. It
was like riding an old subway car through a
Vegas hall of mirrors.

Then I noticed the people.

I'm not inexperienced in the ways of the world,
nor am I a prude, but I suddenly realized why my
query had earned me that curious chuckle from
the telephone operator. Tesseracts was an S&M
club.

The room was quiet, but most of those about
were fetishists of one sort or another. The rubber-
suit brigade was well represented, as were all the
variants of modern primitive, pierced and punc-
tured worse than shredded tires. There was a
lady with her tits squeezed so tight into a cling-
film halter they'd likely stay fresh into the fourth
millennium, and a man with his testicles dan-

gling in a tank of yellow liquid he pushed around in front of him on a little cart. I can't imagine why. Decked out in my beige Dockers, brown Hush Puppies and Members Only jacket, I was the one garnering weird looks from all around. I've never even worn an earring. Not during my worst moment as a youthful outsider had I ever felt so deeply out of place.

A woman approached me. She was wrapped head-to-toe in material I can only describe as pink bunny-slipper fur. There were cut-outs for her eyes, mouth, nipples and — most disturbingly — her pudenda. Her labia had been pulled open and out and pierced with pearl studs which were affixed to the bunny-slipper fur. I suppose it was her idea of sexy, but you would have had to nail my dick to a post to make it hard at the sight. Of course, given the environs, I'm sure that could have been easily arranged.

"How ya' doing," I chirped. Not exactly Dorothy Parker material, I admit, but what the hell would *you* say confronted by a broad with her exposed pussy lips tacked to pink bunny-slipper fur?

Apology accepted.

She didn't answer — or if she did I couldn't hear her through the material — she only beckoned to me with a crooked finger.

"Maybe later," I said, looking around for some help.

Then she held out a banana. I got the message.

I followed her past more of the flashing neon and several acts of degradation I'd not believed imaginable in the American Midwest, much less

Ideaville. I wondered if my dad knew about Tesseracts, and feared that he probably did. For all I knew he might be a founding member.

The Pink Lady took me down a hallway done up in cheap polystyrene dungeon effect — like cast-off props from an old *Star Trek* episode — and up a half-flight of stairs leading to a big door. My guide's thighs made whooshy corduroy sounds as she walked. She rapped on the door, but there was no response. She did it again, still without reply, then looked pleadingly at me.

The thing is: you can't really knock on doors too well with bunny-slipper fur wrapped around your knuckles.

I glanced heavenward, then knocked myself. I heard a buzz, then a click and the door popped open. The woman took my hand — I have to confess, the bunny fur felt kind of nice against my skin — and led me inside.

A Man and his monkey sat side by side on matching, black leather, vibrating Laz-E-Boy recliners.

The Man wore a one-piece, canary yellow Spandex body suit; so did the monkey.

The Man wore an enormous yellow straw hat, big as a sombrero; so did the monkey.

The Man smoked a long, fat Cuban cigar; so did the monkey.

The Man smiled and licked his lips at the sight of the woman in pink; so did the monkey.

The Man gestured for her to come close and she sidled up to his chair. He stuck out the immaculately manicured index finger of his right hand. The woman thrust her pelvis forward and . . .

I looked away. Only to see the monkey standing there with its little brown finger similarly outstretched.

I really didn't want to see this.

The woman sidled up to the monkey. As it reached for her, she leaned over and held out the banana. For a moment the monkey was torn; it looked at her labia, then the banana, then her labia. It looked up at the Man from YellowHat, who nodded.

The monkey snatched the banana.

I feel we were all relieved.

"Thank you, Meg," YellowHat said. Though he was thin as Minny the Moocher's heart, he had a fat man's phlegmy voice. "Please tell Charles to prepare The Black Thing for when we're finished here."

She nodded and then walked off in her whooshy, pink way. I heard the lock click when she closed the door behind her.

"Meg and her brother run Tesseracts," YellowHat explained. "They are *god*sends to this community."

I nodded, uncertain if he was referring to Ideaville, or men who owned kinky monkeys, or . . . something worse. I sure wasn't about to ask. The monkey was eating its banana in a particularly obscene manner, and watching a naked woman on a giant video screen that hung on the wall. The black-and-white film was in Swedish with subtitles — could the monkey read or was it Scandinavian? — and seemed pretty old. I assumed it was porn, but it looked tame and vaguely familiar.

"*I Am Curious (Yellow),*" the Man told me.

I had, indeed, seen the film years before. There was a time, hard to believe now, when it had been the cutting edge of risqué in America. These days the monkey might be watching it on the Disney Channel.

"It's his favorite," YellowHat added, patting the monkey's head. "Along with *Mighty Joe Young*. The original, of course."

"Of course. I used to dig the *Planet of the Apes* films," I said. I lowered my voice to a bass rumble: "*Ape has killed ape.*"

"Excellent!" YellowHat agreed. The monkey gave me a big thumb's up. It did look a little like Roddy McDowall.

"I got your message," I said. I pulled the banana skin out of my pocket and tossed it at the monkey. It caught it cleanly, sniffed it briefly, then tossed it aside. The action in the movie was hotting up. The chimp exuded that same musky odor I'd detected in my room. And the mediciney scent, I realized, was my mouthwash.

"Very good, very good. We had feared that you might not be sufficiently insightful to follow up on our little calling card."

"Insight, I got. Like you got subtlety. So who used my mouthwash — you or J. Fred Muggs?"

The monkey scowled at me, but YellowHat burst out into an entirely unconvincing fit of laughter. "Excellent, excellent. You are a character, sir."

"Ain't we all. So what's going on here? What's the play?"

"Oh, no play, I assure you of that. Or rather, *all* play. That is our business, after all, is it not?"

"I don't know how you know my business. Or why my business would be any business of yours."

"Please, sir. Do give us just a little credit." He leaned over and spoke to the monkey. "May I?"

The monkey didn't look happy — actually, I confess that I don't know exactly how a happy monkey looks; I just don't *think* it's anything like he looked at that moment — but the chimp handed the remote control to YellowHat. The Man punched a couple of buttons, then gestured at the screen with the dingus. The naked lady was replaced by crisp color video taken inside the Los Bros offices. I watched myself riding the elevator up to see the brothers.

"How'd you get this? The Robustos must be losing their touch."

"Channels, my good boy, channels. The brothers aren't half so clever as they like to believe they are."

YellowHat punched another button and the picture changed: me again, but this time being unceremoniously dumped from Roach's limousine several days prior. I don't care what anyone says, the camera definitely adds ten pounds. The Man tapped the remote and the Swedish honey reappeared, moaning her way to another improbable orgasm. The monkey clapped his hands. Hell, she deserved it.

"So, are you angling to represent me or something?" I asked. "Going to make me into a video star?"

That evoked a fresh bout of fake "bwah-ha-has" from The Man. He held his stomach as if in pain from the hysterics. Monkey see, monkey do.

"By gad, sir, I like you. I admire the cut of your jib."

"I get it pre-cut at Jibs 'R' Us. I'll give you the address."

More hilarity. The Man had to reach for a tissue to dab at his eyes. A particularly saucy encounter was taking place on the screen; the monkey, too, grabbed for a tissue, but he dabbed at something else. Man, the smell.

"Let us lay our cards on the table," YellowHat declared.

"By all means."

"You're a bit of an enigma to me, sir. I have made numerous inquiries as regards your purposes, but no one seems to know your name."

"Why should anyone know my name? I'm just a guy, passing down these mean streets. Not himself mean, either. At least, not without good cause."

"And would you have such cause?"

"Maybe. Maybe not."

"Allow me to be frank."

"Which would make him Sammy," I said, pointing to the monkey. It had suddenly become a very tough room.

"You arrived in town less than a week ago and have been seen in consultation with both Blackwell and the brothers Robusto. In that time, the slightly warm cold war between those great houses — and my own — has rather intensified. Within the hour, an anonymous source plastered the code to Blackwell's new gaming engine on sites all across the Net. Within minutes thereafter, the Los Bros web site was nuked and replaced with streaming video of late Mother

Robusto's autopsy. I don't suppose you would know anything about these events?"

"Accidents will happen," I said and shrugged.

"Really, sir, you insult us both."

Not that tough a trick, I thought, as The Man and the monkey simultaneously folded their arms across their chests and huffed at me.

"What do you care?" I said. "Seems to me that you should be lapping this up. Lie back and enjoy and all that jazz. Trouble for Black X and Los Bros can only be good for you. Surely the enemy of your enemy is your friend." It worked with the Robustos, so what the hell?

"Perhaps. But alliances have a funny way of breaking down in this town, in our oh-so-combustible business. One cannot always tell who is a friend and whom an enemy. And one must take pains to avoid getting caught in the crossfire when alliances shift."

"Your concern is touching."

"I have no concern. Other than for the continued well-being of YellowHat Software. For my monkey and for myself."

"Well then, maybe you do have something to worry about," I said. I pulled a disk out of my pocket and tossed it at The Man. The monkey flew out of his chair and plucked it out of mid-air. He was faster even than Francisco. Not as endearing, though. (Or as hairy.)

The Man wheeled his chair over to a console and popped the disk in a drive. A flat screen on the wall blinked on. YellowHat booted up the lone file on the disk without my prompting and quickly scanned the pages.

"Good God," he whispered. The monkey, reading over his shoulder, collapsed to the floor like James Brown at the end of a three-hour performance. "How do you come to possess this?"

I casually examined the chewed ends of my fingernails, polished them on my shirt. "Piece of tamale," I said.

"Those crazy bastards," The Man said, standing up. No one had brought him a cape from offstage, but the monkey got up, too. "They gave this to you?"

"Yeah, but Roach showed it to me first."

"Impossible!" YellowHat yelled.

"And a kid in a schoolyard offered me a copy, too. Traded it for a Norm Cash baseball card. Why, is it . . . *confidential*?"

The Man let out a roar. The monkey leapt up onto his shoulder and pounded its chest. Apparently it had seen *King Kong*, too.

The disk contained part of what Sandy had sent me, courtesy of Den. It was nothing less than YellowHat's corporate accounts and current financial plan. I had no idea how Den managed to get a hold of it, but my respect for the gangly gamer shot up by the day.

"I knew it. I knew they were combining forces against us." The Man turned to the monkey. "Didn't I tell you? Didn't I predict this would happen?"

The monkey, looking somewhat abashed — obviously he *hadn't* seen it coming — grudgingly nodded.

"It's Fester."

"Sorry?" I said.

"Fester. Our new VR release. They're both of them terrified of what it will do to the market. The game makes Hieronymous Bosch look like Barney the Dinosaur. They've joined forces to sabotage me before it's too late, haven't they?"

I hadn't heard a thing about Fester, but I can go with what works. "They do seem concerned about it. Roach started sweating when we talked about it, and even Francisco crossed himself when José mentioned the title."

"I knew it! They think they can make a monkey's uncle out of me."

Nephew let out a horrific screech, the hairs on the back of his neck standing straight up.

"Sorry, old friend," The Man said. The monkey nodded, but didn't look mollified. "What's your stake in this, sir? What do you want? And what, precisely, do you know?"

"Not much really. Though I do know why the caged bird sings." I sketched a little target circle in the air over YellowHat's heart. "It sings for *thee*."

"Mother of mercy," he groaned, lowering his head into his hands. The monkey aped his actions. Just then the door opened and the Bunny Lady, Meg, stuck her head inside.

"The Black Thing will have to wait," The Man From YellowHat cried. The monkey beat its breast.

Gotcha! I thought.

It was so late when I got back to the Anchor, that even Mr. Ricky was gone from the lobby. I dragged myself up to my room and the comfort of my semi-lumpy bed. Police sirens woke me up a couple of times during the night — things were definitely hopping in town; good news for the home side — but while I slept, it was the sleep of the just.

The rest of my meeting with The Man couldn't have gone any better if I'd planned it. Of course, to some extent I had; the tenor, at least, if not the specific timing. My luck had been extraordinary so far, though without Den's inside track — and Sandy feeding it all to me — I'd have been nowhere at all.

"Seems to me," I'd told The Man, "that you can either take the others down, or get took. The law of the jungle, no offense."

The Man nodded, but looked nervous. "What's your stake in this?" he asked.

"Does it matter? Let's just say that every man has his monkey to feed."

He seemed to understand that. The monkey nodded, too.

We parted company having agreed that I'd go on the YellowHat consulting retainer, continuing to feed The Man whatever lowdown on Roach and Los Bros I could get. He promised to stir things up in his own way.

"We'll go ape on them," were his parting words, spoken without a trace of irony.

What a town.

I woke up bright and bushy-tailed the next morning, determined to stir up more trouble wherever and however I could. I'd need to spend more time online, but thought I could use some real stimulation first; sinkers and coffee at Ulysses' Diner.

I don't know why, but I sort of looked forward to seeing Mr. Ricky in the lobby on my out. He was the closest thing I'd found to a friend so far in Ideaville — Sandy notwithstanding, of course, though I still couldn't be sure exactly how much Sandy might be willing to stand for. As I came down the stairs my mild disappointment at the old man's absence was dramatically overwhelmed by the vastness of my surprise at who was sitting in Mr. Ricky's chair in the hotel lobby.

My father, the Czar, was waiting for me. He looked even worse outside the confines of his miserable office than he did within.

"When there's no more room in hell, the dead shall walk the earth," I said.

"Still a wit, eh, boy?"

"Take my wife, please. Oh, sorry, that was your line, wasn't it? Who'd have guessed old man Blackwell'd take you seriously. Laugh riot, ain't it?"

"You live too much in the past, boy. I told you that."

"Maybe I wasn't listening. What the in the name of generic gin are you doing here, anyway? How'd you even find me?"

"Had a hunch," he said and shrugged. "Used to be a cop, you know. And I asked around."

"People still talk to you, do they? I mean without you paying to bang 'em after?"

"This still ain't that big a town. And I provide a certain amusement value for various of the locals."

"You're a fucking fun fair, Pop. A tilt-a-whirl, cotton candy, freak show all wrapped up in an eighty-proof package. A regular barrel of monkeys. Yellow hats not included."

He ignored me. "You leaving town today?"

"Should I?"

"Funeral's today, ain't it? You got some reason to stick around?"

The funeral. I'd been so busy scheming and planning — so delighted by the fact of Sandy's continued existence — that I'd forgotten all about it. It wouldn't do for me to miss it at this point. He may not have meant to, but the old man'd done me a big favor reminding me.

"I'm thinking now I might stay on another day or two. I hear it's father-son day at the ballpark this weekend. Thought maybe you and me'd catch a game together, have a dog and a beer. Maybe you'll snag a foul ball for me, huh? Wouldn't that be a thing?"

"You don't fool me, boy."

"Huh?"

"You can play the wounded pup all you want, but it don't wash with me."

"Neither does soap and water from the stink of you."

"That's all right, get your digs in. I've taken lots worse than you can dish out. It don't bother me no more. I'm here to tell you that you'd best clear out when all's said and done today. There's nothing else for you."

"Who sent you here?" I asked.

"Ain't no one sent me, I come of my own accord. I'm just doing my fatherly duty so-called."

"You don't even lie well anymore, Pop, you're too far gone. Your upper lip sweats and your left eye twitches. And you wouldn't have crawled out of your dark little hole in the wall unless someone stuck a mighty sharp stick up your ass. Was it Roach?"

"Don't know what you mean," he muttered. But now he was having trouble looking at me, and his hands shook.

"Things are starting to happen in Ideaville, aren't they? Los Bros are on the warpath and YellowHat's got some nasty ideas of his own. Blackwell have big plans, don't they, and Roach is worried about anything that rocks his comfy little boat. Well, baby, you can quote me on this one: this town is due for a tidal wave."

The Czar looked scared now. The shakes had spread across his body. "You don't know who you're messing with, boy. I knew you was up to something here, knew you wouldn't have come all the way back here for some whore's funeral. You can't be doing this, though. You got to leave things be."

"Why, Pop? Why not stick my hand in the hornet's nest? You never know who might get stung."

"There's things you don't know. If you ain't learned nothing in these years, you must at least have figured out that you was never half so smart as you thought you was. As we let you think you was."

"You're right, that was an early lesson, and a painful one. You and Mom did me no favors letting me grow up like you did, believing what I believed. You should have told me there's a thousand — ten thousand — little towns like ours, each and every one with its own smartest kid in the world. I grew up thinking I was brainier than all the other boys and girls and the adults. But you knew that wasn't true. I was maybe a bit of a prodigy, yeah, but you let me believe I was the Mozart of the Midwest. You were tossing up gopher balls for me to whack out over the short fences of one tiny town. The first fastball to come along damn near tore my head off and I've been shy about stepping up to the plate ever since."

"You're still swinging."

"Yeah, but that's no thanks to you. Now I'm back. And I've learned how to throw a few pitches of my own. You'd best watch out for my fastball, Pop."

"You're making a mistake."

"Why stop now? I've had a lifetime of practice, starting with being your son. And what do you care, anyway? Didn't you tell me just the other day how you'd like to see it all get burned down, right to the ground? The whole damn town?"

"I didn't mean nothing by that, it was just talk. Nobody listens to me anyway, ain't for years. And I'd been drinking . . ."

"Sorry, Pop, you used that excuse up long ago. You got to be careful what you wish for old man, you just might get it. You wanted a fire? Well, maybe I'm going to give you one. This town's a tinderbox and I got me a big book of matches. Happy Father's Day!"

"No," he cried, but there was nothing in it; barely even a breath. He lowered his head into his shaking hands and started to blubber. If I gave a shit, I might have felt sorry for him.

I merely felt sick.

"Best buy yourself a fan, old man," I whispered into his ear, "'cause things are about to heat up."

I left him sitting there, crying.

I dashed back up to my room to put on some better clothes. The Czar was gone when I came back down and Mr. Ricky was just settling into his spot. He didn't see me, but I slipped over to the machine and got him a cup of hot chocolate. I plunked it down on the table in front of him as he sat down in his chair.

"Nothing like a little sugar rush to get the day in gear," I said, and winked at him.

"Oh, mighty kind, young feller, mighty kind. Say, you're looking spiffed up this A.M. Don't suppose you'd care to join me in a repast?"

"Can't right now. Got things to see and people to do. I'll take a raincheck, though. Honest."

"You know where to find me," he said with a wave.

I had an hour to kill before the funeral and decided that, as originally intended, I'd head over to the doughnut shop. I grabbed a copy of the morning paper on the way, did a little happy dance up the sidewalk when I saw the headlines about tit-for-tat troubles at various Black X, Los Bros and YellowHat properties the previous night. Things were stirring up right nicely.

No cops in Ulysses' Diner when I walked in, though the joint was jumping. The same chicken-necked goober was working the counter, aided by a couple of high-school girls waiting tables and

working the checkout. The doughnut machine was
spitting out sinkers like the U.S. Mint makes pen-
nies, and they were selling as fast they fried.
Seemed like everyone who walked into the joint —
men in business suits or coveralls, kids on their
way to school, secretaries in skirts and sneakers
— went out carrying a grease-stained brown bag
of hot, sugary splendor. Damned if they didn't all
leave with smiles on their faces, too, despite it
being the start of a working day. I do believe that
if you could stick a Ulysses' on every block in the
country (instead of a Starbucks, though I love
Frappaccino much as the next guy) labor strife
might become a thing of the past.

Fortunately, most of the trade was take-out, so
I got a table no problem. I ordered up the Oedipus
Special — two fried eggs that stared back at you
like plucked eyes, and a big sausage that . . .well,
you figure it out — and the obligatory plate of
sinkers. I spread out my newspaper and tucked
into breakfast with a ferocity that surprised me
until I realized that I hadn't eaten anything substantial since before my visit to Los Bros the previous afternoon. I'd been so busy scheming and
running around, I simply forgot to eat. Of course,
the visit to Tesseracts was enough to put anyone
off their clams.

By the time I polished off the last of the
sinkers and my fourth cup of joe, Ulysses' had
cleared out. Rush hour evidently happened early
in Ideaville, and to their scattered cubicles everyone had gone. I had just turned to the funnies —
that Marmaduke just cracks me up; who says this
isn't the golden age of the comic strip? — when

the cop tapped me on the right shoulder. A second uniform stood behind me on the right.

"Sorry guys," I said, "I ate all the sinkers."

"Up," the first cop said.

"Now," the second added.

"I haven't read *Family Circus* yet."

They grabbed me under either arm and yanked me to my feet. I got a nasty case of pit burn as they hauled me toward the door.

"I haven't paid," I complained.

"Charge it to the Chief," the first cop yelled to the counter man. I saw him shake his head and look to the skies before they dragged me outside.

They shoved me toward a dark sedan parked in a handicapped-only spot along the curb. My old pal Dink, wearing a shiny houndstooth sport jacket, sat in the back seat. He didn't even look up as the patrolmen shoved me inside, just stared at the back of the front seat.

"I sure hope you've got a sticker to park here," I told him. "One-armed bank guard might come along and get pissed."

He lashed out and slapped me across the chops. It didn't especially hurt, but the mere fact of it shocked the hell out of me. He hit me! Dinky!!

I'm not a tough guy — that much should be obvious to anyone — but I responded in the only way I could.

I laughed.

"Oh, Dink. What's become of you?"

As he glanced at me, I could see that *he* was no tough guy, either. I don't know if he was performing for the sake of the beat cops standing outside, or out of some pitiable self-delusion, but one look in his eyes told me he was far more scared than I was.

"It's time for you to go," he said. His voice cracked a little.

"Hey, you dragged me in here."

"Out of Ideaville, I mean. I want you out of my town."

I failed to stifle another chuckle. "Dinky. Ideaville is a lot of things, most of them pretty awful, but the one thing it most certainly is not and never will be is *your* town."

"You've had your visit, more than enough time to say your good-byes or whatever you've come for. Now you have to leave."

"Or what?"

He was staring fixedly at the seat-back again. "Or I can't be responsible for what happens."

"You mean like you're responsible now?"

"I'm the Chief."

"Uh-huh. I'm sure you've got a bronze plaque on your desk that says so. Probably a nice hat, too. And maybe you even get to blast the siren in the Fourth of July parade. But Dink old friend, you are not in charge of Jesus Squat. Roach pulls your chain as sure as God makes little green apples."

"But God doesn't make little green apples," Dink squeaked.

"Shit. You ever been in Indianapolis in the summertime? It pisses with rain."

"You've still got to go."

"You're the second person to tell me that today and it's barely nine o'clock. Makes a fellow worry he's got B.O. or something. Do I offend?"

"What? Who else told you to go?"

"The Czar," I said.

"Oh," Dink piped. "That's bad."

We sat there quietly for a while.

"You still walk around with your eyes on the ground, Dink?" I asked.

"What? What's that?"

"In the old days you were always looking down, remember? You said you never knew when you might walk past a really good dead thing. Said there was nothing you wanted to see up high anyway."

"I haven't thought about that in years."

"I remember. I remember everything, Dink, you must know that. And I remember how they'd laugh at you, the kids and the adults, walking up and down the streets, staring down, searching for god alone knows what. But I always walked with you, Dink. I was always there at your side and I never laughed."

"I remember," he whispered. He cleared his throat. "But Roach . . ."

"Roach's days are numbered. One way or another. There's a harvest coming, Dink; a cold, hard harvest of the brown mountain of shit that this ugly burg has been built on. A cleansing of the poison that's eaten away at the soul of the place. Ideaville may be nothing more than a little signpost for what's happened to America, but that doesn't mean we have to like it or take it. It's high time somebody did something. Made a stand, no matter how small. What the hell, it might as well be me who does it. What else have I got? You just don't want to be standing in the way when the scythe comes whizzing down from on high, or you'll be wearing brown earmuffs for life. You don't want to be looking down now, Dink. Keep your eyes up this time."

Typically, Dink was staring at the floor, but I could see tears forming in his eyes. The beat cops standing outside studied us curiously.

"You take a message to Roach for me. You tell him that the old days are back, that it's shirts versus skins."

"What?"

"He'll understand. You tell him that and you ask him if he ever learned how to hit the curve ball. 'Cause Sandy taught me her best. And I finally — *finally* — understand what she meant."

He didn't try to stop me as I got out of the car. The two cops got in the front and with a gesture from Dink, they drove off. I went back into Ulysses' Diner.

"I want to pay for my breakfast," I said.

The counter man grinned, doffed his white paper hat and wrote up my check. I was about to pay when I saw her sitting in the corner, nibbling at a sinker and scribbling away in her composition notebook: the woman I'd run into in Dunn's then seen in The Boxcar. The writer for *Spy*. She caught me looking at her and waved. I walked on over.

"You're a popular fellow," she told me.

"How so?"

"Meeting with the Chief of Police. The Man From YellowHat. The brothers Robusto."

I frowned. "How do you know all that?"

"Oh, I've got a little route that I follow, keeping an eye on things. It's my job, remember?" She tapped her open notebook with her pencil. I glanced down and managed to read a bit of what she was writing:

... SAD, BUT NOT TOO AWFUL-LOOKING IN THAT SELF-CONSCIOUSLY GEEKY WAY. BUT WHY, OH WHY, IS IT THAT THE BOYS ALWAYS HAVE TO ...

She slammed the book shut, and wagged a finger at me. "A reporter's notes are sacrosanct. I lost my notebook once, and you wouldn't believe the trouble it got me into. I'll never let that happen again."

"Exactly what story are you reporting?"

"There's only one story in town: the software wars."

"I thought there were eight million stories in the naked city."

"Maybe, but seven-million nine-hundred ninety-nine-thousand nine-hundred-and-ninety-nine of them are dishwater dull. And Ideaville only thinks it's a city."

"So who's winning the war?" I asked.

"I thought you could tell me."

"I don't know nothing."

She giggled. "Can I quote you on that? Or how about on Blackwell's plans to go public?"

"How's that?"

"Oh, puh-lease. Like you don't know that Blackwell Unlimited have plans for a major share offering. What else are these wars all about?"

In fact, I didn't know that Blackwell was looking to go public. It explained a lot, though, especially Roach's desire to see the back of me and any trouble. A bad word in the wrong ear could cost him millions — hell, tens of millions — on the share offering. Very interesting.

"Maybe I should get a little spy route of my own," I said.

"It's a living," she said.

I paid the check — hers, too — and walked out.

I had a funeral to attend.

X. The Big Sleep

The funeral service was short and sweet. Some rent-a-prayer minister gave the usual spiel about brief lives, God's mercy, and ashes-to-ashes yadda-yadda-yadda. He did all right until he had to look down at his notes when he forgot Sandy's name. Francisco Robusto, sitting in the row in front of me, cursed in Spanish when he did it and started to reach under his black duster — did they have ones for every occasion? — but José stayed his hand. The preacher must have noticed it, though, because he didn't make another mistake through the rest of the ceremony. Sweated a lot, though.

The minister then called on Roach to deliver the formal eulogy. To a smattering of applause from his hangers-on (and one particularly inappropriate Arsenio-vintage woo-woo), Roach stood up and swaggered his way to the podium. He wore a sharp, black suit and didn't remove his trendy sunglasses. He looked out over the assembly the way a pig farmer studies the occupants of his sty.

It wasn't a big crowd, but there were more people than I'd expected. Roach's coterie — there no doubt to provide a suitably receptive audience — made up the bulk, but the Robusto boys had brought along a few of their henchmen, too. Dink was there and foppish Farny took a seat for the service, along with a handful of sallow, tear-

flecked young women who, based on their somewhat skimpy attire, I could only assume were
Sandy's fellow working girls. There were a few
faces I couldn't place at all, reporters most likely,
drawn by the presence of the bigwigs. And Den, of
course. And me.

"Sandy was always a good kid," Roach began.
It came out as pure pontificating. "We known
each other a long time, ever since we was little.
We didn't always get along perfect, but she come
around in the end. Oh yeah, she come." He ever so
slightly emphasized the word "come," evoking a
chuckle from his lackeys. A regular George Jessel.

"Sandy, well, it's no secret she had a rough
time of it these last years. Her old friends, we
tried to help her out, show her the way to a good
and decent life. I offered her I don't know how
many jobs, but she couldn't make none of them
work. I tried to get her into rehab, off the stuff
and onto the straight and narrow. I offered her
the full resources of Blackwell Unlimited, 'cause
there's nothing I wouldn't have done to . . . for her.
But people will be people and you can't go and
change them however much it hurts you to see
how they live."

Roach took off his shades and stared straight
at me.

"I think some of Sandy's troubles started way
back. The bad influences she was exposed to as a
kid. And not just TV and stuff. We used to talk
sometimes about it and Sandy she used to always
try to apologise for who she was and the stuff that
she did. I tried to tell her, 'Sandy, forget about it;
what's done is done, you got to look ahead of you.'

But she never got over what she done in her past. Those bad influences.

"Sandy's expiration is a terrible thing. We all know that. A terrible loss. Tragic, even. But maybe there's something we all can learn from it. If only she had listened to me, taken the . . . hand I extended to her in friendship, things would be different. We wouldn't be here like this today. If only she had listened to me."

He put his shades back on.

"Think about it."

Another subdued smattering of applause came from his peanut gallery as he took his seat. The rent-a-priest looked a little stunned. I knew how he felt. There was an uncomfortable silence until he walked back to the podium.

"Sandy" was to be cremated right there at the funeral home. Before sending the coffin into the flames, the minister asked if anyone else cared to say a few words. José Robusto looked like he wanted to say something, but Los Bros were clearly doers, not talkers. The hookers were too busy being distraught and trying to look sexy as they did it. I glanced at Den, sitting right up front, and saw him pop something into his mouth. I thought perhaps they were pills, then spotted the "value size" M&M bag sticking out of his jacket pocket.

Though Sandy wasn't really dead, another girl was. I couldn't bear the thought that Roach's self-serving words should be the ones that sent *any* soul off to their final resting place.

"I'll say something," I volunteered, before I could think better of it. The minister, looking relieved, waved me up to the podium.

I gazed out over the assembly and considered the opportunity and my words. Roach, clearly unhappy to be reduced to an opening act, glowered at me through eye slits thin enough to shave with. Francisco was bouncing up and down in his seat like a jumping bean and again had to be restrained by his brother. The hookers preened and pouted, but then so did Farny. Den stuffed another handful of M&Ms — peanut — into his mouth. He winked at me (but then, so had Farny).

"I knew Sandy for a long time, too," I began.

Just then the back door whooshed opened and everyone turned around. The Man From YellowHat and his monkey walked in, outfitted in identical black suits, with black shirts and black ties. The only traces of their usual attire were tiny, surprisingly tasteful, YellowHat tie clasps and matching cuff links. The chimp looked especially uncomfortable in his monkey suit and kept scratching his ass; though also looking out of sorts, The Man, to his credit, did not. They took their seats in the otherwise empty back row.

"Sandy was maybe the only thing in this world that could have brought me back to Ideaville," I continued. "When we were kids we started out as rivals, as so many boys and girls do, but we soon learned that we were more alike than we were different and became best friends."

Roach performed an exaggerated, highly theatrical yawn. His lackeys followed suit.

"Sandy taught me a lot of things at a time when I thought I already knew everything there was to know. She taught me that there was more to life than books and facts, that living is about experiencing the good and the bad first-hand, unmediated." I smiled to myself. "She tried to teach me how to throw a curveball, though I could never toss one like she could.

"Sandy, more than anyone else, taught me that I didn't know any of the really important stuff in life. Some of those lessons were hard — very hard — on both of us. I didn't realize it at the time, but I was asking a lot of a young girl, more than was fair to ask. But then I was a difficult and unreasonable young man. If I could talk to Sandy now, I'd apologize to her for being such a pain; ask her to forgive me for not recognizing and appreciating what a gift she was to me, what a precious gift. And I'd beg her grace for not ever telling her how I really felt about her. If I could go back, I'd tell her that she shouldn't settle for second best or for what other people tell her is good enough. I'd tell her to be her own woman and not be shaped into what others want her to be, need her to be. Whether that person is me or anyone else."

Roach turned around in his chair and took a long look around the room, then conspicuously studied his watch. I focussed my gaze directly at him.

"I'd tell her that there is no inevitability to life. Just because things *are*, doesn't mean that's how things have to *be*. There's always room for maneuver, always an angle left to play. If you think you're up against it, you have to find a way to use that to your advantage; press the leverage you've got.

"You've got to know when to throw that curve-ball."

Roach was watching me closely again; obviously my message to Dink had already been relayed.

"Because no matter how big and tough they are — or think they are — you can still strike 'em out, put 'em in the dirt, with the right pitch."

I nodded to the minister, who now looked even more puzzled, and took my seat. He said a few final words, then we all stood up and watched the coffin as the machinery came on and it disappeared into the black hole in the wall. The working girls were a bit sniffly, but the only actual tears I could discern dribbled down the cheeks of YellowHat's monkey.

But then maybe it was just the cut of his suit.

I wanted to talk to Den, but given all the information he'd been channelling to me, I thought it best not to approach him where we could be seen. As the crowd of mourners broke up, Den remained in his first row seat, staring at the empty space where the coffin had lain, chomping his M&Ms. Roach went up and offered the gamer a crocodile pat on the back before exiting with his entourage, Dinky nipping at their heels. The Robustos crossed themselves before departing through a side door, followed close behind by YellowHat and his monkey. I walked out with the hookers, who traveled in a pack, wailing and chattering like some pantomime Greek chorus.

Once outside, I was brought to an abrupt halt by a sight I never expected to see: YellowHat, Los

Bros and Roach — the Bad, the Worse and the
Ugly — standing in a tense triangle in the funeral
home parking lot. Actually it was only José and
The Man in conference with Roach; Francisco and
the monkey waited off to one side, sitting on the
hood of Roach's Continental and playing a vigor-
ous game of Rock, Paper, Scissors. The Monkey
was getting the better of the contest.

   Their various henchmen and bodyguards were
nowhere in sight, and the conversation grew very
intense indeed. At one point the three of them
turned to watch me walk to my car and I half-
expected a hail of gunfire to follow. But they just
turned back to one another and resumed their
conversation. I'd have loved to be a fly — or a
monkey — on the wall, but there was no way I
could get closer without seeming any more suspicious than I already was. Instead, I got into my
Pacer, started her up and hit the road.

   I spent the rest of the afternoon in my room,
tapped into the Net. Knowing that Blackwell had
plans to go public provided another opportunity
to foster a little havoc, for where Black X went,
Los Bros and YellowHat couldn't be far behind. A
few carefully planted stories about their various
operations, attached to lines of program code that
could only have been provided by an insider,
would prove too enticing not to make headlines in
all the right places. Ah, what Matt Drudge and
his ilk hath wreaked! I used every contact I knew,
fair and foul, to help spill lie and counter-lie, half-
truth, full-truth, and just plain bad craziness all
across the Net. Some of it looked like it came

directly from Black X; some would get traced to
YellowHat or Los Bros; some would just appear as
if from the ether, the mercurial hand of god trac-
ing foul rumor in flames on the virtual walls of
the World Wide Web.

By the time the markets closed in New York
there was talk of an impending FTC investigation
into irregularities in the computer gaming industry. I'd probably wiped millions off the value of
any near-term share offering. Ha!

By nightfall the sound of sirens racing back
and forth across town was constant and flames
rose into the darkening skies from the vicinities
of the YellowHat and Robusto headquarters.

My work here was done.

With Roach knowing where I lived, and wary
of what information about me might have passed
between the big boys in the course of their chat
outside the mortuary, I slipped out of the hotel
the back way and got into my car. I figured I
should lay low for a while as events ran their
course. I needed to get out of town.

I wanted to see Sandy.

Beyond the burgeoning suburbs of Ideaville,
there was no one on the road as I headed for Blue
Moon Lake. There's nothing like driving on the
open road on a fresh night. The dashboard glows
like fairy lights on a Christmas tree and the rush
of air through the open window fills your lungs
like the breath of life itself. You can empty your
mind on a quiet road at seventy miles per hour,
refresh your very soul. I think angels flying
through heaven, if such a place exists, must feel

the flush of power, of joy, that comes with the exertion of speed in the comfort of still darkness. No
one in front, no one beyond; just you and the night.

The lake was pitch dark, but the lights were
on in Sandy's bungalow.

Den stuck his head out the door, offered me a
wave of his bony hand when he heard my car door
slam. I'd stocked up on supplies on my way out of
town — beer and pretzels mostly — grabbed the
bags off the back seat and schlepped them into
the kitchen where Den stood slaving over a hot
hot-plate, the floor around him littered with crin-
kled candy wrappers. Some kind of stew bubbled
in the pot. Den's hands shook as he stirred the
contents, though it smelled pretty tasty.

"I brought some stuff," I said. I pulled a fam-
ily-size package of Almond Joys out of a bag and
tossed them to him. He fumbled the catch, but
caught the package between his knees on the way
to the floor. He gave me a shaky thumbs-up and a
weak smile.

"Those disks Sandy sent me — the code for the
gaming engines — pretty impressive stuff. How'd
you come by it?"

"I'm one of those invisible people," Den said.
He crammed an Almond Joy in his mouth. "I do
my job, don't make a fuss, take what they pay me.
No one even notices me. I'm a ghost."

"Well, they just might start paying a little
more attention after today. I've put it all out
there. With the fuses I lit, the big boys are all
going to be looking for who sprung the leaks in
their boats."

"Sometimes you feel like a nut, sometimes you don't," he said and shrugged.

"I'm just saying you want to be careful. Maybe keep your head down till we see how this all plays out."

"Don't you worry about me. I walk between the cracks in the sidewalk. I'm Claude Rains, baby. I'm Ralph Ellison."

"Maybe, but I appreciate your help and I don't want to see you get burned on account of it."

"Nothing I wouldn't do for her, man. Nothing. She keeps me together, dig?"

I nodded. "She in her room?"

"Went out."

"Out? Where did she go?"

Den shrugged. "Just out. She does that, you know? She lives, she breathes, she walks. We all gotta live."

He unwrapped another piece of chocolate, offered one to me. I shook my head, opting for a beer instead.

The screen door slammed. I turned around and my heart froze like a Dreamsicle in my chest.

Sandy stood in the kitchen doorway, soaking wet, a towel fastened under her arms and around her middle. Her hair was wet and wild, dripping down her pale shoulders. Her bare feet were muddy — she'd tracked some into the house — the chipped nails of her stubby pigeon-toes painted bright pink. A fat drop of water dangled from the tip of her nose.

For a moment I was transported back in time, to that Fourth of July Sunday and the road not taken. Sandy was sweet sixteen and I was a horny kid. She wasn't wearing a towel, but a too-small bathing suit; night was day, the air was electric and life was about to begin.

"I saw your car," she said.

"Huh?"

"Your car. I saw your car, knew you were here."

The past receded into memory, like the picture on an old TV slowly diminishing to a tiny white dot.

"I drove it here," I said.

"Yeah, so I figured. You don't usually see chauffeured Pacers."

"I drove here," I repeated. Seeing her standing there like that, my head had gone all funny. I wasn't even sure what I was saying. Sandy laughed.

"I'd better go dry off."

"You've been swimming," I spat out. I didn't want her to go; didn't want her to move from that spot, from the way she looked standing there.

"I love swimming in the lake at night. The water's cold — so's the air — but you get used to it after a while. There's no one else around, just the bugs and the birds and they don't even make a lot of noise at night. I swim out and float on my back and pretend there's nothing else in the entire world, just me and the water and the stars in the sky. And at night I can skinny dip."

I swallowed. "Skinny?" I said.

"Why not? It's so much nicer. And who's there to see? Or care if they did?"

Me, me! I wanted to scream. I kept my trap shut.

Sandy turned around and started toward her room. As she took a couple of steps down the dark

hall, the towel came loose and slipped to the floor
and I saw that she was, indeed, naked underneath. She quickly bent down (from the knees) to
scoop it up and resecure it, but in that moment I
saw the thickness that had grown about her middle, the stretch marks on her legs, the telltale cel-
lulite chunkiness of her ass.

I'd have given everything I owned to kiss it.

I glanced over at Den, saw that he'd been
watching me carefully. For the first time, his
slack features looked tight, his fuzzy eyes narrowed into a scowl of disquiet. He could not have
missed the look of longing that surely graced my
own face at the sight of Sandy's naked flesh.

I ventured a brave smile. "So how's that dinner coming?"

"Nothing I wouldn't do," Den muttered. He
unwrapped another chocolate and stirred his
stew.

The beef was on the gristly side, but Den was
a good cook. We gathered around the rickety
kitchen table to eat. I got the chair, Sandy sat on
a three-legged stool, and Den perched on an
upended computer carton. They only had two
plates, so Den dished out portions to Sandy and
me and ate his straight out of the pot. I'd bought
a loaf of Wonder Bread — it's what I've always
eaten; builds strong bones and bodies in twelve
ways — but Den cut up a fresh French stick
which complemented the stew in a rather more
flattering way. I drank another beer, while Sandy
went straight for a bottle of Scotch. Den had a big
glass of Yoo-Hoo.

"This is really good," I told him, dabbing the last bits of gravy from my plate with a crust of bread.

"Chocolate," Den said.

"Sorry?"

"Chocolate's the secret."

I glanced down at my plate with a frown.

"You can't exactly taste it," he explained, "but just a hint of chocolate in the cooking gives it that extra bit of flavor. You find it a lot in Mexican food."

"Really?" I've been to more than my share of Taco Bells, but I don't recall the chocolate chimichangas.

Den nodded. "For stews and casseroles I use Reese's Pieces."

"Huh," I said. Sandy let out a loud and unladylike belch. It brought a smile to my face — and Den's; the chef clearly accepted the compliment — because she'd been doing it ever since she was a kid. Her old man used to find it hysterical (I think he'd secretly wanted a boy: thus the curve ball), but her mom would get apoplectic.

We talked briefly about what I'd been up to on the Net that day, but there hadn't been a lot of chat over the meal, which was a good thing, because I was having a hard time concentrating on anything substantial. Shoveling stew into my mouth was as demanding a chore as I was able to carry out. Sandy had dressed for dinner by throwing on a heavily worn and faded man's oxford shirt and a pair of white athletic socks. Oh, yeah, and a thin gold anklet on her left leg with a pair of charms which jingled like tiny reindeer bells

whenever she moved. The shirttails draped down
to her thighs — could it possibly be one of her
dad's old shirts? After all these years? — and
though I couldn't tell for certain, I strongly suspected she wore nothing else underneath. With
the top three buttons undone, I could tell that she
was braless. Feeling like a cherry fifteen-year-old
again (though it was a strangely wonderful feeling), it required vast reserves of restraint not to
stare down the gap every time she leaned over
her plate to take a bite. Reserves which, I fear, I
don't possess.

If Sandy noticed she didn't acknowledge,
through word or expression.

Den glared at me through the entire meal,
though, stabbing at the chunks of meat in his
stew as if he was clubbing baby seals.

I started to get up to clear the dishes, but Den
pushed me back into my chair. "My job," he
declared. "I'll make some coffee, too. Mocha?"

Sandy poured a generous shot of hootch into
hers, while I settled for milk. Den also took his
straight, but topped it off with an extravagant
swirl of shake-it-up whipped cream from the noz-
zled can. He brought out an impressive selection
of after-dinner mints and proceeded to eat them
all on his own. He made little growly happy-
noises as he ate them, like a dog at his bone. I
don't believe I've ever seen anyone over the age of
eight who so loved their sweets. It might have
been endearing if not for the fact that he looked
so cadaverous, and it was hard not to reconcile
the peculiarity of his various appetites with his
mournful appearance.

Sandy added another jolt of Scotch to her now coffee-free mug and slugged it down. I cracked open another beer.

"I wonder if you'd excuse us for a while, Den," Sandy said.

The gamer had been making daisy chains with the bright colored foil from his mints. He froze in mid-fidget, didn't say a word.

"We have some things we need to talk about. In private."

Den looked up at her, seemed to think about it for a moment, then sighed and tossed the wrappers aside. He stood up and headed toward the room containing his gaming gear.

"I mean *very* private," Sandy said.

He slowly turned around, his jaw visibly dropping as he turned. Such blood as there was drained from his ashen cheeks.

"Perhaps you could . . . go out for a while."

Den stared at Sandy, visibly heartbroken. His drooping, lower lip began to quiver. You'd think someone had just shot his yearling.

"Ow-ow-out?" he whimpered.

"You don't mind, do you?"

Excuse me, sir, you don't mind if I hack off your testicles and feed them to my goat, do you? There's a good fellow!

"You want me to go out?" Den said. He looked as if he was about to shatter into a million pieces and clatter to the floor. I studiously read the label on my beer.

"Go on," Sandy said.

Have a seat, kid; it's only thirty thousand volts.

"'Kay," he said. But he didn't move.

"Thanks, Den. You're a brick."

I hazarded a peek and saw him standing there, looking lost and broken. He didn't say anything, but the volume of his pleading all but filled my head. Sandy smiled at him in that thin way that says: I own you. God how I know that look. Roach had shown it to me that day he got out of his limo and offered to send my regards to "Mom." I felt goose bumps run down my arms and retreated further to my beer label. Cold filtering — fascinating!

Den must have stood there for a full two minutes before finally moving. He started toward the door and stopped. He looked at Sandy again, who was still offering that Nanook of Ideaville smile that I prayed she'd never flash at me. Den shuffled into his room and rooted around for a minute, then came out with a set of keys in his hand. He didn't stop this time or even look at Sandy. He did pass me a glare — thank God that looks can't kill — as he went out the door. I heard the car start on the third or fourth try, then a squeal of rubber as Den sped off . . .

Somewhere into the night.

It was just Sandy and me. Alone at last. Again.

Sandy poured herself another healthy shot of Scotch and held the bottle out to me. I started to say no, then figured what the hell. I nodded and she half-filled my coffee cup. I took a slug, felt the fire going down, and coughed. Sandy passed me my beer and I chased it back.

"Smooth," I gagged.

"Only the best around here." Sandy drained

her mug in a single swallow, didn't so much as blink.

"You've had practice at that," I said.

"I've had the time. And the inclination." She refilled her cup, but only took a tiny sip from it. She swirled the liquor around, staring into it. "Apology accepted," she announced.

"Pardon?"

"Your apology. I accept it."

I shook my head.

"My eulogy today. Den told me you got up to say a few words after Roach spoke, that you were the only one. He said you apologized for the way you treated me, begged my forgiveness. I'm saying that the apology is accepted. Though it would have been better if you'd said it to my face. My *living* face."

"I am sorry, Sandy. I thought I did tell you that."

"Did you?"

"I'll say it again if I didn't. Or if you couldn't, or wouldn't, hear me. I. Am. Sorry. If you want, I'll find a judge and legally change my name to it."

"Not necessary," Sandy said.

"Does it make any difference? Being sorry?"

Sandy thought about that. She took a longer drink of drink.

"Sure. Why not?" she said.

"You don't sound very convincing."

"It's my face. No one ever believes this face."

"There's nothing wrong with your face, Sandy. It's a beautiful face."

"Ha! I guess your eyesight went with your IQ."

"I mean that. And I've always had perfect vision."

"So why could you never see what was in front of you?"

My turn for a slug. "Because my perception sucks. I only ever saw what I wanted to see. What I could stand to see."

"And now?"

"Now my doors of perception open a lot wider."

"That's very Jim Morrison of you."

"Jeez, Sandy, I'm trying to make the effort here."

"But why? Why are you making the effort? That's what I don't understand. I can believe you came back here with some romantic notion of revisiting and revising the misery of the past, but what's the point? You can't change any of it. You can't rewrite the stories of our lives no matter how many times you read them. What do you want? Why are you still here?"

"I love you, Sandy."

That shut her up.

She stared at me. Started to open her mouth. Closed it again. Stared some more.

"I've always loved you. Always. And I love you still," I said.

"Oh, Christ," she moaned. She closed her eyes and lowered her head to the table.

I took a sip of scotch, but found I couldn't swallow it. I had to spit it back into the cup. Sandy just sat there with her forehead pressed against the unsteady Formica table top, slowly shaking her head no.

"Sandy?" I whispered.

She was sobbing. Softly, quietly sobbing. I stood up and walked around the table, touched my hand to her back.

"Sandy?"

She suddenly sat up straight, her eyes red and teary. "Do you know how many men I've screwed?" she yelled into my face.

"Sandy . . ."

"Do you know how many cocks I've sucked? How many have spurted between my legs and up my ass? Sometimes two at a time. Do you know?"

"I don't care."

"No? What about this?" She tore open her shirt and practically shoved her left tit in my face. "You see that?"

I saw the golden light of heaven, but little else. "I don't . . ."

"There!"

I saw a jagged scar that ran halfway around the aureola. It hadn't healed well.

"Roach," she said. "He tried to bite it off one night. Then he wouldn't let me go to a doctor until he was finished with me. You want me to show you some of the other scars he's left?"

I shook my head no. She tucked herself in and rebuttoned her shirt.

"You love me, huh? Buddy, you don't even know me. You're in love with your own ideas of the past. You're in love with the memory of who you used to be and can't be anymore, the little boy genius who everyone adored. You look at me and you see a chance to reclaim something you thought was gone forever. A little piece of the glory that once was. You don't see what's in front of you, the here and the now. You don't see the ruin that you created. You don't see me at all."

Sandy tried to shove me away. I put my arms

around her and she scratched at my face. I let her. I could feel blood dripping down my cheek, but I just held her until she stopped fussing. The loamy scent of the lake on her skin filled my nose. I could feel the heat of her trembling body through the thin fabric of the old oxford shirt.

"So I guess maybe my apology isn't *entirely* accepted," I said.

She shoved me away. I don't know why — I certainly had no right — but I suddenly felt angry.

"You betrayed me, too," I said.

"What?"

"Didn't you."

"I don't know what you're talking about," Sandy muttered.

"The case that brought my father down, the case against Roach's dad. You were the one who fed me the leads . . . the false leads. You were the one who set us up so the Blackwells could swat us down. Or had you forgotten?"

The temperature in the room dropped twenty degrees. Sandy poured herself a very chilled scotch. It didn't last long in the cup.

"How long have you known?"

"Always. I've always known."

Sandy nodded her head sadly, her shoulders slumped as she stared down at the floor. Fucked up the ass again. And without even a deuce to show for it.

"That's not true," I said.

She raised her eyes.

"I didn't know until the other day. Roach told me. To gloat, of course. He couldn't believe that I

didn't know, and he got a very big laugh out of it.
The fact is it would never . . . did never occur to
me that you could have betrayed me. In spite of
. . . everything."

Sandy started to cry again. I reached up my
hand, but she swatted it away.

"Don't!" she yelled.

She got up and ran into the bathroom, stum-
bling, slamming the door behind her.

I drained my cup, poured out what little
Scotch was left in the bottle and drank that. I
heard water running in the bathroom. It stopped,
but the door didn't open. I stood up to collect the
dirty mugs and put them in the sink, and discovered that I was very drunk. I sat back down. The
bathroom door clicked open and Sandy came
back into the kitchen. She dragged the stool over
to the corner and stood on it to open up a high
cupboard. As she reached for an object on the top
shelf, her shirt rode up and her naked ass was
exposed to me again. She half-fell off the stool,
just managing to land on her feet. In her hands
she held an old metal lunch box: The Banana
Splits.

She put the lunch box down on the table, sat
in Den's chair. Opening it up she withdrew a
dented flask with Fleegle's image plastered on
the sides. She unscrewed the top and pulled out a
cellophane bag.

"You smoke dope?" Sandy asked.

"You mean . . . Mary Jane?"

She flashed me a you-have-*got*-to-be-kidding
look. I was. I smiled to prove it. She still looked
doubtful.

"I've been known to inhale," I said. "I like college interns, too."

Sandy nodded. "This is Den's stuff. It's . . . different."

"Like Den."

"Don't you talk about him!"

"No offense meant."

Sandy rolled a pair of joints — big ones — with well-rehearsed ease. She stuffed the baggy back in the thermos and the flask back inside the lunch box. She lit up the first joint, took a deep drag and passed it over. I took a more tentative hit and found it harsh — though not quite so harsh as the generic Scotch — and held it in my lungs.

The stuff went right to my head. It always does.

"What do you think?" Sandy asked.

"Damn," I said. "Fleegle knows his shit."

She nodded and giggled. "Den sprinkles it with something."

"Sprinkles? What? Belgian chocolate?"

"He won't tell me. But that's what makes it . . . different."

It had been a good few years since I'd smoked any dope, in part because it does go right to my head, but in larger part because it had been a long time since I've had anyone to light up with. And getting high by yourself is second only to masturbation for the depths of post-event depression. I can hate myself enough by jerking off, thank you very much.

We finished off that first joint sitting there in the kitchen. When it was too small to pass Sandy said, "Now this roach I'm happy to eat," and popped it into her mouth.

We both started to laugh.

"Let's go outside," Sandy said. She lit up the second joint, stuck it between her lips and wandered out the door. It took me a couple of tries before I could successfully stand up and follow her. I stopped, too, to admire just how really beautiful that old kitchen was. Uh-oh.

Sandy walked down the path toward the road. I trailed her, a dozen paces behind, as she crossed it to follow the dirt track that led to the lake. A three-quarter moon and a ballet of dancing fireflies provided the only light. The other houses were dark, and there were no sounds but the delicate lapping of the lake on the shore and the thin breeze in my ears. Sandy turned a clumsy pirouette as she neared the edge of the water and giggled into the night. I laughed and felt my heart expand inside my chest.

Sandy tore her shirt open and off. The buttons flew through the air, catching glints of moonlight as they tumbled and fell into the water, too small to even make a splash. She shook out her long hair, and raised her arms above her head. She looked up at the stars, waved at them, and laughed. Her body was a streak of white in the surrounding darkness, shadows delicately draped about her as if drawn on by some censor's black marker.

Though the night air was cool, she ran out into the lake, stomping furiously like a kid in a mud puddle. Droplets splashed up as high as her chin, then she threw her arms out and fell over back-

ward into the water. A moment later, squealing
with the cold, she was back on her feet, the water
and moonlight caressing her splendid form. Legs
spread wide in some conquering pose, one arm
raised to the heavens, the other tucked behind
her head, Sandy stood like some alabaster Grace
brought to supernatural life by the magic of the
night.

"You coming in?" Sandy called.

She only had to ask me once.

I fell over trying to take my shoes off as I ran,
landed on my ass and laughed like a loon. I tossed
my shoes and socks over my shoulder, shucked
my shirt somewhere else and got to my feet as I
tussled with my belt. I tripped again as I pulled
one pants leg off, rolled onto my back and bicycled
the air until I was rid of them. I tore my briefs off
and flung them away. Sandy was in hysterics
watching me, floating on her front, then her back
and spitting a tiny geyser of lake water out of her
mouth. I stepped into the water — or on top of it,
for all I knew — my penis pointing the way to
Sandy like some quivering, fleshy divining rod.

The water felt cold — very cold — but it was a
wonder it didn't turn to steam at the heat ema-
nating from my body. A shudder passed through
me as I dove into the water, but I had only Sandy
on my substance-altered mind. She teasingly
darted away from me as I drew near, swimming
languorous, elongated figure-eights in precise,
measured strokes. I'd never really learned how to
swim, and so dog paddled after her like some bull-
dog who'd sniffed a bitch in heat. I was out of
shape from too many hours in front of computer

monitors and too few doing any physical exertion; Sandy could have led me a merry chase all night.

She didn't.

She swam back to the shallows and stopped, floating again on her back. Her hair spilled out around her, billowing like anemones on the waves we made. Her heavy breasts bobbed atop the water, her big nipples hard as diamonds from the cold. The moon's gentle white light made her shine, glow like the bobbing fireflies that dotted the shore. I swam up beside her and started to stand. The water wasn't deep enough so I sank to my knees in the lake's muddy floor. I put my arms out beneath her, let her float to me, cradling the small of her back, the fleshy underside of her thick thighs. She poked the tip of her tongue out and gently licked at her lips, her brown eyes reflecting the bitten disk of the bright moon.

I kissed her.

I felt my heart race as our lips touched. I heard a sizzling in my ears, like fatty steaks on a barbecue: it was blood thrilling through my veins. A surge in my loins left me aching with stiffness. Our tongues entwined, embracing like stripes on a twirling barber pole, as we feverishly tried to devour each other. Sandy threw an arm over my shoulder, raising herself out of the water to press herself tighter against me. The feel of her breasts tight against my chest, her erect nipples digging into my flesh like pebbles in a shoe, drove me to deeper passion. I slipped my hand between her thighs, pressing my palm against her sex, heated like some black smoker beneath the cold water. She pressed herself against me then opened her legs wide until I plunged my fingers inside her tender depths.

"Devour me," she whispered into my mouth, and I bit gently at her lips and tongue, buried my face in the gentle curve of her neck.

"Be in me," she asked.

One hand still inside her, the other under her back, I stood up, lifting her out of the water as I strode toward the shore. Sandy lolled back her head and flashed a broad, dopey smile at the sky. With one hand still draped around my neck, she reached out beneath her with the other finding the length of my straining cock, cupping my pulsing balls.

"Oh, that's what I like," she murmured. "God help me."

I carried Sandy to a patch of wild grass and laid her down. She splayed her fingers through her hair, then threw her arms out above her head. She raised her mouth for a kiss, her tongue extended, the tip curling and uncurling in a sirenic tease. I sucked it hard, felt it dance and swirl about the inside of my mouth, gave back as good as I got, exploring the recesses of Sandy's teeth. I drew away and she offered a tiny frown and a disappointed moan, so I quickly kissed her cheeks, her chin, bathed and lapped and nipped at her neck.

Sandy ran her hands down the length of her body and I followed her lead. I dappled her white shoulders with my tongue as I touched the backs of my hands along her sides. I brought my mouth to her chest and kissed the space between her splayed breasts, brushing the edges with the

curves of my palms. She raised her chin and
arched her back until I attacked her nipples with
my lips and tongue. I mashed her tits together,
until the hard nubs of her nipples were an inch
apart, and tried to stuff them both in my mouth
at once. It made her laugh.

I let go long enough to throw a leg over her,
straddling her middle between my thighs. My
absurdly stiff penis bounced off her tummy, elicit-
ing a further chuckle of delight. She reached
down and took hold of me as I fastened my fingers
to her nipples, pinching each between a thumb
and forefinger. It made her squeeze my cock so
hard that I nearly lost control and had to gently,
if reluctantly, prise free of her loving grip.

As I backed off, she opened her legs to me and
I gratefully fell between them. I rested my sweaty
cheek against the thick mat of her pubic hair and
luxuriated in the rich odor that trailed from her
cunt. I rolled my mouth and chin across her wet
fur, then lay a line of gentle kisses down her
meaty thighs. She raised her legs into the air as
I pressed my palms against the undersides of her
thighs, my thumbs softly stroking her labia.

I rode the elevator to the basement.

Sandy groaned loudly as my lips found hers. I
sucked a moist flap of labia into my mouth and
gave it the tenderest of chews. I skipped my
tongue across and within the cascading folds of
her inner skin, sucking down her salty wetness. I
painted the letters of the alphabet, then an array
of Chinese characters, across her pulsating pussy
with my tongue, lavishing care to the sunflower
seed of her clit as she writhed and groaned and

rocked beneath me. Her fingers were locked in my hair, pressing me deeper against her. As I tried to pull away, she forced me back.

"Eat. My. Clit," she moaned.

A good little boy does as he is told.

At the point of no return I pulled away again and Sandy practically shrieked. I wagged a finger at her, then I wagged something else.

She spread herself as wide as she could go.

If there is anything as sweet in this life as the moment in which you first slip into your lover's most private, secret embrace, you'd need Bill Gates' money to pay for it. As I penetrated Sandy, slipping into her heat and filling her even as she filled me, the bonds of time and the shackles of age dissolved like sugar in hot tea. The past two decades disappeared — they'd never happened. As I rose and fell above my beloved, slipped in and out of her with the slickness of a Rolls-Royce piston in its chamber, we were young again; innocent again. All the horrors, all the mistakes, all the nightmarish wrong turns up one-way streets didn't matter. It was just Sandy and me and the perfection of the three-quarter moonlit night.

"Oh," she groaned.

"Oh, my sweet girl," I shuddered as I exploded inside her. It went on and on as if my very soul were being spent in the warmth and delight of her. I know the French call orgasm "the little death" — the big froggy creeps — but I admit, I'd have happily died in that moment. What more could there be?

"More," Sandy groaned. And I realized: not done yet.

Sandy continued to push against me. I was still inside her, still hard (but fading fast). I pressed against her, continuing the motion, rubbing myself against her while there was still something left to rub. I reached down and felt for her with my hand. Down to bone against bone, I touched the nub of her clit with my finger and pressed the magic button.

"That's . . . .that's . . . ." Sandy let out a yell into the night.

And we collapsed into each other's arms.

"Sandy . . ."

"Shhh."

The last thing I remembered was the heat of her breath on my neck, and a loving, fleeting kiss brushing my lips.

I slept.

The morning poked me in the eye like a Three Stooges *manqué*. Someone had stolen in during the night and driven twenty-penny spikes through the middle of my face, nailing my head to the tacky floor. I blinked, but the noise was unbearable, so I didn't repeat the experiment. I closed my eyes, deciding that unconsciousness is underrated and gave it four gold stars in my little black book.

What floor? something unpleasant in the back of my brain had the temerity to ask *You fell asleep in the grass!*

I could have done with a forklift, but through a determined act of sheer mental will, I prised my eyes open again.

I lay on the floor of the bungalow's "fun room";

the room in which I'd slept all those years ago,
where Sandy had snuck under the covers of my
bed to hide from her mom. The room was mostly
unused now, with some of Den's old computer
equipment stowed in the corner. I knew that's
where I was because an ancient paint-by-num-
bers, fake-wood cigar store Indian plaque,
"crafted" by Sandy's dad, still hung on the wall in
my field of vision. How the hell did I get here?

I put my mind to it. The last thing I could
remember was making love to Sandy in the tall
grass by the side of the lake. I remembered coming inside her — and smiled — and her coming
against me. I remembered all the beer and Scotch
I drank, Den's special dope that we smoked.

Which likely accounted for the metal spikes in
my face.

I remembered a funny dream I'd had: I was
sitting on a bench in Baltimore. Which is funny,
because I've never been there, though *Homicide* is
my all-time favorite television show. A woman
came and sat down beside me. She wore a pink
bunny-fur suit, but it wasn't Meg from Tesseracts
and instead of displaying her spread sex, a little
monkey's head poked out through her open fly.
The monkey wore a bright yellow sombrero and
laughed and laughed. I asked the woman if she
knew a man named Carroll or a boy named Sue.
But all she said to me was: "Nevermore." She
then turned into a raven and flew away.

Christ, the things we carry around in our
heads.

I managed to raise myself an inch off the floor
without throwing up. I raised my left hand up

and touched it to my brow: I felt very hot, very sweaty. I rubbed my eyes. When I tried to raise my other hand, the better to keep my aching head from exploding, I discovered that it was already clutching something else.

I looked at it: it held a cable.

A printer cable.

I followed the length of it.

The bulk of the cable was wrapped around Sandy's neck.

I shot bolt upright.

"Sandy?" I choked. My throat was as dry as a Mormon's liquor cabinet.

I let go of the cable, reached out and touched my finger to Sandy's naked leg. She felt cold. So cold.

I screamed.

My head still pulsing, my limbs barely responding to my needs, I scampered into the corner of the room and stared at Sandy's body. There was no movement at all. I could hear whimpering, but couldn't figure out where the noise was coming from.

I tracked it down to the back of my throat.

"Sandy!" I cried.

I crawled back over to her, prodded her gently with my hand. Then a little harder, and harder still.

She didn't move. She'd never move again.

I got to my feet, looked around for my clothes. They were scattered around the kitchen and living room, though I had no recollection of how they got there. I had no recollection of anything at all, certainly not . . .

I couldn't see straight, couldn't think clearly. I slipped into my things, bouncing off chairs and walls as I pulled my pants on, needing three tries to get my shoes tied. I ran out of the house into the bright light of morning. There was no one around, nothing moving on the lake. Birds chirped, bees buzzed; high above me a jet left its fuzzy contour trails like chicken-scratchings in the sky. It was so far away I couldn't even hear the engines.

A perfectly normal, sunny fall day.

And I'd killed the only woman I'd ever loved.

XI. The Big Knockover

When I was a *little* kid — before Sandy moved to town; before I'd ever encountered Roach and his cronies; before Boy Detective was even an idea in my precocious, crew-cut head — my dad was just a patrolman and we lived in a small rented house on the outskirts of town. My parents were trying to save up enough money to buy the home that I grew up in, so we lived a little below our means. We had one set of neighbors, a big family named Allen, who were always trying to be buddy-buddy with my folks, probably because they knew my dad was a cop and it never hurts to know a cop because who can say when you might need one? My mom always referred to the Allens as "earthy." This was her polite way of acknowledging that we lived next door to white trash. Roseanne, at her fattest and most working class, wouldn't have had anything to do with this bunch. The Allens had a mess of kids, of course, all of whom were *messy*. My mom wasn't real thrilled with having me play with them, but they did live next door and one of them, Digger, was my age, and we sort of got along in a nothing-better-to-do way, and kids will be kids so what are you going to do?

One day, me and Digger were playing out in the yard, tossing around an old football that had been cast off by one of his older siblings. It was far

too big for our hands, and neither of us knew how
to throw or catch it, but it made us feel like big
boys and it was fun and what the hell do little
kids care, so long as they're having fun? The
trouble was that the football had a tiny leak in its
bladder — no doubt the reason the older Allen
had tossed it away — and constantly had to be
pumped up to be of any use at all. Fortunately, I
had one of those small hand pumps, the kind
that's attached to the brace bar of a bicycle, which
I'd found among my dad's sports stuff. So we
could play with the ball for ten minutes or so
before it would deflate and have to be pumped up
again. It took a big effort for two little kids to
pump up a football, but that was kind of fun, too,
and what do you have but time when you're knee-
high to nothing with nowhere to go?

We were pumping up the football one day,
trading the job back and forth to share the effort,
when two of Digger's older brothers showed up.
Gary and Larry had gained some notoriety for
their bullying ways — Roaches in the making; the
type is ubiquitous — though they'd never bothered me. Having a policeman for a dad can be a
very handy thing sometimes. Nonetheless, they
were bullies through and through and we were
younger boys so they couldn't resist having *some*
fun with us. Gary snatched the football from Digger, and Larry grabbed the pump out of my hand.

"I lost a pump just like this," he said, studying
it. "Looks like I found it again. Har-har."

"That's mine," I squeaked.

"Can you prove it?" Larry asked. He held the
pump up in the air, out of my reach.

"It's mine. You know it is."

"Ixnay," Gary told his brother. "His oppay's an opcay. Ememberray?"

I hadn't yet mastered the subtle conjugations of pig Latin, and judging from the look on Larry's face, he struggled with it, too. He worked it out, though, because he put his arm down and let me get a hand on the pump. Then he snatched it away again.

"Don't be upidstay," Gary warned. Larry waved him off.

"Want to see something really cool?" Larry asked me. He didn't wait for an answer, just walked off toward the back of the yard, still holding onto my bicycle pump. Digger tossed the half-inflated football away and followed him. I tagged along.

Larry got on his hands and knees by the filthy patch of stagnant water that the Allens sadly referred to as their "pond." I didn't much like going near the pond because of all the bugs, but Larry had my pump and I did want to see what was so cool. Larry darted around in the mud, thrusting his hands into the water and cursing. He'd put the pump down in the grass, and I thought about picking it up, but Gary beat me to it. Finally Larry let out a hoot as he came away with a green frog trapped between his fingers. It didn't make any noise, though the little bulb in its throat was pulsing away. It was about the size of a penny-pinky ball.

"You like balloons?" Larry asked me. I nodded; who didn't? "Well, check this out. Hold out your hands."

I was one of those kids who didn't much care for worms or frogs or slimy things of any kind, but I didn't want to look chicken. I didn't trust the Allen boys, either, but I held out my cupped hands. Larry placed the wet frog in my palms and told me to hold on tight. I didn't hold it tight enough, though, because it instantly squirted out and Larry had to dive to catch it before it could disappear back into the water. He held it out to me again.

"Hold it tight now, nitwad," he commanded.

I obeyed.

"Good," he said. He turned to his brother. "Doctor, the instrument."

Gary handed Larry the pump. Larry examined the needle at the end of the hose and nodded his approval.

"Hold him tight around the front, but open up your hands a little in the back," Larry said. Gary was starting to laugh, though I didn't know why.

I did as I was told and Larry took the needle and prodded the frog in the rear with it.

"Tighter!" Larry insisted. It was tough, because the frog was a squirmy little thing. You'd be, too, if someone tried to stick a hose up your ass.

"Got it," Larry said. He told Digger to hold onto the end of the hose attached to the rear of the frog. Digger moved fast, knowing the consequences of not doing exactly as his brother told him to.

"Here we go," Larry said. Gary had taken several steps back. "Now hold that sucker tight as you can."

Larry pulled back the plunger and then forced it in. I heard the air whistling through the needle and into the frog, some of it escaping out the side. The frog tried to jump and for the first time, made a froggy noise.

Larry continued to pump.

The needle came out a couple of times, but Larry neatly reinserted it on each occasion, giving a Digger a slap across the back of the head each time for screwing up. Finally, he got a solid rhythm going. Gary was now a good ten steps away.

At first, I thought it was really cool. I could feel the frog inflating in my hands, expanding just like a balloon. Digger and I both giggled at the sight of it. The frog's tiny eyes were popping out of its head, but it had gone silent again. Until it made a high-pitched squeal, less like a frog than a wounded kitten.

"Gary?" I said.

He just kept on pumping.

"You're hurting it," I cried, but I didn't let go. The frog had blown up bigger than a softball, and had turned a different, darker shade of green.

"Frogs got no feelings, turd breath. No nerves."

He pumped and pumped. I looked at Digger, who looked at me. He dropped the needle and I was just about to let go, when Larry completed one final thrust of the pump.

The frog exploded all over me.

Digger caught a bit of it, too, but most of the poor frog's innards burst all over my face and shirt, and in my hair. I didn't even realize at first what had happened, but then I felt something in my mouth and when I spat it into my hand, saw that it was a teary little frog eye.

I screamed and burst out crying.

I never played with Digger again, and Gary and Larry kept their distance from me, especially after my dad paid a visit on Allen Senior. We bought our real house soon after and moved away. I don't know what became of the Allens. Digger never attended school with me so perhaps they moved on to a fresh patch of trailer park America.

But I never forgot the feeling of that frog exploding in my hands; the horror of having participated, however unknowingly, in the torture and death of that tiny creature. Ever since, I've shooed flies out the window rather than kill them; let a spider be when I see one in the corner of the room. I don't like hurting things, killing things, could never again participate in the kinds of bug and animal torture that fascinated other kids I knew.

So how could I have killed Sandy?

I drove myself back to Ideaville, though I don't remember anything about the ride. Blame it on the drugs, blame it on the booze — hell, blame it all on Auntie Mame, I don't know — it's just a big blank to me. The first thing I knew I was sitting in a line of cars at the town limits, waiting at a police roadblock. *They're looking for me* I thought, before some semblance of sense returned and I realized that there was no way they could even know yet.

Was there?

One car after another was getting turned back the way it came. The drivers looked angry but there was no clue as to what it was all about. It took ten minutes before I reached the front of the line. A bored looking cop in uniform stuck his head in my window as I stopped.

"Some trouble up ahead, no one gets through," he said.

"I have to get to Ideaville."

"That's what they all say. Turn around, buddy."

"I have to get to Ideaville."

"Listen, Mac: don't make a fuss. Town's closed today, okay? Just like Christmas. Now be a dear and turn your ass around before I drag you out of there and we play police piñata."

"I have to get to Ideaville."

"That's it." The cop hauled open the car door. Just as he did it, I stepped on the gas. "Hoo-o-o-o . . ." he screamed, spinning down to the dirt behind me. The door swung shut on its own.

I jammed on the brakes when I saw two more police cars completely blocking the road in front of me. The cops had their shotguns drawn and pointed right at me.

"What gives here? What . . . ?"

I saw Dink running up the road from behind, wearing an ill-fitting uniform. A broad smile took over his face when he leaned down to look at me. He waved to his officers to lower their guns.

"All the chicks coming home to roost today, yes sirree. Where you been?"

"I have to get to Ideaville," I said. It was all I could think.

"We got a little anarchy in town at the moment. Those Robusto boys have popped their corks. Martial law, don't you know. Wouldn't recommend a visit."

You can guess the nature of my response.

"Your funeral," my old pal told me. He didn't seem much saddened by the prospect and cleared the way for me.

I sped on without looking back.

The first sign of trouble came as I rounded Dead Man's Curve and caught sight of smoke trailing out of the Black X headquarters. A dozen fire crews scampered around the grounds aiming their hoses every which way, including at each other. All of the glass on the street side of the glass-and-steel structure had been blown out, and millions of pinpoint shards dusted the grass like a glistening layer of morning snow. The charred and fractured remains of a van could be seen wedged in the ruins of the building's main entrance. A car bomb, I reckoned, courtesy of Los Bros Motors.

Welcome to Ideaville, the West Bank of the Midwest.

I gunned it up Commerce Street, only to have to jam my foot Fred Flintstone style on the brakes and cut the wheel, as a quartet of cherry-tops came roaring up the road toward me in a diamond formation running both sides of the street. I jumped my Pacer up the curb with a grinding squeal, taking out a No Stopping sign in the process.

The cops raced past without giving me a second look.

I pulled back out onto the road with a deal more caution. Gunfire sounded in the distance, but I couldn't tell where it was coming from — perhaps everywhere. Columns of smoke billowed into the sky from various points around town. On a whim, I headed for one especially dense black cloud like some mad tornado-hunter, skirting the center of town as I drove. I wasn't surprised to find that it trailed from the smoldering ruins of the YellowHat factory. The plant was alive with fire and small explosions regularly sounded from within. A handful of security guards in bright yellow YellowHat uniforms, the monkey's smiling face decaled on the backs, dejectedly watched the disaster from a safe distance, pointing and shaking their heads as the place burned. A chunk of roof as big as a football field collapsed into the flames while I watched, with a roar like stampeding buffalo. There were no firemen here; not so much as a dalmatian with a weak bladder.

It would seem that Roach had Ideaville's fire service wrapped up near as tight as the local police.

The streets were quiet, as the good — and not so good — citizens of Ideaville took the hint and kept to their houses. I did pass several more squads of racing police cars — they zipped back and forth across town like latter-day Keystone Kops — but none paid me any mind. I felt like a ghost riding those empty streets, as hollow within myself as I was invisible to those without. Ideaville — the whole world — existed for me only at a great remove. Nothing really mattered: the flames that licked at the morning sky, the bullets that intermittently ricocheted around me, the should-have-been delightful sight of my corrupted little town literally going to hell. My plan to sow the seeds of suspicion and discontent had succeeded perfectly, but it was all just background music, incidental detail; nothing more than the well-rendered but inconsequential mise-en-scene for a computer game that had no effect whatsoever on the play. I was reaping my money's worth but it was still Game Over.

Sandy was dead. Again. What else could possibly matter?

I tried in my mind to reconstruct the events of the previous night at Blue Moon Lake. I tried but I failed. I could summon up flashes of detail: the burnt orange color of a carrot in the stew; the tiny sound made by the brushing of a shirttail against Sandy's thigh; the neatly folded foil mint wrappers that littered the table; the taste of Sandy's sex against my searching tongue; but I couldn't bring them together to tell a coherent story. A story that could explain the sight that dominated all the others; that filled my head with horror and my heart with a pain as vast as the Great Plains: Sandy's body lying dead on the floor. The computer cable wrapped around her neck . . . and entwined in my fingers.

It was unthinkable that I could have killed her; there was nothing Sandy could have said or done to drive me to that. I love . . . loved her. The unpleasantness between us was all in the past. At last. We'd both lived lives of desperation attempting to escape what went before. But we'd finally gone past it and come back together again last night. If I closed my eyes, I could smell her, feel her, see her too-beautiful-for-me face. Even taking into account the mix of booze and drugs — Den's mysterious magic dust — and the hours of blackness that followed our lovemaking, it was impossible to believe that I could have hurt Sandy. *Especially* after our lovemaking.

It had been the high point of my entire, miserable life.

Without meaning to do so, I'd driven back to the center of town. It was well into normal business hours now, but the shops were all shut tight. Even Panchito's Bagelteria — open 24-hours a day, 365 days a year, supposedly, so even Santa could stop by for lox with a shmear — had the steel shutters down. I parked the car and dropped a couple of quarters into the meter. Maybe Panchito was unreliable, but never put anything past a professional meter maid. Though there was no one else on the streets, though Ideaville was exploding around me, I began to walk.

Up Franklin Street, down Dixon Road, a quick whirl around McFarlane Terrace. I walked through the park, past the school, across Mile End Creek and back again. I walked and I walked until my feet hurt and my back ached and I wanted to just collapse to the ground in a big heap of misery. And still I walked.

As I turned up Dahl Road, a black Blazer, stuffed to the rafters like a clown car with duster-clad Robusto minions, came tearing around the corner. The bad boys were shooting their guns up into the air like it was Cinco de Mayo, howling and shrieking like a pack of hemorrhoidal ban-

shees on a bad trip. The driver screeched to a halt
when they spotted me, and they all got out and
turned their weapons on me, licking their lips,
ready to rock and roll. I turned to face them, with
nothing standing between me and my fate but the
thin sheen of tears that washed down my face.

They lowered their guns, got back in their car,
and quiet as monkish church mice, departed the
way they had come, well within the speed limit.

On Centerburg Avenue I beheld a tiny miracle:
Ulysses' Diner was open for business, a police car
parked out front. Wiping my face on my sleeve, I
went inside.

One uniformed cop waited nervously at the
counter while the Bard of the Sinker fiddled with
his persnickety doughnut maker. He yelled at it
and shook it and finally took to pounding its side
with his fist until it started spitting out its gems.
It wasn't until he filled three big bags that he
handed them to the cop.

"Put it on the Chief's tab," the policeman said.

The counter man yanked the bag away.

"Hey!"

"No credit today," the counter man said. He
nodded toward the door.

The policeman's hand slid down to his holster
before he reconsidered and pulled out his wallet.
He paid, harrumphed, took his doughnuts and
ran back to his car. He turned the siren and flash-
ers on and hauled ass.

"Help ya?" the counter man asked. As if it was
just any other day.

"Cuppa joe," I stammered.

He happily obliged. "Sinker with that?"

I shook my head; I felt sunk enough.

"Can't let it get you down, friend." I shot him a look. "YellowHat?"

"What about it?" I muttered.

"You work for YellowHat? That the problem?"

"No. Why?"

"Pssh. Figured a fellow out on the streets today'd be a fellow in the know."

"I don't know shit."

"They got The Man. Monkey, too."

"Who did?"

"Los Bros. Those hombres have gone plum loco. Even for them. After they heard that YellowHat and Black X agreed to join forces in a hostile takeover, they just went wild. Sent The Man to yellow heaven on a thirty-ought rowboat. And that poor little monkey, somebody ought to call the ASPCA for what they done. Who you think's been shooting up the town all night, anyhow?"

"Roach . . . "

"Blackwell is running scareder than a luau virgin on marry-the-volcano night. Got himself holed-up in that big old manse of his with a mess of Blackwell U's best guns. Riding out the storm best he can."

"What about the cops?"

"Haw-haw. They couldn't find their asses with Mr. Whipple leading the search party. 'Sides, lots of 'em's been taking money on the Robusto pad, too. They been half shooting at each other when they ain't been running for their lives. No sir, the big boys have pulled their plonkers out and now it's a pissing contest."

"Aren't you a little scared being out in the middle of it all? Keeping your business open with all this . . . yellow rain coming down?"

"Aw hell, friend, we never close. And you got to know that this is the safest place in town. Ain't you understood?" He flashed me a sly grin: the cat who'd eaten the canary cream doughnut. "*Everybody* loves my sinkers."

I polished off my coffee, tossed a buck on the counter and walked out. I hardly even blinked when I heard an explosion from around the corner, saw a rainbow hailstorm of silver DVDs cascade down on the street in front of me. I picked one up: SimHolocaust.

Just another judgment day in Ideaville.

I know I wasn't thinking straight; after all I was half in shock. But even if I'm not the smartest ex-kid in the world anymore, I do reckon myself to be a few watts brighter than the average bear. So why it didn't occur to me straight off, I can't really say. But when it hit me, it dropped on my head like a safe in an old cartoon. You could have opened the combination on the door and seen me inside, goggle-eyed, with little stars circling around my head. As the realization set in, my sorrow turned to anger, my pain to a hunger for revenge. I was a man with a mission once again.

Den.

The cord that strangled Sandy might have been wrapped in my hand, but at that moment I knew — as surely as I knew anything in this world — that I hadn't been the one to kill her. No drink, no drug could do that to me; it wasn't in my nature. Den, on the other hand, had every motive. I flashed back to the look on his face when Sandy asked him to go, the crushing blow it must have been to the slender threads of his weak ego. He'd seen Sandy through the worst of times, after all, from her life on the street right through to her "death." It was clear from the way she spoke to him and his response to her that he was entirely in her thrall; that he was slavishly devoted to her.

But you can only whip even the most loyal dog so hard before it'll turn on its master.

Or mistress.

I had to find him. He might still have been back at the lake, but somehow I didn't think so. Den was too weak-willed to hole up at the scene of the crime. Far more likely that he did the deed, then ran back to town. He must have had a place here, but I'd never heard either of them mention it, had no idea where to start looking. Where the hell would Den . . .

Then the anvil dropped from the top of the cliff: two Looney Tunes epiphanies, no waiting. I knew exactly where to look.

I walked into it on Couffignal Street.

There's no telling what happened in the moments before, how events had played out as they had. Did Los Bros screw up? Or was this some desperate last stand they were making, knowing they'd come to the end of their particular, insane road?

I saw the car first: the Robusto's primo '57 Caddy, cobalt blue with fins that could give Steven Spielberg nightmares. The last time I'd seen it was in the Los Bros parking lot, watched over by two armed guards. It had been immaculate.

Now, tires blown, half-riding the curb, it was a wreck. The driver's side was smashed in and the glass all shot out. The fuzzy dice that had dangled from the rear-view mirror had come up craps on the crunched-up hood. The dice lay next to the head of the Man from YellowHat's monkey, which had been impaled on the hood ornament as a sick trophy.

Curiosity clearly killed more than just the cat.

The brothers themselves, decked out in ponchos and bandoliers, stood in front of the ruins of a discount software store. José clutched a shotgun in one hand, a pistol in the other. Francisco held matching Uzis. A pair of their duster-wearing henchmen, also with shotguns, one man bleeding profusely from the head, stood beside them, while another half-dozen of their posse — all out of the game — lay in bloody pools in the street.

Across from them, guns at the ready, stood a small army of Roach's rent-a-cops. Two score of them stood in the street, another dozen aiming down at Los Bros from the rooftops.

The tableaux was frozen as I turned the corner. Francisco waved his guns back and forth at the forces lined up against them. It held the cops in check, none of them brave enough to fire the first shot. The duster boys looked scared — hell, they were only on payroll, and the Robustos didn't strike me as big perk employers — but the brothers were positively giddy. Francisco was bouncing up and down, while José had a big grin plastered across his face, his eyes alight with excitement. As he took in the mass of forces arrayed against them, he started to laugh. Francisco joined in a few seconds later. The boys' laughter broke the silence in an eerie way, and I saw it coming before the rent-a-cops did. I dove for cover behind a cement trash bin.

I guess the boys hadn't been kidding back at the funeral home: Los Bros really *were* born ready to die.

Francisco opened up with the Uzis.

To the extent that I was brave enough to look, I saw things in slow motion. The cops went down in a row, as if choreographed for *Riverdance*, only with fountains of blood exploding out of them, and musical accompaniment courtesy of Smith & Wesson. The rent-a-cops shot back and the massacre was on.

One of the duster boys took a volley of bullets in the chest, sending him hurtling back through the software shop's big plate glass window. Even before he had fallen all the way through I saw the other duster go down from a single shot to the center of his forehead. His shotgun flew up into the air as he fell, going off as it hung there in space. The hand of God (or the devil; the difference, after all, is only in the details) must have pulled the trigger, because the bullet hit the rear of a squad car which exploded on contact, taking out a whole cadre of Roach's men.

José was shooting at a group of cops attempting an assault from the left, while Francisco turned his Uzi fire at the snipers on the roof. Francisco had been hit several times, and his poncho dripped with blood, but he didn't stop until both clips were empty. When they were spent, he rolled to the ground, slapped another pair in, and was on his feet firing before you could say "Arnold Schwarzenegger." Sadly, he needed an action hero with a shorter name, because it was still enough time for a marksman on the roof to draw a proper bead. The shot hit a shell on his bandolier and detonated it, setting off the strip of cartridges like a mat of cheap firecrackers.

A five-hundred-piece jigsaw puzzle would serve as a suitable tribute to what was left of Francisco.

One Bro to go.

"Hermano!" José screamed when he saw Francisco go down (and up and out and all around). He, too, had taken a series of messy hits and could only stagger to the spots where his brother now lay. There were still a dozen or more rent-a-cops lined up against him, emptying their weapons as madly as they could. José took bullet after bullet, but kept on standing. He dragged his bloody self over to the wreck of the Caddy and managed to pop the trunk open. The rent-a-cops seemed to sense that they had him now and, throwing caution to the wind, advanced on José at close range, guns blasting.

José pulled a small satchel out of the trunk, flicked a little switch on the top. A red LED suddenly flashed green.

Exit stage left, I thought, and scrambled to my feet, running as far and as fast as my smelly feet would take me in the opposite direction.

"CUMBRE DEL MUNDO, MAMA," José yelled.

I heard another spray of bullets.

The impact lifted me off my feet and sent me flying through the air before I heard the explosion.

And it was a loud motherfucker.

Fortunately, I landed in a flower bed, my only injuries inflicted by the big-as-noses thorns on a pink rosebush. A tower of flame and smoke rose from gutted Couffignal Street where the confrontation had taken place.

"Vaya con dios," I said, snapping off a salute to the violent memory of Los Bros Robusto.

José and Francisco, YellowHat: three down, one to go. Not long now to find out who'd be last man standing.

The first three places I tried were closed, as well they should be. Then I stumbled across Montgolfier's, a seedy VR and games arcade on the Anchor's side of the tracks. The place was a true gamer's dive. The mere fact that it was open with all that was going down in Ideaville testified to the nature and quality of the clientele; the arcade equivalent of one of those nameless backstreet bars that pour unbranded bourbon with Rheingold chasers to barflies who've long since drowned the last vestiges of their circadian rhythms.

The place was full of guys who looked just like Den. And one fat broad.

It was dark inside, the only light coming from the banks of glowing video screens offering the latest in slam bam shoot-'em-up action. The simple video gamers aren't too bad — thin and pasty or fat and ruddy, having in common only the desperation in their eyes and the emptiness of their souls — so long as you aren't fool enough to engage them in conversation. They just sit there in front of their screens like so many hamsters idly spinning away their lives in those little metal wheels. Their fists full of dollars to drop into the machines, they generally can't talk about anything other than what level they're on or which combination of buttons and joystick jerk-offs are needed to remove the spines of their pixel-based foes.

The VR addicts — like Den — are much more unpleasant.

In the dimness of the arcade, and underneath their bulky VR goggles, helmets and gloves, the gamers all looked exactly alike. VR-types are always junkie-thin; addiction is addiction. The floor in the VR section of Montgolfier's was littered with candy wrappers, sugar packets and empty cola cans. Small video screens are attached to each VR setup so interested third-parties, who and wherever they might be, can watch the fantasy world the gamer is immersed in. The arcade's selection seemed particularly pedestrian to me: flying dinosaurs, dull Tolkienesque role-playing worlds, goofy golf . . .

There had to be more to a place like Montgolfier's.

A black beaded curtain, straight out of some Haight-Ashbury hash house circa 1969, fluttered at the very rear of the VR room. A weasly attendant wearing a torn I ♥ Lara C. T-shirt intercepted me as I approached it.

"S'private, bud," he simpered.

"I'm looking for someone," I said.

"No one back there."

"I'm a pal of Den's."

He narrowed his eyes at me and sniffled. He gestured me through with a jerk of his pointy head.

The back room featured another half-dozen VR setups. I'd been to places like Montgolfier's before and knew what to expect. Not everyone is interested in playing Tom Bombadil in Hobbit happy-land when VR offers the possibility of so much more. Every new technology turns to sex first, though there are limits to what you can do with gloves and goggles. Until they come up with a way to steam-clean those full-body VR suits, you'll only get so much sensation from virtual play.

The VR rigs in back didn't feature separate viewing screens, but sure enough the goofball in the first cubicle stood there rocking his hips back and forth in a way that meant he was either fucking something or learning to hula-hoop. Or both, I suppose. I walked on by.

The next two cubicles were deserted, but the fourth was occupied — with no room to spare — by an immensely fat young woman who sat on the floor. She wore VR gloves on both hands and reached out into the empty space around her, plucking God knows what out of the air and pushing it into her mouth. She pantomimed chewing, though I don't know why; it's not like they've invented a data-gullet. Was it a crazy sex thing? Some weird food fetish?

I didn't want to know.

The fifth cubicle was marked "out of service," but in the very last rig, bigger than the others, I spotted Den. He lay on his stomach on a small, stiff bed, of the type you see in a doctor's office, but which slowly shifted up and down courtesy of some silent hydraulics. Pretty fancy stuff for a dump like Montgolfier's. Den wore a set of goggles which strapped around his head and completely covered his ears. He also wore gloves along with a pair of wired slipper-shoes which looked like the feet on a pair of Dr. Denton's. He stretched his arms out to either side and rolled with the gentle movements of the bed. The look on his face was that of a big grinning kid.

I yanked off his headset.

"Noooo," he groaned, blinking like Mr. Magoo. He looked angry until he saw it was me. Then he looked scared.

"Hey, Den. Having fun?"

"You, you shouldn't do that, you know. Just pull a person out like that. It can be very upsetting."

"Is that right?"

He blinked and took off the gloves. As he started to bend down to remove the VR slippers, I grabbed his shoulder and made him sit up.

"Where you been, Den?" I asked.

"Whuh? I been here. You know: gaming."

"Where you been all night?"

"Night?" He seemed genuinely confused by the question. His eyes bounced around in his head like the little ball in a slowing roulette wheel. He had it bad.

"Where did you go last night?"

"Out, man. Sa-Sandy . . . she sent me away. You were there."

He reached into his pocket and pulled out a packet of mini peanut butter cups. I swatted them out of his hand and they scattered across the floor.

"Awww, man."

"You went back to the bungalow, didn't you? You snuck back and watched us. You saw it all."

"I di-didn't see a thing. I didn't see you . . . why would I . . . what did you do?"

He pulled a $100,000 Bar out of his other pocket. I let him unpeel the wrapper before I slapped it, too, onto the floor.

"What is your trip? I . . . really need a pick me up, you know?"

As he leaned over to pick up a piece of dirty chocolate, I slapped him hard across the face, straightening him up. I think it surprised us both.

Den started to cry.

"What do you want from me!" he bawled. "Didn't I help you? I gave you all that data, wasn't that enough? You had to have her, too? It's not fair, man. You got everything I have. Everything. Don't you have enough yet?"

His cries sounded in my ears like my mother's plaintive wails to my father all those years ago ("My pooper! My pooper!"), and it evoked nothing but the deepest fury in me.

So I hit him again. And knocked him clean off the still-rocking bed.

"You miserable piece of shit. You killed her

didn't you? You came back in the night and you
choked her to death? How could you do it? How
could you hurt her after the way she treated you?"

"She *fucked* you, man. She treated *me* like her
dog," Den cried. He reached out for a mushed
peanut butter cup and I stomped on his wrist
with my heel. I could hear a bone snap and Den
screamed. I glanced around, but no one came running. The proprietors at Montgolfier's probably
heard a lot of funny noises from the back room.

"That's not what she told me," I said. "She said
that you two looked after each other. That you
were the only person in Ideaville that she could
trust, who really cared about her. Who loved her."

Den had been clutching his broken wrist, rocking over it like the dude with the virtual hula-
hoop. He suddenly stopped. "Sh-she said that?"

I nodded.

He let out a fearsome scream.

"What did I do?" he yelled. "I did go back. I
saw you. And her. And I . . . I couldn't stand it. I
couldn't bear it. I have no-nothing without her."

Before I could say anything Den collapsed to
the floor, rolling onto his back and kicking his
legs like a baby throwing a tantrum. His feet
were still jacked-in and I saw the hydraulic bed
go into contortions attempting to respond to the
wild movement of his feet.

He was gone; completely hysterical. This was-
n't what I'd expected and I didn't know what to
do. I wanted to flail out at him, beat him, hurt
him for what he'd done to Sandy. But he was too
pathetic. Den screamed and thrashed, tore at his
face with his fingernails, doing more damage

than I likely could or would have done. He kept yelling Sandy's name, screaming it till he went hoarse.

"Oh, Den," I whispered. "Why did you have to kill her?"

"He didn't," a voice croaked from behind.

Den was still screaming, but I whirled around and was eyewitness to the impossible. The illogical, inexplicable, wonderful . . . impossible.

Sandy stood there in the cubicle doorway; alive, like Joe Hill, as you or me.

XII. The Cleansing of Ideaville

"Whaaaaah? Huuunnnhh," I said.

"Hey, yourself," Sandy croaked. She didn't sound good. She didn't look too good, either: pale, even for her; her eyes red-rimmed with big black circles around them. She looked weak, haggard, exhausted . . .

But damn good for a woman now *twice* dead.

"Sandy," I cried.

Den stopped his caterwauling. He'd been clawing at his eyes, but now peered through the cracks between his blood-drenched fingers. He lay on his back, but ceased his rocking, his legs frozen in the air above him as he took in the sight of her.

Den screamed and rolled into a ball.

"Sandy," I repeated, and ran over to her. I hesitantly reached out with my right hand, wanting to, but afraid to touch her for fear that she'd pop out of existence again, like a floating soap bubble. She nodded at me, and offered ever-so-weak a smile. I traced the edge of her cheeks and chin; I reached up and cupped her face between my hands, touched my thumbs to her lips. She pursed them, offering up the ghost of a kiss.

I took her frail form in my arms and I kissed her lips. I held her tightly to me and she returned my embrace. I didn't want to let her go, but she pulled away.

"How?" I sputtered. "What . . . how . . . ?"

"Den," she wheezed. She could barely speak, but even amid the bleeps and blips and bursts that emanated from the front of the arcade, her thin, damaged voice boomed across the room.

Den curled more tightly into himself as he crawled away from her. He'd trapped himself in the corner of the VR cubicle, but didn't realize it. If the molecular alignment had been just right he might have passed right on through the walls. I'm certain that he would have liked to.

"You were dead," I said. I reached out to touch her again. "I saw you, I touched you, I . . ."

"You didn't check my pulse," Sandy said.

"But the cord. Around your neck. And your eyes . . ."

"Den," she said again.

The gangly gamer looked up at her this time, terror in his eyes. He was trembling like a wounded bird in your hand, his head shaking so badly I doubted he could see straight. He tried to say something, but he couldn't bring his lips together. I saw him bite his tongue in the effort — a tiny jet of blood spurted out like spittle — but he simply could not form the words.

"He tried to kill me," Sandy said. She was speaking to me, but staring down at the quivering, pale mass in the corner. "He came back in the night."

"That's what I guessed."

"You didn't even stir. I tried to talk to him, explain to him about us, but . . . what could I say. I am sorry, Den."

"*You're* apologizing to *him*?"

Tears fell from Sandy's eyes now. She clutched at herself, wrapping her arms about her middle, and leaned against the wall for support. I stepped toward her, but she shook me off.

"I tried to tell him. That I still loved him. That he'd meant so much to me, all he'd done, the way he'd stood by me when no one else would. But your return . . . changed things. Confused things. Confused me. You and I were meant for each other. I'd always thought that, knew that. Even after what you did to me, after you left. Through all the years, with Roach, and all the others. Through everything. I thought we were . . ."

"I know," I said. "Me, too."

"I tried to tell him, but it made him crazy. He'd seen us . . . together. Den and I, our relationship wasn't . . . he was the only one I *hadn't* . . . I should have known better. It's like we were living as childhood sweethearts, in some impossible, schoolgirl's dream of innocence. Maybe it was just one that I conjured in my mind, but I liked it. I thought he did, too. I was foolish."

"You can't blame yourself when someone tries to kill you, Sandy."

She looked at me and blinked. It was weird, talking about Den and what had happened as if he wasn't lying there in a puddle at our feet.

"He was crying, hysterical. He tried to kiss me, force himself on me. Then I tasted it on his breath and knew there'd be no reasoning with him."

"Tasted what?"

"Hershey's syrup. When things are really bad, he drinks it straight from the can. It makes him crazy. He usually knows better."

"What?"

"When I pushed him away, he freaked. We bounced around the room, as I fought him off. You were snoring away on the floor."

Ever the hero.

"I think I may have kneed Den in the groin at one point, but I definitely remember stomping on a package of Reese's Pieces that fell out of his pocket. It made him nuts. The next thing I remember Den ripped a cable out of the back of the computer and began winding it around my neck."

Sandy had been wearing a brightly colored silk scarf. She unfastened it and tilted her head back, and I saw the quarter-inch-thick line that snaked around her lovely throat: the impression left by the printer cable.

"But why aren't you dead?" I asked. We both turned toward Den, who had uncurled a bit and was flexing and unflexing his fingers.

"There but for the grace of Carpal Tunnel Syndrome go I," Sandy said. "Den's fingers just aren't strong enough. All those years of gaming and typing and mouse play. He simply hasn't got it in him. Do you Den?"

Den buried his face in his weakened fingers and began to sob. I could see that Sandy half-wanted to go to him, to comfort him. But she couldn't truly forgive him, either. Who could blame her? She cried, silently watching him.

"Sandy, I . . ."

Den leapt to his feet. I wouldn't have thought he could move that fast, but he darted between us and out of the cubicle before either of us could respond. He shoved me out of the way and I tumbled over onto my ass, but he paused just long enough to wrap an arm around Sandy and spin her through a half-swirl of a dance. Then he ran out.

"Den!" Sandy yelled, her voice like a blender full of rusty nails. She took off after him. As I started to get up to follow, my hand came down on Den's discarded VR goggles on the floor. I had to go after Sandy, but that cursed quest for knowledge got the better of me and I paused long enough to take a peek at the virtual world Den had been visiting: it was, indeed, a dream of flying, though all I could see was the handle and frame of a parasol that carried me through a gay blue sky above a Victorian London landscape. It had an appeal — not unlike a spoonful of sugar — but there was no time to enjoy it.

I ran out into the video arcade just in time to see Sandy exit through the front door. A rush of explosions from the speakers of a video game behind me — NaPalm Springs — was drowned out by the sound of a real-life battle coming from the open door. I ran to it just as Sandy ducked back inside Montgolfier's, pulling me down to the floor. A second later, a line of bullets tore out the plate glass which exploded on top of us.

"Coo-uhl," someone in the arcade exclaimed, then went back to their game.

I brushed the glass off of us — no damage done — and cautiously crawled over to peer out the door, Sandy right behind me.

Den stood in the middle of the street, shaking like a leaf and looking very confused. On one sidewalk stood two groups of Roach rent-a-cops, handguns drawn and leveled; on the other a trio of wounded, Robusto duster boys, armed to the teeth. The two sides had been shooting it out until Den somehow wandered between them. Everyone froze, not sure what to do, and there was an utter, eerie silence.

"De-e-e-en!" Sandy screamed. I clamped my hand over her mouth to stifle the cry, but it was too late.

Den turned to look, and I'm not sure, but I think he even managed a tiny smile at the sight of her.

Both sides let loose with everything they had.

Den had been trembling so badly that, at first, nothing seemed to change.

The trembles became jerks, the jerks turned into spasms.

We watched, Sandy screaming, as Den performed a grisly dance of death on the black tarmac, hails of large caliber bullets tearing him to shreds. Minutes later the duster boys were dead, too. The remaining rent-a-cops moved on without a glance back.

Sandy had collapsed to the floor, not even cognizant of the shards of glass that cut into her arms and legs. I reached down toward her when movement in the street caught my eye.

"Look!" I said.

Sandy followed the direction of my quaking finger.

Den, blood spilling out of him and snaking down the street into a filthy drain, somehow raised himself to one knee. He reached into his shirt pocket and fumbled for something inside. He struggled — it must have taken a superhuman effort for him even to move — but managed to pry two fingers into the pocket. They came out with something silver and round. He slumped back to the tarmac, but held the silvery disk in his outstretched hand. His bullet-pulped face lit up at the sight of the thing, then a cascade of brown blood gushed out of his open mouth and the life fled from his eyes. As he collapsed for the last time, the disk sprang from between his fingers and flew through the air toward us. It bounced on the street — once, twice, a third time — and, as if sentient and determined to reach us, jumped up the curb and onto the sidewalk in front of Montgolfier's Arcade. Sandy scrambled to her feet and dashed out to get it before I could stop her. I ran to follow.

Sandy picked the little disk up and immediately began to cry. She fell to her knees and sobbed like a baby.

"What is it?" I asked.

She held it out for me. I extended an open hand and she dropped it into my palm.

A York Peppermint Patty.

Sandy's wailing abated as quickly as it came over her. She looked long and hard at Den's broken body in the street, then casually went over to the fallen Robusto men and picked up a handgun that lay beside them. With the deftness of an NRA camp counsellor, she checked the clip, then rocked a round into the empty chamber. She spied a second gun, checked it, and slipped it into her waistband.

"All this must end," she said. "Let's do it."

Her face was perfectly composed, her hands and raspy voice as steady as a salesman's smile. But her eyes betrayed a hideous thirst for vengeance.

There comes a time, I realized. A reckoning, a final act, an end to all unfinished business.

A harvest.

"Roach?" I asked, knowing the answer.

"We've had the sex and the drugs," Sandy replied. "Now let's rock and roll."

My natural caution, honed to a state of near-catatonic reticence over a sedentary lifetime, again got the better of me as we approached Roach's stronghold. I suggested a low-profile reconnoiter, but Sandy had in mind exactly what she wanted to do and was in no mood to discuss it.

"Go for it," she told me. She held one gun in hand and braced herself out the car window.

"Huh?" I replied.

"Hit it!" she said, and reached out with her left leg to force my foot down firmly on the gas pedal. "Go for the gate."

My old Pacer doesn't do zero-to-sixty in any clockable time, but Sandy wouldn't let off and there was no turning back now. Three of Roach's clowns lounged in front of the gate, quite reasonably not having taken any notice of an AMC car coming up the street at them. Threat, what threat? It was only as we screamed (well, whined) our way up the cutout in the curb that they realized we were trouble. By then it was much too late.

The first one bounced off the right fender and went flying into the bushes. I saw the second guy fumble for his gun, but Sandy took him out with one clean shot to the middle of the chest. The third rent-a-cop tried to get out of the way by climbing up the gate, but inasmuch as I used the car to smash through it two seconds later, you'd have to call that poor judgment. The front end of my Pacer crunched and folded as we made contact, and I naturally went for the brakes, but Sandy just screamed at me and kicked at the accelerator again.

Another pair of Roach's men came running up the driveway, guns drawn. They both dove to the left at the sight of the oncoming car, which also proved unwise: two more shots from Sandy and they were done for.

"You just killed those guys," I said. I felt surprisingly calm, and somehow managed to keep driving up the winding path.

"Probably," Sandy said. "I think *you* mushed the dude on the gate."

"It was an accident."

"So were mine. If anyone asks, I was cleaning my gun. But I don't think anyone will be around to ask."

"Sandy . . ."

"Do you have the balls for this or not?" she hissed. "I told you that it ends here. Today. Us or him. Can you handle that or do you want to run away? Again."

I didn't even have to think; I floored it in response. And then jammed on the brakes because Chez Roach loomed directly ahead.

Sandy was out of the car before I could slip it into park.

"Better let me take the lead," she said.

I wasn't going to argue.

That second pair of guards must have been covering the porch, because there was no one else in sight. Sandy didn't trust the front door, though, and keeping low and close to the wall, gestured to head around the side of Chez Roach. As we crept along, she slipped the second gun out of her pants.

"Can you shoot left-handed?" I whispered.

"Never too old to learn."

Just as we came around a corner of the house, a spray of bullets tore up the flower bed that we trampled. I ducked back behind the jutting edge of the building and covered up, but Sandy tucked and rolled across the open expanse of lawn like some supercharged croquet ball, the spray of gunfire tracking behind her by mere inches. I couldn't even figure out where the assault was coming from, but Sandy was already back on her feet, both guns blazing.

A thick body dropped out of a tree. Sandy zigzagged her way over to it, putting a just-in-case bullet into the back of the shooter's head. It took me a minute, but I recognized him as Duke K., one of our childhood nemeses.

"Shit," I muttered.

Sandy was quickly back at my side, Duke's Uzi clutched under her arm.

"Take it," she said.

"I don't . . . I can't . . ."

"Just hold it for now. I may need it."

The gun was still warm — whether from firing or just from being held in the late Duke's hand, I didn't know — I gripped it gingerly, the barrel pointed at the ground. I was afraid to let my finger stray anywhere near the trigger. Sandy cocked her head, indicating we'd better keep moving.

"Where, when . . . who taught you how to shoot like that? How to *move* like that?"

"You don't hang with bad boys like the Robustos without learning a few moves," she said. "You don't live like I've lived if you can't look after yourself around the rough crowd. You learn or you die, buddy boy. Them's the facts of life."

And I thought I was slick for teaching myself C^{++} at home.

Sandy led a faster pace through the garden and around the back of the house. She took out a second sniper on the roof of the garage and two more beefy goons who were playing hackey-sack with a doll's head on the rear lawn. She took the three of them out with only four shots.

A whole group of rent-a-cops were huddled around the patio and on top of the sundeck where I'd seen my mother sitting when last I'd visited Chez Roach. They must have heard the gunfire, but they sat tight. Two on the deck and four more at ground level. They looked jumpy and there was a lot of hardware on view. One of them was speaking into a small walkie-talkie.

"We need a distraction," Sandy whispered.

"We need an army," I said.

Sandy checked her clips, then shook her head. "These'll do." She took a good look around, then gently tapped a drainpipe that snaked down the side of the building. "I'm going up," she said.

"What about me?"

"When I give the signal, you start shooting."

"Wait! I don't think . . . the guy on the gate was an accident . . . I don't know if I can just shoot these guys in cold blood."

Sandy looked angry, started to say something then bit it back. She poked her head out for another quick peek at the rear patio. "You see that big bay window? Just aim at that. I'll handle the rest."

And up she went, shimmying the drainpipe like some Sherpa squirrel.

"What's the signal?" I whispered up after her.

She'd already made the roof and hung her head down over the side, her long hair trailing. She suddenly looked to me just as she had all those years ago, when I'd come calling for her and find her up in the treehouse her dad had built in the big elm in their yard. She even had the same goofy smile on her face. "You'll know it when you hear it," she said.

And she was gone.

I hovered there at the corner of the house, ducking my head out every so often to keep an eye on the rent-a-cops. I glanced at the Uzi which now felt cold in my fingers. It's a nasty looking piece of work, designed to *do* nasty work. I mentally rehearsed what I would do when Sandy gave me the sign, pictured myself stepping out into the open and letting rip with the Uzi. As I ducked out for another glance, I caught sight of her dancing across the rooftop of Chez Roach. Sandy stood there, right out in plain sight, on the shingled eave ten feet across from and just as high above the sundeck. If any of the rent-a-cops happened to turn around and look up, she was dead meat. Surely this was when she needed the distraction.

"ALLEY-ALLEY-OXEN-FREEEEEEE," she screamed, and with a mighty spring, launched herself off the roof and toward the sundeck.

At that moment I darted out and sprayed the big picture window with Uzi fire. I had rehearsed the action perfectly in my head, but forgot to account for the recoil. The gun bucked wildly in my arms and though I did manage to shatter the glass, the Uzi simply spasmed out of my sweaty hands. It proved distraction enough, though, because the startled guards on the ground started firing at the broken window and not at me. I dropped to the grass just in case, not even thinking to pick up the gun, but it didn't matter: from there on it was all Sandy.

She was amazing, unreal: Chow Yun Fat's whiter, older sister. Sandy was a killing machine with the speed of a jackrabbit, the grace of a swan and the ferocity of a prodded wolverine.

Now I knew precisely why even the Robustos had chosen not to fuck with her. Those boys might have been crazy, but they weren't stupid.

As she tumbled through the air, she had both guns drawn and was firing even before she landed neatly on her feet between the two guards. They went down before they knew what had hit them.

One of the dim bulbs below was still shooting at the busted window, but the other three were firing up at her through the slats of the redwood deck. I saw a tiny spurt of red erupt from Sandy's left thigh as a bullet nicked her. It only made her madder though, because stuffing the guns back into her waistband, she took a running jump toward the edge of the wooden deck, and hooking her hands back over the rail, somersaulted right over the top. As she tumbled down in a diver's neat tuck, she pulled out the guns and again started to fire. Two of the guards went down right away, one of them wiping out a third man with his trailing fire as he fell.

Sandy hit the grass hard, but went straight into another roll and came up face to face with the remaining goon. They each held their guns out in front of them, pointing straight at the other's head, no more than three feet between them.

They held the pose, staring each other down. The rent-a-cop looked scared, Sandy just smiled. She pulled the trigger.

The gun went "click."

Now the rent-a-cop smiled an ugly smile. He drew the gun back — as if to take perfect aim, then extended it again. There was a roar.

Roach's man wasn't smiling anymore; Sandy had shot him in the nuts with her other gun, and he collapsed to the ground. A second, very clean head shot put him out of his newly neutered misery.

Sandy tossed the empty gun away and nodded at me. I ran over to her side.

"Are you all right? You got shot." I bent down to examine her leg, but she wouldn't have it.

"It's nothing. Let's keep going while we can."

Sandy did a quick check of how many rounds

were left in the clip, then slid open the big glass
door and walked into the house. The French doors
led into a huge dining room, bigger than my
whole apartment. The room was dominated by an
immense mahogany table of the type that two
people who really don't like each other can sit at
and still share a happy meal. All of the furniture
in Chez Roach was dark and heavy and half-past
the tasteless side of ornate.

Sandy wheeled at a rattling sound to our left.
A door shuddered slightly on its hinges. She
waved me over to the hinged side, while she
hugged the wall by the knob. She gestured for me
to open the door. I did so and ducked out of the
way as Sandy went in gun first.

The old nurse and the young maid in her I-got-
thighs uniform — stilettos and all — came tumbling out of the narrow closet.

"Get out of here," Sandy told them. "Now!"

The maid, still wobbling on those heels, didn't
need to be told twice, but the nurse glanced up, as
if she could look through the ceiling at her charge.

"I'll take care of her," I said. "She'll be fine."

The nurse nodded, then dashed out the back
door after the maid.

Sandy sniffed at the air. "I think it's just the
three of us, now," she said.

I don't know how she could tell. I sniffed, too,
but all I could smell was the lingering eau de
bimbo. I didn't question Sandy, though. Nor
would I again.

"Let's get the bastard," I said.

It was my fault.

I think, sometimes, those are the words that will be engraved on my tombstone: words to live by, words to die by.

Words that killed Sandy.

We checked the ground floor of Chez Roach and found it clear of everything but empty beer bottles and crumpled take-out bags from Ulysses' Diner. Telltale trails of powdered sugar proved that Roach's rent-a-cops might not be good, but they were true to their calling. Sandy indicated that we should head upstairs where Roach, no doubt, awaited.

Sandy led the way, gun drawn, cautiously climbing the gaudy staircase that spiraled up from the front foyer. The risers were carpeted, but even so, Sandy ascended without making a sound. I followed several steps behind, keeping an eye out behind me for any remaining guards. Sandy moved like a cat — sleek, elegant and silent — but I proceeded cautiously, on tippy-toes. Just as she reached the first floor landing and turned to offer me an encouraging grin, her eyes glinting with a predator's glee, I took a flat-footed step in the middle of a stair.

It creaked, loudly, like an old rocking chair bearing a fat man's weight. The sound echoed through the house and Sandy's grin drooped as her eyes widened.

Out of nowhere, Roach emerged onto the landing, a heavy silver gun in his meaty fist. He opened his mouth and let out a gurgle of a foul laugh.

He fired twice.

The first shot caught Sandy in her left shoul-

der, spinning her around. Sandy looked shocked
rather than hurt, her mouth gaping open in a big
O of surprise. She struggled for her balance,
swaying on the top step of the staircase.

The second shot was right to the head.

I screamed, though Sandy didn't make a
sound. She appeared to float there for a moment
at the top of the stairs, as Roach continued to
cackle. Perhaps it was just my imagination —
wishful thinking — but I could swear that she
looked down at me, reached out for me with her
final gesture.

The she went tumbling past me all the way
down to the bottom of the stairs. I stood there,
horror-struck at the sight of her broken body
sprawled on the floor a dozen steps below me. I
glanced back up, but Roach was gone leaving
behind nothing but the mocking echo of his cruel
laughter.

A savage fury consumed me. I saw Sandy's
gun lying on the next-to-top step. I took another
look back at her crumpled form. I ran up the
steps, grabbing the gun as I passed, screaming at
the top of my lungs: "ROOOAAAACCHHHHH!"

I kicked at every closed door down the hallway, gun at the ready, murder on my mind.

Nothing. Every room empty. Where the hell
had he gone?

At the far end of the hallway, the final door
opened on to a narrow, low stairway leading
to the attic. A funny scent drifted down the
stairs, like mothballs and lavender and Dentu-
grip and . . .

It was an *old lady* smell.

A reverberation of Roach's laugh came down the stairs and for a moment my anger dimmed as my terror swelled. Though I'd always bested Roach when we were kids, I knew in my too-few moments of self-honesty that I'd always lived in fear of him. He was the *ur*-bully representing, from the day we first met, everything I was not. Roach acted on feeling and instinct, not on intellect and rationality. Roach was physical, carnal, dominated to the core by his desires and wants; I was cerebral, tentative, acting only after due consideration, sublimating desire as the better part of valor. Roach had always been, and still was, everything I failed to be; feared to be: the supercharged id to my inflated superego. If Roach was not the better part of me, he was at least *another* part of me. I'd been avoiding him, one way or another, for the best part of my life, fearing what facing up to him — and the part of me that he represented — might mean for how I live.

I would avoid him no further.

"I'm coming motherfucker," I shouted and took the stairs at full charge, Sandy's gun held out in front me, my finger on the trigger. I burst through the door at the top of the stairs ready to face the story of my life.

I came out in a tiny attic. The low ceiling sloped down beneath the house's eaves, making the room claustrophobic. A single bed was set against one wall, a night stand covered with medicine bottles beside it. An old, familiar quilt was neatly arranged on top of the mattress, a hand-stitched rug bearing the emblem of a bald eagle in the center of the floor. I recognized it from my parents' room. My mother had made it by hand. It took her more than a year and had been her pride and joy. She chose the eagle design because she thought it signified all that my father repre-sented. I was stunned to see that she'd kept it.

My mother was there, too, looking so small in her wheelchair. A blanket covered her legs, though her bare feet poked out from underneath. She squinted at me and blinked, so I couldn't tell if she recognized me. She fumbled in her lap for her glasses, but they lay out of reach atop the pil-low on her bed.

Roach stood directly behind her. He still held the big gun in his hand, but now the barrel was directed squarely at the back of my mother's grey-haired head. He was grinning like a jack-o'-lantern on Halloween night.

"Drop it," Roach told me.

I thought about it. I held my gun steady in front me, pointing straight at Roach's chest. If I fired, there was a chance I could take him out and be done it with it all. Forever.

Or I might miss and watch him blow my mom's head into a million bloody bits.

I dropped my piece.

"Pussy," Roach snarled. "Same as it ever was."

He walked out from behind my mother's chair and kicked the gun on the floor under the bed. He gestured for me to sit down on the mattress. Mov-ing slowly, I followed his instructions. I glanced at my mother, but she just looked confused and I wondered if she even knew what was going on. I hoped not.

"You had a nice little run, you and the snatch.

She fooled me good with that car crash, I got to admit. I sure thought she was toast. Still, you can't much murder a dead girl, so no sweat about killing her now."

"Somehow I don't think you'd lose sleep over it anyway."

"No, you're right about that. Sandy was a decent lay, but no twat is worth all that trouble. Which reminds me."

Roach smoothly swiveled the gun away from me and pointed it at my mother. There wasn't even a second's hesitation as he pulled the trigger.

My mother let out the tiniest of gasps as the bullet hit her, but didn't otherwise make a sound. I jumped to my feet — I think I may have screamed — but Roach had the gun trained back on me before I could take a step toward him. My mother slumped forward and fell out of her chair and onto the floor. The eagle rug soaked up the blood that dribbled out of her.

"Cleaning house today," Roach said. "I swear I don't know what the old man ever saw in her, but I did promise him I'd look after her. Enough is enough, though."

I couldn't speak, couldn't move, could barely breathe as I watched my mother — however distant and divorced, she was still my mother — dying on the floor at my feet.

"Oh, gee, I suppose that officially makes you an orphan," Roach said.

I managed to stir myself to look up at him.

"Yeah," he said, with mock sympathy, "I'm afraid the Czar has been deposed. Vive la révolution and pass the gin."

Had Roach killed my father, too? Is that what he was saying? I found that I couldn't seem to understand simple English. My brain could not properly function.

A last, best joke.

"The town's a right old mess for the minute, but really I should thank you," Roach said. "Los Bros are no longer hale and hardy; The Yellow Man has gone to monkey heaven. You done good, my son, better than I gave you credit for. Dink and his boys — I mean, *my* boys — will clean it all up in a few days, plenty of dead guys to blame for the troubles, and then it's clear sailing for Black X from here on out. So let me show you my full appreciation."

Roach smiled and took careful aim at me. I saw his finger tighten on the trigger, then briefly relax.

"Oh, yeah: you'll take the posthumous rap for offing the pair of cunts," he said. He winked at me. "You're welcome."

He closed one eye, raised the gun and grinned.

The bullet tore a piece of his scalp off.

Roach didn't shoot. He looked kind of surprised, and touched his hand to the top of his head. He looked *really* shocked when a hairy flap of skin came away in his fingers. A fountain of blood began to pump down the side of his head.

The two of us turned our heads toward the stairs like a pair of synchronized swimmers.

Sandy stood in the doorway like some bloody, avenging angel. I swear I could see the fire of God in her eyes as surely as I saw the damp, red stains spotting her clothes. A bleeding circle marked a spot on her scalp where Roach's bullet had struck her . . . and apparently ricocheted off the bone in a glancing blow. One shot in a million.

Sandy had more lives than a Ray-O-Vac battery.

"Oh," Roach said. The gun slipped from his hand and clunked to the floor. He turned and took a step toward Sandy as the blood spurted from the hole in his head. "It's you."

Sandy limped her way across the room toward Roach. Her left arm dangled uselessly at her side and she had to walk practically on the side of her twisted right ankle. But I don't think a platoon of marines could have held her back.

She came right up to Roach, who still looked surprised. She brought her face within inches of his, staring directly into his fuzzy eyes. They all but embraced.

She raised up the gun in her hand and pressed it against his belly.

She only stopped shooting when there were no more bullets.

Sandy kicked his body with her good foot at least a dozen times to make sure he was really dead. Then she threw away the gun and collapsed to the floor beside him.

The sight of her falling finally snapped me out of shocked lethargy. I knelt down beside her, saw that she was still breathing. The bullet hole in her shoulder seemed to go clear on through to the other side, but for the moment at least, wasn't gushing. I hated to let her out of my arms, but I heard a voice calling to me from across the room.

My mother had managed to roll herself onto her side. A deep pool of blood had formed around her, more than her old rug could soak up: the eagle was drowning in red stuff. So deep was my concern for Sandy, that I might just have ignored her, but she called out my name.

My true name.

I crawled over to her through the blood and laid her head atop my thigh. She looked up at me through glassy eyes and reached out her hand to stroke my cheek. At the touch of her fingers, cold as they were, I felt transported back in time. For a moment, I was a boy again, living in a happy household with a strong, brave daddy and a loving, all-knowing mom. I swallowed hard and could swear I tasted Vito's pizza and icy Dr. Pepper.

I couldn't help myself; I started to cry.

"Faaaa . . ." my mother tried to say. I wiped my eyes against my shoulder and bent down to try and make out what she was saying. "Naaa . . . faaaa . . . thaaaaa . . ."

"Father?" I whimpered. "Dad? What about him? What is it?"

My mother managed to nod her head. Suddenly Roach's taunt about the Czar came back on me. He, too, was now dead; of that I felt certain. Why would my mother even want to think about him in what could only be her final moments.

"Naaaa . . . aaaaa . . . faaaaa . . . thaaa . . ." her words became a gurgle as blood trickled out of her mouth. With trembling, dying hands, my mother painfully reached inside her collar and pulled at a gold locket she wore around her neck. I recalled the locket from years before: it had held pictures of my father as a young man and me as a boy.

"Daaa . . . Tuuhhhhh," my mother said.

And then she said no more.

I wailed like the lost child that I was. I screamed and bellowed my rage and pounded on the floor. For a time, I believe, I ceased to be a human being.

Sandy brought me around.

She called out to me, called the name my mother had used, and dragged me back from the pit of loss. She had hauled herself up and leaned against the bed. She was breathing hard, but miraculously she was still alive.

"Better get out of here," she wheezed.

I knew she was right. But where to go? Sandy needed help, but how could we trust any hospital? Even with Roach gone, his rent-a-cops would still be roaming the streets. I didn't believe good old Dink had what it took to run Ideaville without Roach behind him, but things were likely to remain ugly for the next few days.

I helped Sandy up and held her tightly, at a loss about what to do. The first step was to get out of Chez Roach. I took one last look at my mother and . . .

The locket glinted in her hand. Reaching for it had been her last gesture, its contents her last mortal thought.

I couldn't leave it behind.

I gently lowered Sandy onto the bed. I knelt down beside my mother's body and touched my hand to her now cold cheek. I stifled back a sob.

It was hard, but I pried the locket out from between her wrinkled fingers. The soft metal held the very last of her body heat. There really wasn't time to be fussing with such things, we had to get moving, but I couldn't resist the temptation to open the clasp and look inside. I owed it to her, and even to my father, bastard though he might have been.

I nearly fell to the ground at what I saw.

I recognized the tiny photograph of myself: it had been taken at a summer cottage we rented when I was five. I sat atop a white Styrofoam float in a kiddie pool, wearing a pair of dark trunks and a sleeveless undershirt. I squinted up into the sun and the camera, cute, as I think even Roach would have had to admit, as the very Dickens.

The other photo, however, was not at all what I remembered; not the snapshot of my father in his sharpest, bluest Police Chief's uniform.

In fact, it wasn't a picture of my father at all.

The man in the photograph was handsome in a rugged way, with sharp, hard features, a square block of a chin and a steely glint in his eyes. I was certain I'd never seen this picture before, or the man, though there was something annoyingly familiar about him. I looked harder at the honed edge of that blocky chin, the birdlike fierceness of his nose.

And the world exploded around me.

I knew, as surely and certainly as I'd ever known anything in my life, who this man was, what my mother tried to tell me with her last gasps of life.

And what the fact of his picture in my mother's locket meant. It all became clear in a blinding, life-altering flash of satori.

I knew, also, what then to do and precisely where to go.

God help me — or pity me for that light of understanding — *I knew.*

XIII. Whosis Kid

My Pacer didn't look too good what with its front end crunched, a thug-sized dent in the fender and assorted blood stains marring the powder blue paint work, but God bless the American Motors Corporation because it started up with the first turn of the key. I could hear sirens in the distance again and even the shoooosh-shoooosh-shoooosh of a helicopter overhead, but nothing was going to stop me. I gunned the engine and made for the gate. So determined was I to get where I wanted to go — so locked in on the image in my head — that I didn't notice running over something until I felt the bump.

It was the body of one of Roach's goons.

"Whuzzat?" Sandy muttered as the car lurched. She had begun to drift off.

"Nothing," I told her. "Just some garbage in the road. You sure you're all right?"

Sandy shook her head; not in denial, but to keep herself awake. She slapped her cheeks with both hands — hard. She glanced in the vanity mirror at the bleeding hole in her head and shuddered.

"I'm fine," she insisted.

She'd have to be: a walking dead woman pretty well had to maintain a low profile.

"We can go to a hospital, Sandy. It might be tough to explain later, but . . ."

"No."

"You're sure?"

"I want to see this. I want to follow it all through to the end."

She turned on the radio and flipped through the dial. She stopped when she heard the Stones singing "Brown Sugar," and cranked the volume. I drove us back to the other side of town; back across the railroad tracks to the Anchor Inn.

The revolving door in front was locked. I peered through the glass panels at the side, but the lobby was dark. And empty.

I drove around to the back of the hotel and parked. The rear entrance was locked, too, but someone had left a small window in the stairwell open a crack. I dragged a Dumpster over and flipped the lid closed. Climbing on top of it, I was just able to pry open the window and squeeze through the narrow passage. I walked back down half a flight of stairs and opened the door for Sandy. She'd been leaning against the side of the building, breathing hard and looking pale. I reckon she'd used up at least eight of her lives by now. I took her hand and half-carried her into the Anchor.

As we opened the door into the dim lobby, we ran into good old D. Sturdy on his way out. He had a bag slung over his shoulder and a pastier-than-usual look. He practically jumped in the air when he saw us.

"Hotel's closed. C-L-O . . ."

"Fuck that shit," I said, and grabbed him by the collar. I may not be much of a tough guy or have anything like Sandy's moves, but even I could play rough with an eightball like this.

D. Sturdy gasped, dropping his bag.

"Mr. Ricky. Which room?"

The desk jockey shook his head. "That information is confidential. P-R . . ."

I slapped him across the face. Then I did it again because it was fun. I could get into this routine.

"Mr. Ricky," I repeated. "Where is he? And if you spell it, I'm going to shove that suitcase up your A-S-S PDQ."

D. Sturdy swallowed. He had to concentrate very hard, but he said it plainly: "Top floor. It's the only room. Owner's suite."

Owner?

Of course: it all made perfect sense to me now. I let Sturdy go with a halfhearted shove. He smacked into the wall with the back of his head.

"Owww," he whined. "O-W-W . . ." He caught himself, looked at the suitcase, looked at me. He ran out of the place leaving his bag behind.

Sandy shot me a puzzled look.

"Don't ask," I told her.

I took her hand and we limped upstairs. There were four floors of rooms and not a sound from any of them. At the end of the corridor on the fourth floor, eerily reminiscent of the layout of Chez Roach, a narrow stairwell led up. The sound of music came drifting down the stairs along with the woody scent of pipe tobacco. Still holding onto Sandy's hand but taking the lead, I started up the stairs.

The door at the top was half-open, and warm

yellow light spilled out from the room. I rapped
gently on the door and it swung open with a creak.
Music filled the room: the scratchy old 78 sound of
muted horns playing a slow dance hall number in
the Thirties style. You could almost see couples in
evening dress dancing cheek to cheek in the wee,
wee hours. The tobacco smell hung in the air, but
it too lent a warmth to the place — a feeling of
lived-inness and comfort and coming home.

The room was big; far larger than any of the
Anchor's regular rooms, I felt sure. The walls
were lined floor-to-ceiling with bookshelves
crammed with leather-bound hardcovers and
pulpy paperbacks and sheafs of paper of different
sizes and colors. More piles of books and brown-
ing, messy columns of manila files and old newspapers were stacked untidily along the floor and
leaned precariously in every corner. A plush vel-
vet sofa occupied the middle of the room across a
glass coffee table from a matching, overstuffed
armchair with filthy antimacassars attached by
safety pins. The coffee table, too, was cluttered
with books and documents, and a thick photo
album lay open atop the heap. Half-drunk cups of
tea were liberally sprinkled about the room.

Clearly, Mr. Ricky had lived at the Anchor for
a very long time.

I wandered over to examine a shelf holding a
series of framed objects. Awards, mostly, from the
Chicago Police Department: citations for bravery,
certificates of merit and three medals of valor. A
photograph of Mr. Ricky being congratulated by a
smirking Mayor Daley. "Little bit of law" my ass:
he'd obviously been quite a cop.

"Hey," Sandy said. It was more of a whisper, really. She was leaning over a glass cabinet set against the far wall, and beckoned me over with a crooked finger.

The bottom shelves of the case were filled with leather-bound books — collector's items, perhaps, or volumes of special esteem or value. The top shelf displayed a mixed batch of knickknacks: a snow globe from the 1939 World's Fair containing a miniature Trylon and Perisphere; a chipped Toby jug with a square chin that looked suspiciously familiar; a series of other small curios and mementos that were junk to the uninformed eye, but which no doubt represented key moments in a life to the old man who'd lived it and who treasured them. Every home has something like it, after all.

It was the shelf below the knickknacks that had attracted Sandy's attention and that now utterly commanded mine. It held nothing but four small photographs in matching silver frames. The first was of a woman I'd never seen before: she had a round face with an angular chin and short, blond hair tucked under a stylish hat. With her long eyelashes and coquettish look, she radiated the grace and elegance of an old-time film starlet.

The second picture meant nothing to me either. The print was an old one: though in color, it had that wan and faded look of chemical processes enacted long ago. A husky young man in an army uniform, cap in hand, grinned for the camera with a cocky look that said the world was made for and belonged to him. There was no physical resemblance, but something in the attitude reminded me of Roach as a kid.

The subjects of the last two photos I knew all too well.

The third frame held a picture of my mother. I'd never seen the shot before, of that I was certain, but there was no mistaking her pretty young face, that mock Veronica Lake hairstyle she wore when I was just a baby. I'd seen it in so many other photos, but I definitely couldn't place this one. Before the horrors of their divorce, I remembered my mother as a happy person. But I don't think I'd ever seen her look so happy — so radiantly sensuous — as she did in this picture.

The last photograph I knew as well as the image in my mirror, for that was what it was. The silver frame held a photograph of me as a boy. It was taken from a newspaper, though it didn't appear to be newsprint that was framed, from the time that I was given the key to the city for solving the Case of the Nutty Gnat. It was my first big breakthrough as a Boy Detective and secured my reputation around town. I had a dopey, slightly embarrassed smile on my face, but I could remember still the pleasure of that moment: the pride, the exultation, the unadulterated joy of cracking my first mystery.

"I like that picture very much. You look so happy."

Sandy and I turned around. Mr. Ricky, wearing a grotesque and very tatty satin smoking jacket, stood in the doorway behind us. His thin, black hair was all mussed and askew — he looked like some absent-minded professor who'd just gotten out of bed. He had on plain black trousers, and what looked like a dark polo shirt as well, but wore old brown slippers on his bare withered feet.

"I ran out of tea," he said. "Had to go borrow some from the hotel kitchen downstairs. Would you care for a cup?"

I was dumbstruck. There were many things I'd planned to say — I'd repeated and practiced them to myself on the drive over — but now I couldn't find my tongue.

"That would be very nice, thank you," Sandy replied.

Mr. Ricky nodded, then squinted at Sandy.

"You're hurt," he said. "You'd better sit down."

Sandy didn't need to be asked twice. She limped over to the sofa and all but collapsed.

"She needs help," someone squeaked. Apparently it was me.

"I can see that." Mr. Ricky studied me closely. "I'll take care of things."

He disappeared into the kitchen, where I heard him speaking on the telephone. Then I heard the water run and the sound of a heavy lid being topped onto an iron kettle. A few minutes later it began to whistle. Mr. Ricky popped his head out into the living room.

"You take milk in your tea?" he asked.

"Yes, please," Sandy said.

He looked at me, and for a second I didn't know how to reply.

"And for you, son?" he prompted.

"However you make it, Dad," I replied.

He nodded and disappeared back into the kitchen.

* * *

"I first came here on a case, of course," Mr. Ricky began. He'd taken a look at the hole in Sandy's shoulder, efficiently cleaned it with some Betadyne and loosely bandaged it, then dabbed at the wound on her head. Sandy looked exhausted, but less pale than before. It didn't stop her drinking her tea and eating Mr. Ricky's Danish butter cookies from the big round tin. I don't even like tea, but I sipped mine anyway. And listened.

"Spent most of my life up Chicago way. Think I mentioned that to you before. Got into the law as a young feller, the way the best ones always do."

"And some of the bad ones," I muttered.

"Never can tell. She was a tough old town, probably still is. But that's what I liked about 'er. I had a yearning, you see, a calling if you will. Got picked by the life as much I picked it. Saw an old man shot down in cold blood right in front of me, and a pretty young gal snatched from the streets like some apple off a cart. Swore then and there that the likes of such couldn't be allowed to go on. Not in my town, no sir. Hunted them hoodlums high and low, I did, and took 'em down hard when I caught up with 'em. Found that pretty little gal and — heh, heh — would you believe I married her in the end? Took some convincing, though. That was my Tessie, that was. I joined the force and made it my life's work insuring that no one else would have to suffer like she had. Or if they did, then those responsible would be brought to pay the piper for their foul deeds."

"Is that her?" Sandy asked. She pointed at the picture of the woman next to my mom's.

"That's my Tess. Never was a heart so true. Certainly not my own."

"And the man in the uniform?"

Mr. Ricky got up and walked over to the cabinet. He opened the glass door and took the frame out, gently running his thumb over the glass that shielded the image of the young soldier.

"Our boy, Junior. Richard Junior. Took that picture the day he went into the service. He never come out again, though. Korea. Broke his mother's heart. She wasn't ever the same after that, my Tess. Nothing direct, she just slowly faded away."

"You obviously kept on going," I said.

"You don't stop being a man, son, surely you know that. Don't think I didn't feel the hurt of losing the boy, 'cause the truth couldn't be no further away. But I was still a policeman, still had to uphold the law. Had to keep keeping on. Crime don't stop for tears or woe or even war. I'd put 'em away, but new ones was always coming along. And as the years passed the bad fellers got meaner and stranger. Crime does that to 'em, I think: twists 'em. Or maybe it's the society that's to blame, like the eggheads say. I don't rightly know no more. I swear, the hoodlums come to look as nasty and twisted on the outside as their hearts and souls was on the inside. Make you sick sometimes. But still they'd keep on coming."

Mr. Ricky softly kissed the photo and carefully placed it back on the shelf. He closed the cabinet door and sat back down in his big easy chair.

"I come to Ideaville — or the town it used to be — hunting a feller down. Not one of your big-time hoods, but a feller caused a fair ruckus just the same. Had to liaise with some of the local law, including a young patrolman. Clean looking, all-American type, he was, strapping fellow quick with his wit and his gun. Married to the prettiest young thing I'd ever seen. At least, since my Tess passed."

"So you slept with his wife?" I asked. "Is that the kind of cop you were?"

Mr. Ricky leaned forward and pointed a shaky finger at me. "Things ain't always so cut and dried, sonny, so clear as they seem. Not even your old friends right and wrong. Hell of a thing for a lawman to say, I know, but it's the only whole truth I ever discovered in this long life. You think your boy's a hero, killed by some slant-eyed yellow demons to protect freedom and democracy. Years later you find out he's a victim of something they call 'friendly fire' and suddenly you can't tell the demons from the angels. You think the law's the law and there's no crossing over it, no mistaking the lines what are drawn and you can only be one side or the other. Then the day after he takes a bullet for you on the street, your best friend tells you that, oh yeah, he's on the pad, and would you pick up his envelope for him.

"You think there's good and bad, love and hate, evil and virtue. You think marriage is sacred and cuckolds go to hell and you'd never in your wildest dreams mess with another feller's — another *lawman's* — fine young wife.

"And then you learn he's a nasty piece of work, crooked as a corkscrew and mean as a snake. You hear, from his own lips, how he beats his wife with his hands and feet and laughs about it after. You see that pretty little thing, hurt and lonely and scared as a hungry kitten whose mama's been run over in the street. So you go to her, to comfort her. Tell her things ain't got to be so bad and try to get her to see that the world ain't always such an awful place. That there are good men, loving men, kind men."

"Lonely men?" Sandy suggested.

Mr. Ricky lowered his finger and dropped his head. He nodded.

"Tessie had passed a couple of years previous. The cancer's what they said, but I knew it was Junior catching up with her. I was so lonely, so alone." He looked up at me again. "Your momma did for me as much as I did for her. We was both of us locked into prisons of our own device. Man can't live on law alone. So for a little while there, we handed each other the keys to our cells and flew free. Soared, we did. It was a wonderful feeling, a rare and precious thing."

"She's dead," I said, voice breaking. Sandy took my hand.

"Blackwell?"

I couldn't reply, but Sandy whispered a "yes." She offered a short summary of what had happened at Chez Roach.

"That does grieve me to know, it surely does, though no one will shed a tear for young Blackwell. But, son, your momma passed for me years ago, in spirit if not in flesh. The day she went back to . . . your father. I wanted to take her to Chicago with me, take her away from this awful little town and all what he was doing to her. But

she wouldn't go. Plain refused. It was the times, I
reckon, and the attitudes and . . . well, truth be
known, she had a true heart of her own. Probably
what most drew me to her, being something like
my Tessie. She couldn't leave her husband
because she had betrothed herself to him, she
said. She had taken a vow and wouldn't dishonor
it. No matter what he done."

I uttered a weak and painful laugh. "How
times did change," I said.

"That's nature's first rule," Mr. Ricky said.
"*Human* nature. And it's as inescapable as gravity, with twice the weight."

"Did you know about me?" I asked.

"Not at first. I didn't know I'd left her in the
family way. Had no way of knowing, did I."

"How did you find out? When?"

"Not for years; till after you'd already grown
and gone, left town. Your momma wrote me a letter then, told me all about it. It was a nasty thing
and I burned it; she liked to blame me for her
woes, for . . . sorry son, but for giving birth to you.
It was right after she went off with Blackwell
Senior. I think it was a kind of . . . she was trying to come to terms with her past, how she got
to where she was. I come back to Ideaville to try
and talk to her, but she wouldn't have nothing to
do with me then. I found out all I could about
you, heard about your exploits, your youthful
detecting wizardry. Made me damn proud to
know you was following in the family tradition. I
told you before something about law's in the
blood."

"So's syphilis."

"No, sir. I knew then you was a chip off this square old block. I wanted to tell you, I wanted to track you down, but . . ."

He shrugged.

So much for *my* life. At least he had the decency to look sheepish about it.

"But sometimes they come back," I said, remembering the Czar's words to me from . . . Christ, was it just a few days before?

"You done good here, son. You done what needed to be done and you done it with style. This town become a cesspool, a garbage pit. With Blackwell and the others gone, now maybe it's got a real chance to revive and to be something."

"And the cost?" I asked with a choking laugh.

"The law always comes with a price attached. An old lawman friend of mine — weird little feller, spooky but worldly wise — used to say to me that the weed of crime bears bitter fruit."

I didn't know how to respond to that, but fortunately I didn't have to. There was a knock on the door and . . . my real father got up to answer it. Another stooped old man came in, carrying a black doctor's bag. He was introduced only as "John," and took Sandy into the bedroom for an examination. Mr. Ricky explained to me that while the man wasn't *quite* a doctor — he refused to say exactly, but I got the feeling that John had been a vet — he knew how to patch people up and keep his yap shut besides. My father and I sat in silence until he came back out. He announced that Sandy would be fine, more or less, accepted an envelope from Mr. Ricky, and then departed. Sandy emerged a minute later.

"Are you okay?" I asked.

"His manner was a bit push me, pull you, but he seemed to know what he was doing. He gave me some happy pills just in case."

"So what's it going to be then, son?" Mr. Ricky said, sitting down again in his comfy chair.

"What's *what* going to be?"

"The town, the rebirth of Ideaville."

"What about it?"

"You going to stick around for it? Help it along? A town in trouble can always use some law. *Blood* law."

"I'm no cop," I snorted.

"Maybe, maybe not. Don't have to sit behind a badge to represent the law, though. All it stands for. You was doing it as a boy, though you might not think it this moment. You could do it again, take up the mantle."

"Quarter a case, just like the old days?"

"Lawman don't do it for the money. Not a real lawman. He does it for the job."

A thought suddenly occurred to me. "You engineered all this, didn't you? You knew . . . about all of it. That newspaper clipping I got in the mail back in California with the story of Sandy's car crash. I thought it was Roach or maybe even my . . . the Czar who sent it. To gloat. But it was you, wasn't it? You sent it because you wanted me back here to take on your mantle, clean up the town. Blood law."

"You got a fanciful imagination, son. I'm just a tired old man. How could I have done, how could I have *known* all that? I just sit here in the Anchor and read the news. Watch the world go by.

That's all. My time is past, but yours? You could just be coming into your cups, if you take the opportunities presented to you. Can you do that? Will you?"

Mr. Ricky cocked his head, pointing that sharp beak at me like an eagle in flight that's spotted its prey. He was definitely more than just a tired old man.

"I think I need to take some of those happy pills," Sandy said, breaking the silence between father and son. "And I need some sleep."

"Plenty of rooms here at the inn," the old detective said.

"We'll go down to mine," I said. I took Sandy's hand and led her toward the door.

"You think about what I said here, son. You think hard."

Sandy had already started down the stairs when I turned around and took a step back inside the old man's lair.

"Your boy's name, who died in the war: you called him Richard Junior. That makes you a Richard, too, yeah?"

The old man nodded.

"Richard what?"

He told me. He told me his name.

My name. My true name.

I nodded and followed Sandy down the stairs.

Sandy took a handful of pills and tumbled into bed before she could even get her clothes off. I removed them for her. By the time I got undressed and climbed in beside her, she was deeply asleep.

I watched her for a while as she slept, imagining things as they might have been. How every night could have seen the two of us in bed together — in a home together — sharing our bodies and our lives, maybe with some little ones in rooms down the hall, glasses of water on little tables next to their cosy beds. I traced the line of her cheek with my fingers and stroked her hair while she slept. She didn't wake, though she did make a contented grumble in her sleep and nestled against me. I wrapped my arms around her and held her tight all through the night.

A night in which I didn't sleep at all. I just lay there, holding Sandy, feeling her softness and her warmth. Soaking it up. Enjoying her, reveling in the sensation of her flesh touching mine.

And thinking.

Always thinking.

Sandy slept for ten solid hours. She was stiff and pained when she finally woke up, but she smiled when she saw me looking at her, holding her.

Growing hard against her.

We made love without either of us saying a word. I slid into her easily, perfectly and staring into each other's eyes we made the motion of the ages.

And it was oh so good.

* * *

I went up to my father's room. The door was unlocked, but the rooms were vacant. I walked around them anyway, examining the titles of the books on the shelves, the foodstuffs in his kitchen, the items in his medicine cabinet.

He had high blood pressure and hemorrhoids. Too much salt and too much sitting, I suppose.

I stopped to look again at those four photographs in their silver frames on the shelf of his glass cabinet. I studied Tessie and Junior, both long since gone. I looked at the picture of my younger self in the days of my supposed all-seeing, all-knowing, encyclopedic glory. I was a pretty cute kid. I wonder whatever happened to him?

I couldn't bear to look at the picture of my mom. Or so I told myself. But much as I tried to look away, her image caught the corner of my eye like a fishhook snags a hungry trout. In the end, I opened the case and took the picture out. I cried — bawled like a baby — as I stared at it, then clutched it to my chest.

I wiped away the tears, blew my nose in an antimacassar and gently put the frame back in its place on the shelf.

I left the room without another look back, closing the door behind me.

Closing all the doors.

My father sat in his chair in the lobby. Sandy was there beside him. The hotel was still closed, but there was a sprinkling of activity out on the street. The sirens had faded in the night and I had the feeling that Ideaville was about to get back to something like normal.

Whatever the hell that means.

Mr. Ricky — I feel more comfortable thinking of him that way — nodded at me and offered a hearty good morning. Sandy flashed me a coy smile as I sat down beside her and entwined her fingers in mine.

"I'm leaving," I told the old man.

He narrowed those steely eyes at me for a moment and flared his nostrils, but then his face relaxed and he nodded.

"If that's the way it's got to be."

"It is," I said. "This isn't the place for me. Not anymore."

"Can't go home again, eh?"

"I don't know about that. Maybe it's just the wrong question. Maybe it doesn't matter. All I know is that. . ." — I swallowed hard and looked at Sandy, then back at the old man — "this *isn't* my home. Maybe it never was. I think, though, that what I have to do is find out where home really could be. For me."

Mr. Ricky looked sad; not disappointed, but sad.

"A feller — a lawman — has got to know his own heart," he said. "Most of all."

"A lady, too," Sandy said. She turned to me, looking almost as sad as the old man. "I've got to stay. In spite of everything, Ideaville is my home. I don't think I could make it anyplace else. I think that's why I couldn't ever make myself go. I'm . . . bound here."

My heart went dead in my chest and I wanted to cry all over again. But I knew deep down in the bottomless pit of my soul — detective, remember? — that what she said was true. Painfully, utterly, undeniably true.

"I know," I choked.

The three of us sat there for a while, in that empty, tacky, deadly silent hotel lobby, each of us — even tough old Mr. Ricky — sniffling and trying not to cry. It was a hell of a thing.

"We been talking," Mr. Ricky finally said. He had to cough and clear his throat to get the words out. "The young lady and me."

"Oh?"

"Mr. Ricky thinks I could do some good here," Sandy said. "Given my . . . talents, abilities. Since I once did a little detective work myself."

"Like I told you, son, there's a job in town still needs to be done. If not by you then by someone else."

"What about your . . . accident?" I asked. "You're still officially dead, you know."

"Could be an advantage," Mr. Ricky said. "No one comes looking for a dead woman. Give's you a whole new kind of freedom to do things, range about. Especially if you got the right resources, a little help from a friend. A gal like Sandy, hell, she could bring a whole new spirit to this old town."

"Do you think?" Sandy said. The question was clearly addressed toward me.

"Without a doubt," I told her and smiled. And squeezed her hand tight. Mr. Ricky nodded his approval.

We sat there a while longer, suddenly enjoying the quiet. Just the three of us.

Together.

* * *

My Pacer looked like shit, but it drove like a dream as I cruised out of town. It would probably cost more to fix the front end than the whole car was worth, but I was determined to have it repaired when I got where I was going.

Wherever that might be.

I was already missing Sandy — and even Mr. Ricky a bit — though I was barely out of Ideaville. I suspected I'd miss Sandy for a long time — maybe forever — but I knew, too, that we'd both come to the right decision. It may have come twenty years late, but we'd had our night together. I'd treasure it always and never forget it, or Sandy, but now we could both, *finally*, hope to move on.

Of course, you can't leave *everything* behind; for one thing, it doesn't work and for another, like the boy who peeps at his sister in the bath, it just ain't right. The past, good and bad, fond and fearsome, is an indelible part of you — a part of everything.

I had come back to Ideaville — Christ, I prayed they'd change the name again with Roach out of the picture — a man who hated his past and dreaded his future. But for all the cruel reminders of a past that I'd loathed, tried to forget or ignore or pathetically disguise, I learned the awful inevitability of it; the foolishness of pretending that history is something other than what it is. We're all of us revisionists of a sort, the Pol Pots of our souls declaring a new Year Zero with every busted flush and broken heart. But that's not what life is, how it works. And it's not

how America works. At least it shouldn't be. Why
not remember the bad, so long as you don't wal-
low in it? How else to learn from what has been?
However painful the memories of the Czar's —
and my own — misdeeds might be, they shaped
me every bit as much as those halcyon lunches
with my mom at Vito's Pizzeria, or those wonderful bicycle rides with Sandy. In forgetting the bad,
you risk losing, too, all that is good.

When I left town the last time, as an angry
and broken man-child, I carried with me only the
bad, having shed my belief in the mere possibility
of good. I wouldn't make that mistake this time.
Or ever again. Finding Sandy, amid the so very
much that had been lost, opened my eyes — and
my heart — to other possibilities, to the existence
and the pursuit of better things. Who can say if
I'll find them? Who knows if any of us ever can —
there sure as hell ain't no guarantees.

But, you know: the way is there, and the possibility is there, and the road forward, potholed
and winding though it may be, can be traveled in
hope. Christ, I never dreamed I'd have even that
much.

And a great car.

The hitchhiker wasn't very good at it; fair
enough, because he looked to be all of twelve years
old. He held his hand high above his head, jabbing
his little thumb out as far as it would go. He had
on a pair of baggy trousers and a black *Buffy the
Vampire Slayer* T-shirt. He practically jumped for
joy when I hit the brakes and pulled up on the soft
shoulder. Definitely a jovial little kid.

"Hey, thanks mister," he beamed as I opened the passenger door.

"Shouldn't you be in school?" I asked him

He froze halfway into the car, a look of panic crossing his face. "Uhhhh. . ."

"It's okay, kid, I won't snitch. Where you going? I'll give you a lift."

"Thanks," he said, and hopped on in.

"Playing hooky, huh?"

"Awww, you know how it is," he told me.

Actually I didn't; I'd never played hooky once in my entire life. That is, until I played hooky *with* my entire life.

"Sure, I know," I lied. "So what's your name?"

"Robert Louis Stein. Bobby."

I glanced at the kid, studied him a bit. I think I made him nervous — he might have figured me for a chickenhawk — and he shot me a hard look back.

"What?" he said.

"Nothing. So where you headed?"

"Meeting my pal J.K. up at Gummy Bear Woods."

"Gummy Bear Woods?" I asked.

"That's just what we call it. You know, 'cause that's where the Gummy Bear Killer got caught and gunned down. It's pretty spooky up there, but it's really cool. Some other weird stuff happened around there years ago. They say it's haunted or something."

"And that doesn't scare you?"

"No way! I couldn't sneak away from my ma in time, so J.K. took off without me. I should be really pissed at her, but she's like a total wizard on the skateboard and she's promised to teach me everything she knows."

"So your best pal's a girl, huh?"

"Why not?" he asked.

"Cool," I said. Why not, indeed? I pulled out onto the road and stepped on the gas. Gummy Bear Woods or bust.

I tell you, kids today!

Acknowledgements

This book owes its genesis to an idea suggested by Rich Klin and Gordon Van Gelder — I just picked up the ball and ran. Special thanks are due to Gordon for nurturing it along and bringing it to fruition. Buy him a beer or six and he'll tell you the whole sordid story.

Thanks, too, to John Oakes for being a publisher of some courage. I hope he never regrets it.

Brown Harvest owes a thuddingly obvious debt to the vast body of work of twentieth century kiddy and teen literature. I believe the name of just about every writer who had a hand in it (and many of their creations) appears somewhere in the body of the text. Find 'em all, win a prize!

A cheeky tip of a battered fedora to Donald Sobol and Dashiell Hammett for . . . Christ, *you* figure it out.

A humble bow to Pat Cadigan, Jon Courtenay Grimwood, Paul McAuley and Kim Newman for Friday lunches in Islington. No coffee for me.

Special thanks to Louis Schechter for yet more unquestioning support.

As ever, love and gratitude to Jane Stokes for . . . absolutely everything else.

And Rosie, if ever you read this goofy book, remember that your dad promises to never be like the Czar, though you'll always be his little czarina.